PRAISE FOR

NEED TO KNOW

"Perhaps there will be two or three readers out there who manage to finish the first chapter of this terrific debut and put it down for more than an hour. But they'll be back. And they'll devour *Need to Know* like the rest of us, skipping lunch, losing sleep, turning pages until the end, where we're all left waiting for more."

—John Grisham, #1 *New York Times* bestselling author

"Prediction: if you read chapter one, you'll read chapter two. If you read chapter two, you'll miss dinner, stay up far too late and feel tired at work tomorrow. This is that kind of book. Superb."

—Lee Child, #1 *New York Times* bestselling author

"Karen Cleveland is the real deal—an exciting new voice in thrillers. Scarpetta would call her a friend."

—Patricia Cornwell, #1 *New York Times* bestselling author

"I am consumed with awe that this is a debut novel. Breathtaking, heart-pounding, it manages to be at once intimate and sweeping, characterful and plot-driven. A really astonishing achievement for any writer, let alone a first-time novelist. I love it!"

—Louise Penny, #1 *New York Times* bestselling author

"I raced through this gripping tale of domesticity and deceit. Cleveland deliciously ratchets up the tension at every turn . . . you won't be able to put it down until the final, stunning page!"

—Shari Lapena, *New York Times* bestselling
author of *The Couple Next Door*

"*Need to Know* carves out a uniquely compelling space among thrillers: high-stakes international intrigue combined with high-drama domestic suspense. These richly overlapping layers of tensions create a fast-paced, relentlessly gripping read."

—Chris Pavone, *New York Times* bestselling author of *The Expats*

NEED TO KNOW

A NOVEL

KAREN CLEVELAND

SEAL BOOKS

Seal Books and colophon are registered trademarks of Penguin Random House Canada.

NEED TO KNOW
Seal Books/published by arrangement with Doubleday Canada
Doubleday Canada edition published 2018

Library and Archives of Canada Cataloguing in Publication data is available upon request.

ISBN: 978-1-4000-2690-6
eBook ISBN: 978-0-385-69091-1

Cover based on a design by Carlos Beltrán
Cover image: © Katya Evdokimova / Millennium Images, UK

Printed and bound in the United States of America

Seal Books are published by Penguin Random House Canada.
"Seal Books" and the portrayal of a seal are the property of Penguin Random House Canada.

www.penguinrandomhouse.ca

2 4 6 8 9 7 5 3 1

Penguin
Random House
SEAL BOOKS

For B. J. W.

When one is in love, one always begins by deceiving one's self, and one always ends by deceiving others. That is what the world calls a romance.

—OSCAR WILDE

NEED TO KNOW

I STAND IN THE DOORWAY OF THE TWINS' ROOM AND watch them sleep, peaceful and innocent, through crib slats that remind me of bars on a prison cell.

A night-light bathes the room in a soft orange glow. Furniture crowds the small space, far too much of it for a room this size. Cribs, one old, one new. A changing table, stacks of diapers still in their plastic. The bookcase Matt and I assembled ourselves, ages ago. Its shelves now sag, overloaded with the books I could recite by heart to the older two, the ones I've been vowing to read more often to the twins, if only I could find the time.

I hear Matt's footsteps on the stairs and my hand clenches around the flash drive. Tight, like if I squeeze hard enough, it'll disappear. Everything will go back to the way it was. The past two days will be erased, nothing more than a bad dream. But it's still there: hard, solid, real.

The hallway floor creaks where it always does. I don't turn. He comes up behind me, close enough that I can smell his soap, his shampoo, the smell of *him* that's always been oddly comforting, that now inexplicably makes him more of a stranger. I can feel his hesitation.

"Can we talk?" he says.

The words are quiet, but the sound is enough to stir Chase. He sighs in his sleep and then settles, still curled into a ball, like he's protecting himself. I've always thought he's so much like his father, the serious eyes, taking everything in. Now I wonder if I'll ever truly know him, if he'll keep secrets so heavy they'll crush anyone close to him.

"What's there to say?"

Matt takes a step closer, puts a hand on my arm. I move away, enough to free myself from his touch. His hand lingers in the air, then falls to his side.

"What are you going to do?" he asks.

I look at the other crib, at Caleb, on his back in his footed pajamas; cherubic blond curls, arms and legs splayed like a starfish. His hands are open, his pink lips open. He has no idea how vulnerabzle he is, how cruel the world can be.

I always said I'd protect him. I'd give him the strength that he lacks, make sure he has every opportunity, keep his life as normal as possible. How can I do that, if I'm not around?

I would do anything for my kids. *Anything.* I uncurl my fingers and look at the flash drive, the little rectangle, nondescript. So small, but with so much power. Power to fix, power to destroy.

Rather like a lie, when you think about it.

"You know I don't have a choice," I say, and I force myself to look at him, my husband, the man I know so well, and at the same time not at all.

CHAPTER

1

"BAD NEWS, VIV."

I hear Matt's voice, words anyone would dread, but a tone that's reassuring. Light, apologetic. It's something unfortunate, sure, but it's manageable. Anything truly bad and his voice would be heavier. He'd use a complete sentence, a complete name. *I have some bad news, Vivian.*

I hold the phone to my ear with a raised shoulder, swivel my chair to the other side of the L-shaped desk, to the computer centered under gray overhead bins. I guide the cursor to the owl-shaped icon on the screen and double-click. If it's what I think it is—what I know it is—then I only have a bit longer at my desk.

"Ella?" I say. My gaze drifts to one of the crayon drawings tacked to the high cubicle walls with pushpins, a pop of color in this sea of gray.

"A hundred point eight."

I close my eyes and take a deep breath. We've been expecting it. Half her class has been sick, falling like dominoes, so it was only a matter of time. Four-year-olds aren't exactly the cleanliest bunch. But today? It had to happen today?

"Anything else?"

"Just the temp." He pauses. "Sorry, Viv. She seemed fine when I dropped her off."

I swallow past the tightening in my throat and nod, even though he can't see me. Any other day and he'd pick her up. He can work from home, at least in theory. I can't, and I used up all my leave when the twins were born. But he's taking Caleb into the city for the latest round of medical appointments. I've been feeling guilty for weeks that I'll have to miss it. And now I'll be missing it and *still* using leave I don't have.

"I'll be there in an hour," I say. The rules say we have an hour from the time they call. Factoring in the drive and the walk to my car—it's in the outer reaches of Langley's sprawling parking lots—that gives me about fifteen minutes to wrap up work for the day. Fifteen minutes less leave to add to my negative balance.

I glance at the clock in the corner of my screen— seven minutes past ten—and then my eyes shift to the Starbucks cup beside my right elbow, steam escaping from the hole in the plastic lid. I treated myself, a splurge in celebration of the long-awaited day, fuel for the tedious hours ahead. Precious minutes wasted in line that could have been spent digging through digital files. Should have stuck to the usual, the sputtering coffee maker that leaves grounds floating at the top of the mug.

"That's what I told the school," Matt says. "School" is actually our day care center, the place where our youngest three spend their days. But we've been calling it school since Luke was three months old. I'd read it could help ease the transition, lessen the guilt of leaving your baby for eight, ten hours a day. It didn't, but old habits die hard, I guess.

There's another pause, and I can hear Caleb babbling in the background. I listen, and I know that Matt's listening, too. It's like we're conditioned to do so at this point. But it's just vowel sounds. Still no consonants.

"I know today was supposed to be a big day . . . ," Matt finally says, and trails off. I'm used to the trailing off, the evasive conversations on my open line. I always assume someone's listening in. The Russians. The Chinese. That's part of the reason Matt's the first one the school calls when there's a problem. I'd rather him filter some of the kids' personal details from the ears of our adversaries.

Call me paranoid, or just call me a CIA counterintelligence analyst.

But really, that's about all Matt knows. Not that I've been trying in vain to uncover a network of Russian sleeper agents. Or that I've developed a methodology for identifying people involved in the highly secretive program. Just that I've waited months for this day. That I'm about to find out if two years of hard work is going to pay off. And if I stand a chance at that promotion we desperately need.

"Yeah, well," I say, moving my mouse back and forth, watching Athena load, the cursor in the shape of a timer. "Caleb's appointment is what's important today."

My eyes drift back to the cubicle wall, the bright crayon drawings. Ella's, a picture of our family, stick arms and legs protruding straight from six round happy faces. Luke's, a bit more sophisticated, a single person, thick jagged scribbles to color in hair and clothing and shoes. *MOMMY*, it says in big capital letters. From his superhero phase. It's me, in a cape, hands on my hips, an *S* on my shirt. Supermommy.

There's a familiar feeling in my chest, the pressure, the overwhelming urge to cry. *Deep breaths, Viv. Deep breaths.*

"The Maldives?" Matt says, and I feel the hint of a smile creep to my lips. He always does this, finds a way to make me smile when I need it most. I glance at the photograph of the two of us on the corner of my desk, my favorite from our wedding day, almost a decade ago. Both of us so happy, so *young.* We always talked about going somewhere exotic for our ten-year anniversary. It's certainly not in the cards anymore. But it's fun to dream. Fun and depressing at the same time.

"Bora Bora," I say.

"I could live with that." He hesitates, and in the gap I hear Caleb again. More vowel sounds. *Aah-aah-aah.* In my head, I'm calculating the months Chase has already been making consonant sounds. I know I shouldn't—all the doctors say I shouldn't—but I am.

"Bora *Bora*?" I hear from behind me, faux-incredulous. I put my hand over the mouthpiece of the phone and turn. It's Omar, my FBI counterpart, an amused expression on his face. "That one might be hard to justify, even for the Agency." He breaks into a grin. Infectious as ever, it brings one to my own face, as well.

"What are you doing here?" I say, my hand still covering the mouthpiece. I can hear Caleb babbling in my ear. O's this time. *Ooh-ooh-ooh.*

"Had a meeting with Peter." He takes a step closer, perches on the edge of my desk. I can see the outline of his holster at his hip, through his T-shirt. "The timing may or may not have been a coincidence." He glances at my screen and the grin fades ever so slightly. "It was today, right? Ten A.M.?"

I look at my screen, dark, the cursor still in the shape of a timer. "It was today." The babbling in my ear has gone quiet. I roll my chair so that I'm turned, just a touch, away from Omar and remove my hand from the mouthpiece. "Honey, I have to go. Omar's here."

"Tell him I said hi," Matt says.

"Will do."

"Love you."

"Love you, too." I set the phone down on its base and turn back to Omar, who's still sitting on my desk, denim-clad legs outstretched, feet crossed at the ankles. "Matt says hi," I tell him.

"Aaah, so *he's* the Bora Bora connection. Planning a vacation?" The grin's back, full force.

"In theory," I say with a half-hearted laugh. It sounds pathetic enough that I can feel color rise to my cheeks.

He looks at me for a moment longer, then thankfully down at his wrist. "All right, it's ten-ten." He uncrosses his ankles, crosses them the opposite way. Then leans forward, the excitement on his face unmistakable. "What have you got for me?"

Omar's been doing this longer than I have. A decade, at least. He's looking for the actual sleepers in the U.S., and I'm trying to uncover those running the cell. Neither of us has had any success. How he's still so enthusiastic never fails to amaze me.

"Nothing yet. I haven't even taken a look." I nod at the screen, the program that's still loading, then glance at the black-and-white photograph tacked to my cubicle wall, beside the kids' drawings. Yury Yakov. Fleshy face, hard expression. A few more clicks and I'll be inside his computer. I'll be able to see what he sees, navigate around the way he does, pore through his files. And hopefully prove that he's a Russian spy.

"Who are you and what have you done with my friend Vivian?" Omar asks with a smile.

He's right. If it wasn't for the line at Starbucks, I'd have logged in to the program at ten A.M. on the dot. I'd have had a few minutes to look around, at least. I shrug and gesture at the screen. "I'm trying." Then I nod toward the phone. "But in any case, it's going to have to wait. Ella's sick. I need to go pick her up."

He exhales dramatically. "Kids. Always the worst timing."

Movement on the screen draws my attention, and I roll my chair closer. Athena's finally loading. There are red banners on all sides, a slew of words, each signifying a different control, a different compartment. The longer the string of text, the more classified. This one's pretty darn long.

I click past one screen, then another. Each click is an

acknowledgment. Yes, I know I'm accessing compartmented information. Yes, I know I can't disclose it or I'll
go to jail for a very long time. Yes, yes, yes. Just get me
to the information already.

"This is it," Omar says. I remember he's there and
glance at him out of the corner of my eye. He's looking
away purposefully, studiously avoiding the screen,
giving me privacy. "I feel it."

"I hope so," I murmur. And I do. But I'm nervous.
This methodology is a gamble. A big one. I built a profile
for suspected handlers: educational institution, studies
and degrees, banking centers, travel within Russia and
abroad. Came up with an algorithm, identified five individuals who best fit the pattern. Likely candidates.

The first four turned out to be false leads, and now
the program's on the chopping block. Everything rests
on Yury. Number five. The computer that was the hardest to break into, the one I had the most confidence in to
begin with.

"And if it's not," Omar says, "you did something that
no one else has been able to do. You got close."

Targeting the handlers is a new approach. For years,
the Bureau's been trying to identify the sleepers themselves, but they're so well assimilated it's next to
impossible. The cell is designed so that sleepers don't
have contact with anyone but their handler, and even
that is minimal. And the Agency's been focused on the
ringleaders, the guys who oversee the handlers, the
ones in Moscow with direct ties to the SVR, Russian
intelligence.

"Close doesn't count," I say quietly. "You know that better than anyone."

Around the time I started on the account, Omar was a hard-charging new agent. He'd proposed a new initiative, inviting entrenched sleepers to "come in from the cold" and turn themselves in, in exchange for amnesty. His reasoning? There had to be at least a few sleepers who wanted to turn their covers into reality, and we might be able to learn enough from the turned sleepers to penetrate the network as a whole.

The plan was rolled out quietly, and within a week we had a walk-in, a man named Dmitri. Said he was a mid-level handler, told us information about the program that corroborated what we knew—handlers like himself were responsible for five sleepers each; he reported to a ringleader who was responsible for five handlers. A completely self-contained cell. That got our attention, for sure. Then came the outrageous claims, the information that was inconsistent with everything we knew to be true, and then he disappeared. Dmitri the Dangle, we called him after that.

That was the end of the program. The thought of publicly admitting there were sleepers in the U.S., of admitting our inability to find them, was already barely palatable to Bureau seniors. Between that and the potential for Russian manipulation—dangling double agents with false leads—Omar's plan was roundly criticized, then rejected. *We'll be inundated with other Dmitris,* they said. And with that, Omar's once-promising career trajectory stalled. He fell into obscurity, plugging away, day after day, at a thankless, frustrating, impossible task.

The screen changes, and a little icon with Yury's name appears. I always get a thrill out of this, seeing my targets' names here, knowing we have a window into their digital lives, the information they think is private. As if on cue, Omar stands up. He knows about our efforts to target Yury. He's one of a handful of Bureau agents read into the program—and its biggest cheerleader, the person who believes in the algorithm, and in me, more than anyone else. But still, he can't access it directly.

"Call me tomorrow, okay?" he says.

"You got it," I reply. He turns, and as soon as I see his back, heading away, I focus my attention on the screen. I double-click the icon and a red-bordered inset appears, displaying the contents of Yury's laptop, a mirror image that I can comb through. I only have minutes until I need to leave. But it's long enough for a peek.

The background is dark blue, dotted with bubbles of different sizes, in different shades of blue. There are icons lined up in four neat rows on one side, half of them folders. The file names are all in Cyrillic, characters that I recognize but can't read—at least not well. I took a beginning Russian class years ago; then Luke arrived and I never went back. I know some basic phrases, recognize some words, but that's about it. For the rest I rely on linguists or translation software.

I open a few of the folders, then the text documents inside them. Page after page of dense Cyrillic text. I feel a wave of disappointment, one I know is nonsensical. It's not like a Russian guy sitting on his computer in Moscow is going to be typing in English, keeping records in English, *List of Deep-Cover Operatives in the United*

States. I know that what I'm looking for is encrypted. I'm just hoping to see some sort of clue, some sort of protected file, something with obvious encryption.

High-level penetrations over the years have told us that the identities of the sleepers are known only to the handlers, that the names are stored electronically, locally. Not in Moscow, because the SVR—Russia's powerful external intelligence service—fears moles within its own organization. Fears them so much that they'd rather risk losing sleepers than keep the names in Russia. And we know that if anything should happen to a handler, the ringleader would access the electronic files and contact Moscow for a decryption key, one part of a multilayer encryption protocol. We have the code from Moscow. We've just never had anything to decrypt.

The program's airtight. We can't break in. We don't even know its true purpose, if there is one. It might just be passive collection, or it might be something more sinister. But since we know the head of the program reports to Putin himself, I tend to think it's the latter— and that's what keeps me up at night.

I keep scanning, my eyes drifting over each file, even though I'm not entirely sure what I'm looking for. And then I see a Cyrillic word I recognize. друзья. *Friends.* The last icon in the last row, a manila folder. I double-click and the folder opens into a list of five JPEG images, nothing more. My heart rate begins to accelerate. Five. There are five sleepers assigned to each handler; we know that from multiple sources. And there's the title. *Friends.*

I click open the first image. It's a headshot of a non-descript middle-aged man in round eyeglasses. A tingle of excitement runs through me. The sleepers are well assimilated. Invisible members of society, really. This could certainly be one of them.

Logic tells me not to get too excited; all our intelligence says the files on the sleepers are encrypted. But my gut tells me this is something big.

I open the second. A woman, orange hair, bright blue eyes, wide smile. Another headshot, another potential sleeper. I stare at her. There's a thought I'm trying to ignore, but can't. These are just pictures. Nothing about their identities, nothing the ringleader could use to contact them.

But still. *Friends.* Pictures. So maybe Yury's not the elusive handler I was hoping to uncover, the one the Agency devoted resources to finding. But could he be a recruiter? And these five people: They must be important. Targets, maybe?

I double-click the third image and a face appears on my screen. A headshot, close-up. So familiar, so expected—and yet not, because it's here, where it doesn't belong. I blink at it, once, twice, my mind struggling to bridge what I'm seeing with what I'm *seeing,* what it means. Then I swear that time stops. Icy fingers close around my heart and squeeze, and all I can hear is the whoosh of blood in my ears.

I'm staring into the face of my husband.

CHAPTER

2

FOOTSTEPS ARE COMING CLOSER. I HEAR THEM, EVEN through the pounding in my ears. The haze in my mind crystallizes, in an instant, into a single command. *Hide it.* I guide the cursor to the X in the corner of the picture and click, and Matt's face disappears, just like that.

I turn toward the sound, the open wall of my cubicle. It's Peter, approaching. Did he see? I glance back at the screen. No pictures, just the folder, open, five lines of text. Did I close it in time?

A niggling voice in my head asks me why it matters. Why I felt the need to hide it. This is Matt. My husband. Shouldn't I be running to security, asking why the Russians have a picture of him in their possession? There's a wave of nausea starting to churn deep in my stomach.

"Meeting?" Peter says. One eyebrow is raised above his thick-rimmed eyeglasses. He's standing in front of me, loafers and pressed khakis, a button-down that's buttoned a touch too close to the top. Peter's the senior analyst on the account, a holdover from the Soviet era, and my mentor for the past eight years. There's no one more knowledgeable about Russian counterintelligence. Quiet and reserved, it's impossible not to respect the guy.

And right now there's nothing strange in his expression. Just the question. Am I coming to the morning meeting? I don't think he saw.

"Can't," I say, and my voice sounds unnaturally high-pitched. I try to lower it, try to keep the tremor out of it. "Ella's sick. I need to pick her up."

He nods, more of a tilt of his head than anything. His expression looks even, unfazed. "Hope she feels better," he says, and turns to walk away, over to the conference room, the glass-walled cube that's better suited for a tech start-up than CIA headquarters. I watch him long enough to see that he doesn't look back.

I swivel back to my computer, to the screen that's now blank. My legs have gone weak, my breath coming quick. Matt's face. On Yury's computer. And my first instinct: *Hide it.* Why?

I hear my other teammates ambling toward the conference room. Mine is the closest cubicle to it, the one everyone walks past to get there. It's usually quiet down here, the farthest reaches of the sea of cubicles, unless people are heading to the conference room or to the Restricted Access room just beyond it—the place where analysts can lock themselves away, view the most sensitive of sensitive files, the ones with information so valuable, so hard to obtain, that the Russians surely would track down and kill the source if they knew we had it.

I take a shaky breath, then another. I turn as their footsteps come closer. Marta's first. Trey and Helen, side by side, a quiet conversation. Rafael and then Bert, our branch chief, who does little more than edit papers. Peter's the real boss and everyone knows it.

We're the sleeper team, the seven of us. An odd bunch, really, because we have so little in common with the other teams in the Counterintelligence Center, Russia Division. They have more information than they know what to do with; we have virtually nothing.

"You coming?" Marta asks, pausing at my cubicle, laying a hand on one of the high walls. The scent of peppermint and mouthwash wafts over when she speaks. There are bags under her eyes, a thick layer of concealer. One too many last night, by the look of things. Marta's a former ops officer, likes whiskey and reliving her glory days in the field in equal measure; she once taught me how to pick a lock with a credit card and a bobby pin I found at the bottom of my work bag, one that keeps Ella's hair in a bun for ballet class.

I shake my head. "Sick kid."

"Germy beasts."

She drops her hand, continues on. I offer a smile to the others as they pass. *Everything's normal here.* When they're all in the glass cube and Bert pulls the door shut, I turn back to the screen. The files, the jumble of Cyrillic. I'm trembling. I look down at the clock in the corner of the screen. I should have left three minutes ago.

The knot in my stomach is twisted tight and thick. I can't actually leave now, can I? But I have no choice. If I'm late to get Ella, it's strike two. Three and we're out; the school has waiting lists for every class and wouldn't think twice. Besides, what would I do if I stayed?

There's one sure way to find out exactly why Matt's picture is here, and it's not by looking through more files. I swallow, feeling sick, and guide the cursor to close Athena, shut down the computer. Then I grab my bag and coat and head for the door.

HE'S BEING TARGETED.

By the time I reach my car, my fingers like icicles, my breath coming in little white bursts, I'm certain.

He wouldn't be the first. The Russians have been more aggressive than ever this past year. It started with Marta. A woman with an Eastern European accent befriended her at the gym, had some drinks with her at O'Neill's. After a few, the woman flat out asked if Marta would be interested in continuing their "friendship" with a discussion about work. Marta refused and never saw her again.

Trey was next. Still in the closet at the time, he'd always come to work functions with his "roommate," Sebastian. One day I saw him, shaken and pale, on his way up to security. I later heard through the grapevine he'd received a blackmail package in the mail—photos of the two of them in some compromising positions, a threat to send them to his parents if he didn't agree to a meeting.

So it's not a stretch to think the Russians know who I am. And if they know that, then learning Matt's identity would be a piece of cake. Figuring out where we're vulnerable would be, too.

I turn the key in the ignition and the Corolla makes its usual choking sound. "Come on," I murmur, turning the key again, hearing the engine gasp to life. Seconds later a blast of icy air hits me from the vents. I reach down, turn the dial so that it's on the hottest setting, rub my hands together, then throw the car into reverse. I should let it warm up, but there isn't time. There's never enough time.

The Corolla is Matt's car, the one he had even before we met. To say it's on its last legs is an understatement. We traded in my old car when I was pregnant with the twins. Got a minivan, used. Matt drives that one, the family car, because he does more of the drop-offs and pickups.

I'm driving by rote, as if in a daze. The farther I go, the more the knot in my stomach tightens. It's not the fact that they're targeting Matt that worries me. It's that word. *Friends.* Doesn't that suggest some level of complicity?

Matt's a software engineer. He doesn't know how sophisticated the Russians are. How ruthless they can be. How they'd take just the smallest of openings, the tiniest sign that he might be willing to work with them, and they'd exploit it, twist it to compel him to do more.

I reach the school with two minutes to spare. A blast of warm air strikes me when I step inside. The director, a woman with sharp features and a permanent scowl, glances pointedly at the clock and gives me a hard look. I'm not sure if it's *What took you so long?* Or *If you're back this early, clearly she was sick when you dropped her off.* I offer a half-hearted apologetic smile as I walk by, though on the inside I'm screaming. Whatever Ella has, she caught it from here, for God's sake.

I walk down the hall lined with kids' artwork—handprint polar bears and glittery snowflakes and watercolor mittens—but my mind is elsewhere. *Friends.* Did Matt do something to make them think he'd be willing to work with them? All they'd need is the smallest sign. Something, anything, to exploit.

I find my way into Ella's classroom, tiny chairs and cubbies and toy bins, an explosion of primary colors. She's in the far corner of the room, alone on a bright red kid-size couch, a hardcover picture book open on her lap. Segregated from the other kids, it seems. She's in purple leggings I don't recognize; I vaguely remember Matt mentioning he'd taken her shopping. Of course he did. She's been outgrowing clothes left and right.

I walk over with outstretched arms, an exaggerated smile. She looks up and eyes me warily. "Where's Daddy?"

Inside I cringe, but I keep the smile plastered on my face. "Daddy's taking Caleb to the doctor. I'm picking you up today."

She closes the book and sets it back on the shelf. "Okay."

"Can I have a hug?" My arms are still outstretched, albeit drooping. She looks at them for a moment, then walks into a hug. I clasp her tightly, burying my face in her soft hair. "I'm sorry you're not feeling well, sweetie."

"I'm okay, Mom."

Mom? My breath catches in my throat. Just this morning I was Mommy. Please don't let her stop calling me Mommy. I'm not ready for that. Especially not today.

I face her and paste another smile on my face. "Let's go get your brother."

Ella sits on the bench outside the infant room while I walk inside to get Chase. The room depresses me as much today as it did seven years ago, when I first dropped off Luke. The diaper-changing station, the row of cribs, the row of high chairs.

Chase is on the floor when I walk in. One of his teachers, the young one, scoops him up before I get to him, cuddles him close, lays kisses on his cheek. "Such a sweet boy," she says, smiling at me. I feel a pang of jealousy, watching. This is the woman who got to see his first steps, the one whose outstretched arms he toddled into for the first time, while I was at the office. She looks so natural with him, so comfortable. But then, of course she does. She's with him all day long.

"Yes, he is," I say, and the words sound awkward.

I get both kids bundled into puffy jackets, hats on their heads—it's unseasonably cold today for March— and then into their car seats, the ones that are hard and narrow enough to fit three across the back of the Corolla. The good ones, the safe ones, are in the minivan.

"How was your morning, sweetie?" I ask, glancing at Ella in the rearview mirror as I back out of the parking spot.

She's quiet for a moment. "I'm the only girl who didn't go to yoga."

"I'm sorry," I say, and as soon as the words are out of my mouth I know they're not the right ones, that I should have said something else. The silence that follows feels heavy. I reach for the stereo dial, turn on the kids' music.

I glance in the rearview mirror again, and Ella's looking out the window, quiet. I should ask another question, engage her in conversation about her day, but I say nothing. I can't get the picture out of my head. Matt's face. It was recent, I think. Within the past year or so. How long have they been watching him, watching us?

The drive from school to home is short, winding through neighborhoods that are a study in contradictions: new-construction McMansions interspersed with older homes like ours, a house far too small for six, old enough that my parents could have grown up in it. The D.C. suburbs are notoriously expensive, and Bethesda's one of the worst. But the schools are some of the best in the country.

We pull up to our house, neat and boxlike, two-car garage. There's a small front porch that the previous owners added, one that doesn't really match the rest of the house, that we don't use nearly as much as I thought we would. We bought the place when I was pregnant with Luke, when the schools made it seem worth the massive price tag.

I look at the American flag hanging near the front door. Matt hung that flag. Replaced the last one when it faded. He wouldn't agree to work against our country. I know he wouldn't. But did he do *something*? Did he do enough to make the Russians think he might?

There's one thing I know for certain. He was targeted because of me. Because of my job. And that's why I hid the picture, isn't it? If he's in trouble, it's my fault. And I need to do what I can to get him out of it.

I LET ELLA WATCH cartoons on the couch, one after another. Usually we cap it at a single episode, an after-dinner treat, but she's sick, and I can't get my mind to focus on anything except the picture. While Chase naps and she's zoned out in front of the TV, I clean the kitchen. Wipe down the countertops, the blue ones that we'd replace if we had the cash. Scrub stains off the stovetop, around the three burners that still work. Organize the cabinet full of plastic containers, matching lids with containers, stacking the ones that fit together.

In the afternoon, I bundle up the kids and we walk to the bus stop to pick up Luke. His greeting is the same as Ella's. *Where's Dad?*

Dad's taking Caleb to the doctor.

I make him a snack and help him with his homework. A math worksheet, adding two-digit numbers. I didn't know they were already up to two digits. Matt's the one who usually helps.

Ella hears Matt's key in the lock before I do, and she's off the couch like a shot, bounding for the front door. "Daddy!" she shouts as he opens the door, Caleb in one arm, groceries in the other. Somehow he still manages to squat down and give her a hug, ask her how she's feeling, even as he's wriggling Caleb's jacket off. Somehow the smile on his face looks genuine, *is* genuine.

He stands up and ambles over to me, gives me a peck on the lips. "Hi, honey," he says. He's in jeans and the sweater I gave him last Christmas, the brown one that zips at the top, a jacket over it. He sets the bag of groceries down on the counter, adjusts Caleb on his hip. Ella's clinging to one of his legs; he rests his free hand on her head and strokes her hair.

"How'd it go?" I reach for Caleb and I'm almost surprised when he willingly moves into my arms. I squeeze him and kiss his head, inhale the sweet smell of baby shampoo.

"Great, actually," Matt says, peeling off his jacket, laying it on the counter. He walks over to Luke and musses his hair. "Hey, kiddo."

Luke looks up, beaming. I can see the gap where he lost his first tooth, the one that went under his pillow before I got home from work. "Hey, Dad. Can we play catch?"

"In a bit. I need to talk to Mom first. Did you already work on your science project?"

There's a science project?

"Yeah," Luke says, and then his eyes dart to me, like he forgot I was there.

"Tell the truth," I say, my voice sharper than I mean it to be. My eyes find Matt's, and I see his eyebrows rise, just the smallest bit. But he doesn't say anything.

"I *thought* about the science project," I hear Luke murmur.

Matt walks back over, leans against the counter. "Dr. Misrati's really happy with the progress. The echo and EKG looked good. She wants to see us back in three months."

I squeeze Caleb again. Finally, some good news. Matt starts unloading the contents of the grocery bag. A gallon of milk. A package of chicken breasts, a bag of frozen vegetables. Cookies from the bakery—the kind I always ask him not to buy, because we can make the same thing for a fraction of the price. He's humming to himself, some tune I don't recognize. He's happy. He hums when he's happy.

He bends down, pulls out a pot and a pan from the bottom drawer, sets them on the stove. I give Caleb another kiss as I watch him. How is he so good at all this? How can he have so many balls in the air and not drop them?

I turn away from him, toward Ella, who's back on the couch. "You doing okay in there, sweetie?"

"Yeah, Mom."

I can hear Matt stop, his movements frozen. "Mom?" he says softly. I turn around, see the concern etched on his face.

I shrug, but I'm sure he can see the hurt in my eyes. "Guess today's the day."

He sets down the box of rice he's holding and wraps me in a hug, and all of a sudden the wall of emotion that's been building inside me threatens to come crashing down. I hear his heartbeat, feel his warmth. *What happened?* I want to ask. *Why didn't you tell me?*

I swallow, take a breath, pull away. "Can I help with dinner?"

"I got it." He turns around, adjusts the dial on the stove, then leans over and grabs a bottle of wine from the metal rack on the counter. I watch as he uncorks it, then pulls a glass out of the cabinet. Fills it halfway, carefully. He hands it to me. "Have a drink."

If only you knew how much I need one. I offer him a small smile and take a sip.

I get the kids' hands washed, strap the babies into their high chairs, one at either end of the table. Matt scoops stir-fry into bowls, sets them down in front of us at the table. He's chatting with Luke about something, and I'm making the right expressions, like I'm part of the conversation, but my mind is elsewhere. He looks so happy today. He's been happier than usual lately, hasn't he?

In my mind, I see the picture. The folder name. *Friends*. He wouldn't have agreed to anything, would he? But this is the Russians we're talking about. All he had to do was give them the slightest opening, the slightest indication he *might* consider it, and they'd pounce.

There's a tingle of adrenaline running through me, a sensation that's akin to disloyalty. That thought shouldn't even be crossing my mind. But it is. And sure, we need the money. What if he thought he was doing us a favor, providing another source of income? I try to remember the last time we argued about money. He came home with a Powerball ticket the next day, stuck it to the fridge under the corner of the magnetic dry-erase board. Wrote *I'm sorry* on the board, a little smiley face beside it.

What if they pitched him, and in his mind it was like winning the lotto? What if he doesn't even know he was pitched? What if they tricked him, if he thinks he's lining up some perfectly legitimate side job, something to help us make ends meet?

God, it all comes down to money. How I hate that it all comes down to money.

If I'd known, I'd have told him to be patient. It'll get better. So we're in the red right now. But Ella's almost in kindergarten. The twins will be out of the infant room soon; we'll save some money in the toddler room. We'll be in better shape next year. Much better. This is just a rough year. We knew it would be a rough year.

He's talking with Ella now, and her sweet little voice pierces through the fog in my mind. "I'm the only girl who didn't go to yoga," she says, the same thing she told me in the car.

Matt takes a bite of his food, chews carefully, watching her the whole time. I hold my breath, wait for his response. He finally swallows. "And how did that make you feel?"

She cocks her head to the side, just the slightest bit. "Okay, I guess. I got to sit in the front for story time."

I stare at her, my fork suspended in midair. She didn't care. She didn't need an apology. How does Matt always find the right words, always know exactly what to say?

Chase is sweeping the remnants of his dinner onto the floor with chubby, food-stained hands, and Caleb starts laughing, slamming his own hands down on his tray, sending stir-fry sauce flying. Matt and I push back our chairs at the same time, off to get the paper towels, to start wiping faces and hands covered in sauce and globs of food, a well-practiced routine at this point, the tandem cleanup.

Luke and Ella are excused from the table and tear off to the family room. When the twins are clean, we set them down in the family room, too, and start cleaning the kitchen. I pause midway through spooning leftovers into plastic containers to refill my wineglass. Matt glances over, shoots me a quizzical look as he wipes down the kitchen table.

"Rough day?"

"A bit," I answer, and I try to think of how I would have answered the question yesterday. How much more would I have said? It's not like I'm telling Matt anything classified. Anecdotes about coworkers, maybe. Hinting around at things, talking around issues, like the big information load today. But it's scraps. Nothing the Russians would actually care about. Nothing they should be paying for.

When the kitchen's finally looking clean, I throw my last paper towel into the trash and sink back down into my chair at the table. I look at the wall, the blank wall. How many years have we been in this place now, and it's still not decorated. From the family room I hear the television, the show about monster trucks, the one Luke likes. The faint melody of one of the twins' toys.

Matt comes over, pulls out his chair, sits down. He's watching me, concern on his face, waiting for me to speak. I need to say something. I need to know. The alternative is going directly to Peter, to security, telling them what I found. Allowing them to begin investigating my husband.

There must be an innocent explanation for all this. He hasn't been approached yet. He has been, but he doesn't realize it. He didn't agree to anything. He certainly didn't agree to anything. I drain the last of my wine. My hand is trembling as I set the glass back on the table.

I stare at him, no idea what I'm going to say. You'd think in all these hours I would have come up with something.

His expression looks totally open. He must know something big is coming. I'm sure he can read it all over my face. But he doesn't look nervous. Doesn't look anything. Just looks like Matt.

"How long have you been working for the Russians?" I say. The words are raw, unprocessed. But they're out now, so I watch his face closely, because his expression matters far more to me than his words. Will there be honest confusion? Indignation? Shame?

There's nothing. Absolutely no emotion crosses his face. It doesn't change. And that sends a bolt of fear through me.

He looks at me evenly. Waits a beat too long to answer, but just barely. "Twenty-two years."

CHAPTER

3

I FEEL LIKE THE FLOOR HAS DROPPED OUT FROM UNDER me. Like I'm falling, floating, suspended in some space where I'm watching myself, watching this unfold, but I'm not part of it, because it's not real. There's a ringing in my ears, a strange tinny sound.

I didn't expect a yes. In saying those words, accusing him of the worst possible transgression, I thought he might admit to something lesser. *I met with someone once,* he'd say. *But I swear, Viv, I'm not working for them.*

Or just righteous indignation. *How could you think such a thing?*

I never expected a yes.

Twenty-two years. I focus on the number because it's something tangible, something concrete. Thirty-seven minus twenty-two. He would have been fifteen at the time. In high school in Seattle.

That doesn't make any sense.

At fifteen he played JV baseball. Trumpet in the school band. Mowed lawns in his neighborhood for extra cash.

I don't understand.

Twenty-two years.

I put my fingertips to my temples. The ringing in my head won't stop. It's like something's there, some realization, only it's so awful I can't wrap my head around it, can't acknowledge it's real, because my whole world will come crashing down.

Twenty-two years.

My algorithm was supposed to lead me to a Russian agent handling sleepers in the U.S.

Twenty-two years.

And then a line from an old intel report runs through my head. An SVR asset familiar with the program. *They recruit kids as young as fifteen.*

I close my eyes and press harder against my temples.

Matt's not who he says he is.

My husband's a deep-cover Russian operative.

SERENDIPITOUS. That's how I always thought of the way we met. Like it was something that belonged in a movie.

It was the day I moved to Washington. A Monday morning in July. I'd driven up from Charlottesville at dawn, all of my possessions crammed into my Accord. I was double-parked, hazards flashing, in front of an old brick building laced with rickety fire escapes, close enough to the National Zoo to smell it. My new apartment. I was on my third trip from car to door, maneuvering a large cardboard box across the sidewalk, when I bumped into something.

Matt. He was dressed in jeans and a light blue button-down, sleeves rolled up to his elbows, and I'd just spilled his coffee all over him.

"Oh my God," I said, hurriedly placing the box down on the sidewalk. He was holding out a dripping coffee cup in one hand, its plastic lid now at his feet, and shaking off his other hand, sending droplets flying. There was a grimace on his face, like he was in pain. Several large brown splotches dampened the front of his shirt. "I'm so sorry."

I stood, helpless, with my hands extended toward him, like somehow my bare hands could do something in this situation.

He shook his arm a couple more times, then looked over at me. He smiled, a completely disarming smile, and I swear my heart stopped. Those perfect white teeth, the intense brown eyes that seemed to sparkle. "Don't worry about it."

"I can get you some paper towels. They're in a box somewhere. . . ."

"It's okay."

"Or a new shirt? I might have a T-shirt that would fit. . . ."

He looked down at his shirt and was quiet for a moment, as if considering. "It's okay, really. Thanks, though." He shot me another smile and then continued on his way. I stood in the middle of the sidewalk and watched him go, waited to see if he'd turn back, change his mind, all the while feeling an overwhelming sense of disappointment, a powerful urge to talk to him just a little bit longer.

Love at first sight, I later said.

The rest of the morning, I couldn't get him out of my mind. Those eyes, that smile. Later that afternoon, with my belongings safely in my apartment, I was exploring my new neighborhood when I saw him, leafing through books at a stand outside a small bookshop. Same guy, new shirt—a white one this time. Totally engrossed in the books. It's hard to describe the feeling that coursed through me—excitement and adrenaline and a strange sense of relief. I'd have another chance after all. I took a deep breath and walked over, stood beside him.

"Hi," I said with a smile.

He looked up at me, his expression blank at first, and then recognition dawned. He smiled back, revealing those perfect white teeth. "Well, hello."

"No boxes this time," I said, and then wanted to cringe. That's the best I could come up with?

The smile was still on his face. I cleared my throat. I'd never done this before. I nodded in the direction of the coffee shop next door. "Can I buy you a cup of coffee? I think I owe you one."

He looked at the awning of the coffee shop, then back at me. His expression was guarded. *Oh God, he has a girlfriend,* I thought. *I never should have asked. How embarrassing.*

"Or a shirt? I think I owe you that, too." I smiled, kept my voice light, joking. *Good thinking, Viv. You just gave him an out. He can laugh off the invitation.*

To my surprise, he cocked his head and said words that filled me with relief and anticipation and just plain giddiness. "Coffee sounds great."

We sat in the back corner of the coffee shop until dusk descended on the city. The conversation flowed so easily, never a lull. We had so much in common: We were our parents' only children, nonpracticing Catholics, apoliticals in a political city. We'd each traveled around Europe on our own, on a shoestring budget. Our mothers were teachers, we'd each had a golden retriever as a kid. The similarities were almost eerie. It seemed like fate that we'd met. He was funny and charming and smart and polite—and drop-dead gorgeous.

Then, with our coffee cups long since drained and an employee wiping down the tables around us, he looked at me, unbridled nervousness on his face, and asked if he could take me to dinner.

We went to a little Italian place around the corner, had heaping portions of house-made pasta and a carafe of wine and a dessert that neither of us had room for but ordered anyway, as an excuse to linger. We never ran out of things to say.

We talked until the restaurant closed, then he walked me home, taking my hand, and I'd never felt so warm, so light, so happy. He kissed me good night on the sidewalk outside my building, the same spot where I'd bumped into him that very day. And by the time I drifted off to sleep that night, I knew I'd met the man I was going to marry.

"VIV."

I blink and the memory is gone, like that. I hear strains of the monster truck theme song from the family room. Babbling. One toy banging another, plastic on plastic.

"Viv, look at me."

Now I see the fear. His face isn't blank anymore. His forehead's creased, those wavy lines he gets when he's worried, deeper now than I've ever seen.

He leans forward across the table, places a hand over mine. I pull away, clench my hands in my lap. He looks genuinely scared. "I love you."

I can't look at him right now, can't bear seeing the intensity in his eyes. I look down at the table. There's a smear of red marker, a small one. I stare at it. It's seeped into the grain of the wood, a scar from some art project, long ago. Why have I never noticed it?

"This doesn't change how I feel about you. I swear to God, Viv. You and the kids are everything to me."

The kids. Oh God, the kids. What will I tell them? I look up, over to the family room, even though I can't see them from here. I hear the twins playing. The older two are quiet, no doubt engrossed in the show.

"Who are you?" I whisper. I don't mean to whisper, but it's what comes out. Like I can't get my voice to work.

"It's me, Viv. I swear to God. You know me."

"Who are you?" I say again, my voice cracking this time.

He looks at me, eyes like saucers, forehead creased. I stare at him, try to read the expression in his eyes, but I'm not sure that I can. Could I ever?

"I was born in Volgograd." He speaks quietly, evenly. "My name was Alexander Lenkov."

Alexander Lenkov. This isn't real. This must be some

sort of dream. This is a movie, a novel. Not my life. I
focus on the table again. There's a constellation of little
indentations where one of the kids banged a fork.

"My parents were Mikhail and Natalia."

Mikhail and Natalia. Not Gary and Barb. My in-
laws, the people my kids call Granny and Gramps. I
stare at the grooves in the table, these tiny craters.

"They died in a car crash when I was thirteen. I didn't
have any other family. I was placed into state care, moved
a few months later to Moscow. I didn't realize what was
happening at the time, but I was placed into an SVR
program."

I feel a pang of sympathy, thinking of Matt as a
scared orphaned boy, and then it's quickly blunted by an
overwhelming sense of betrayal. I clasp my hands even
tighter.

"It was English-language immersion for two years.
When I was fifteen I was officially recruited. Given a new
identity."

"As Matthew Miller." Again, a whisper.

He nods, then leans forward, his eyes intense. "I
didn't have a choice, Viv."

I look down at the rings on my left hand. I think back
to those first conversations. Finding out we had so much
in common. It seemed so real. But it was all made up.
He'd created a childhood that never existed.

Suddenly everything is a lie. My life is a lie.

"My identity wasn't real, but everything else was," he
says, almost as if he can read my thoughts. "My feelings
are real. I swear they are."

The diamond on my left hand catches the light; I look at the facets, one by one. I'm vaguely aware of sounds from the family room. New sounds, louder sounds. Luke and Ella are arguing. I look up, away from my ring, and Matt's watching me, but his head is craned just enough that I know he's listening to the kids.

"Work it out, you two," he calls without taking his eyes off me.

We stare at each other, both listening to the kids. The argument intensifies, and Matt pushes back from the table, goes in to referee. I hear snippets, the kids each trying to argue their side to Matt, his admonishments to compromise. There's a fuzzy feeling in my head. The wine, maybe.

Matt comes back holding Caleb and sits down. Caleb grins at me, sticks a drooly fist in his mouth. I can't force my face into a smile, so I just look back at Matt.

"Who's the real Matt Miller?" I ask. I think of the birth certificate buried deep in our fireproof safe. The Social Security card, the passport.

"I don't know."

"What about Barb and Gary?" I say. I picture the two of them. The matronly woman, the pastel-colored tops that always remind me of something my grandmother would have worn. The man with the belly that protrudes over his belt, his shirt always tucked in, his socks always white.

"Others like me," he says.

Chase starts crying, a distraction that's strangely welcome. I stand up from the table and walk to the family room. He's on the floor near the couch where Luke and

Ella sit, and I can see the outline of a little blue ball wedged underneath. I reach for it, then pick him up, shift him onto my hip. He's quieter now, just little whimpers, the ball tight in his grasp.

My thoughts are a jumbled mess. How could I have been so easily duped? Especially when it comes to Barb and Gary. There were red flags, certainly. I didn't meet them until the wedding. We've only been out to Seattle once, and they haven't visited us. There were reasons, of course. Ones that made sense at the time, that seem so flimsy now. Barb's afraid to fly. We didn't have enough vacation days. We've had one infant after another, and who wants to risk a screaming baby on a cross-country flight?

I felt guilty about it. Seeing my parents so often, his barely at all. I even apologized. "Life has a habit of getting in the way," he said with a smile. A somewhat sad smile, sure, but he never seemed all that bothered by it. I suggested video chats, but they weren't comfortable with the technology, were happy just talking on the phone every couple of weeks. Matt seemed fine with it, too.

And I never pushed it. Did I not push it because secretly I was glad? Glad that we didn't have to alternate Christmases, that we didn't have to bust our budget to fly the family across the country on a regular basis, that I didn't have overbearing in-laws. Maybe even glad that Matt's affections weren't split. That his entire focus could be on the kids and me.

I walk back into the kitchen and sit down at the table with Chase on my lap. "What about all those people at our wedding?" There were at least a couple dozen other relatives there. Aunts, uncles, cousins.

"Same."

Impossible. I shake my head, like it could put all these random facts into some semblance of order. Something that makes sense. I've met upwards of twenty-five sleepers. How many do the Russians have here? Far more than we thought.

Dmitri the Dangle. Suddenly he's all I can think about. He'd said there were dozens of sleeper cells in the U.S. He told us so much that didn't make sense, that made us sure he was a dangle. That the handlers carried the identities of the sleepers on themselves, at all times, when we knew they were stored electronically. The decryption code that didn't match the one we had from other sources. And the outrageous claims. That sleepers had infiltrated the government, were slowly working their way to the top. That there were dozens of cells buried here in the States, when we thought there were no more than a few.

That one wasn't so outrageous after all, was it? And then another realization strikes me.

"You're a spy," I say quietly. I'd been so focused on the lie, on the fact that he wasn't who he said he was, that I hadn't fully comprehended the obvious.

"I don't want to be. I want nothing more than to actually *be* Matt Miller from Seattle. To be free from their grip."

There's a heavy feeling in my chest, like I can barely catch my breath.

"But I'm trapped." He looks so sincere, so pitiful. Of

course he's trapped. It's not like he can just quit. They have too much invested in him.

Chase is squirming on my lap, struggling to break away. I set him down on the floor, and he gets on all fours and starts to crawl away, happy little shrieks trailing behind him.

"You lied to me."

"I didn't have a choice. You, of all people, should understand—"

"Don't you *dare*," I say, because I know where he's headed.

I picture us, so long ago, the little table in the corner of the coffee shop, oversize mugs in front of us. "What do you do for work?" he asked.

"I just finished up grad school," I said, hoping that would suffice, knowing it wouldn't.

"Do you have a job lined up?"

I nodded. Took a sip of coffee. Stalled.

"Doing what?" he pressed.

I looked down at my mug, the little puffs of steam that were rising from it. "Consulting. A small firm," I said, the lie tasting bitter. But he was a stranger, and I wasn't about to tell a stranger I had been hired by the CIA. "How about you?" I said, and thankfully the conversation turned to software engineering.

"It's not the same at all," I say now. "You've had ten years. Ten *years*."

"I know," he says, contrite.

Now Caleb's squirming, too. Squirming and smiling at me, no doubt wondering why I won't smile back. He stretches his arms out toward me, and Matt holds him up and out over the table at the same time I reach for him. He settles into my lap, calm.

"Do you do that kind of thing? Pretend to be someone's relative?" I ask. I don't know why it matters. Why that, of all things, is what I want to know.

He shakes his head. "They wouldn't want me taking a risk like that."

Of course they wouldn't. He's more valuable than that, isn't he? Because he's married to me. And I work for the CIA.

God, the Russians really scored big with him. They must be thrilled. How lucky is that, a deep-cover spy married to a CIA counterintelligence analyst?

And then a jolt of cold runs through me like electricity.

I picture the two of us, in my apartment a few weeks after we'd met. Sitting across from each other at the folding table in the corner of the studio, pizza on paper plates in front of us. "I haven't been completely honest with you," I said, wringing my hands, worried how he'd react to my admission of untruthfulness but relieved to be clearing the air, putting myself in a position where I wouldn't have to lie to this man ever again. "I work for the CIA." I remember his face clearly, unchanged at first, like the news didn't surprise him. Then something flickered in his eyes, and I thought the information just took a moment too long to register.

But it didn't, did it? He knew all along.

My chest is tight. I close my eyes, and I see myself in the grad school auditorium, the presentation from the CIA recruiter. The realization that *this* is what I could do with my life, a way to make a difference in the world, to serve my country, to make my family proud. Time flashes forward, past the application process, the background investigation, the battery of evaluations. To the day, a year later, after I'd all but given up, when I got the letter in the mail, generic government return address. Plain white paper, no letterhead. Just a start date, salary, directions. And the office to which I'd been assigned: the Counterintelligence Center.

That was two weeks before I moved to Washington. And met Matt.

My breath is coming fast now. In my head I'm back in that coffee shop, sitting in that corner, reliving our first conversation, the one where we discovered how similar we were. He didn't just play along, create a persona as he went. *He* was the first to say he was raised Catholic, that his mom was a teacher, that he had a golden retriever. He said it because he already knew it about me.

I raise a hand to my mouth and am vaguely aware it's shaking.

The Russians weren't lucky. They were thorough. Everything was intentional, planned. It wasn't serendipitous at all.

I was his target.

CHAPTER
4

MATT LEANS FORWARD AGAIN, THE CREASES DEEPER, THE eyes wider. I'm convinced he can read my thoughts, that he knows the truth that just dawned on me. "I swear everything I feel for you and the kids is real. I swear to God, Viv."

I've taken classes in detecting deception, and I'm vaguely aware of the fact that he's showing none of the signs. He's telling the truth.

But then, wouldn't he have received the same training? More of it, probably. Wouldn't he know how to convincingly lie?

Hasn't he been doing it for twenty-two years?

Caleb's chewing on my finger, tiny sharp teeth digging into my skin. The pain is strangely welcome, and I don't stop it, because it's the only thing that feels real right now.

"The day we met . . . ," I say. And I can't continue. I can't make myself finish the thought, ask what I want to ask, what I already know deep down. It's too much.

He takes a moment to respond. "I'd been watching

you all morning. When I saw you with that box, I walked in front of you." He looks guilty when he says it. At least he looks guilty.

I think of how many times I've told the story of our first meeting. How many times he's told it. How we've each laughed in all the right places, jumped in with our own perspectives.

It was all a lie.

"You were my target," he says, and my breath catches in my throat. The fact that he'd say it—that's proof he's being honest. It has to be proof. But that's the wife in me speaking, isn't it? The counterintelligence analyst in me says he's telling me what I already know. The oldest trick in the book, a way to try to make himself seem more truthful than he really is.

"But then I fell in love with you," he says. "I fell deeply, deeply in love with you."

He looks sincere. And of course he loves me. You don't spend a decade married to someone you don't love. I shake my head. I don't know what to believe anymore. And the thought that he might actually *not* love me is more than I can wrap my head around.

"At first I couldn't get over how lucky I was. It wasn't until much later I realized how awful it is, that our relationship is built on a lie. One that I can't share, because if I do, everything will come crashing—"

He stops abruptly and focuses his attention on a spot behind me. I turn and see Luke standing silent in the doorway. I wonder how long he's been there. What he's heard. He looks from Matt to me, his eyes serious, reminding me so much of his father's.

"Are you fighting?" he asks in a small voice.

"No, sweetie," I say. And my heart breaks for him, though my mind can't fully process why. "We're just having a grown-up conversation."

He says nothing, just watches us, and for the first time I realize I can't read his expression, can't tell what he's thinking. He's Matt's son, he's always going to be Matt's son. Maybe I'll never know what he's thinking, whether he's telling me the truth. I have an unsettling sense that my whole life is slipping through my fingers and I'm powerless to stop it.

"Dad, can we play catch now?" he asks.

"Not now, buddy. I'm talking with Mom."

"But you promised."

"Buddy, I—"

"Go," I say, interrupting him. It's what I need now. Him gone. Time to think. I stare at him evenly, then add more quietly, "You wouldn't want to *lie* to him."

A wounded expression crosses his face. But that's what I intended, right? Let him be hurt. It's nothing compared to the hurt I feel.

And I stare evenly back. Suddenly I'm angry at him. So angry. He betrayed my trust. Lied to me, for a decade.

He looks like he's about to say something, then stops. Still has the hurt expression on his face. He stands up wordlessly, walks around the table, over to where I sit. I continue staring straight ahead, at the wall now. He hesitates next to me, then puts a hand on my shoulder. A shiver runs through me at his touch.

"We'll talk about all this," he says. His hand stays on my shoulder a moment longer, and then he drops it, follows Luke out of the room. I stay at the table, staring straight ahead, and I listen to them put on jackets, round up mitts and a ball, walk outside. I wait until the door shuts behind them, then I get up, shift Caleb to my hip, and walk over to the sink. I watch them out the window. Father and son, tossing a baseball back and forth in our backyard, dusk settling around them. A perfect snapshot of America. Only one of the two isn't American.

And then it dawns on me, hits me with such force I grip the edge of the sink to steady myself. This isn't just betrayal. This isn't something that's going to be solved by a fight or a conversation or anything like that. It's not solvable, period. I need to turn him in. He's a Russian spy, and I need to turn him in. The anger seems to melt away, morph into a river of despair.

My gaze drifts to my phone, sitting on the counter. The one that holds an endless chain of texts with Matt, countless pictures of our family, our life together. I should be picking it up. I should be calling Agency security right now. The FBI. Omar.

I look back outside. He's smiling at Luke as he winds an arm back, slowly, and lets the ball fly. So relaxed, so comfortable. And it's wrong, all of this is wrong, because sleepers run. They try to get on planes back home before the authorities can stop them.

But Matt's not running. He's not going anywhere.

Caleb yawns, and I shift him in my arms so he can lay his head against my chest. He snuggles down and lets out a little sigh.

I continue to watch Matt through the window. I see him show Luke how to keep legs loose and bouncy, bring the arm back just so. He looks completely normal.

He finally casts a glance back at the house, at the kitchen window, right at me, like he knew I'd be there. I meet his gaze and hold it until he turns away, back toward the game. Then I look at the cellphone again. He knows I'm in here, alone, with the phone. A sleeper wouldn't let that happen. A sleeper would protect himself. All the more proof this is Matt. My husband, the man I love. Someone who'd never run.

We'll talk about all this. His words ring in my head. That's what I need, isn't it? I need to hear what he has to say. And then I have to turn him in.

I turn away from the phone. I can't pick it up. Not now. Not until I've talked to him.

And he knows that, doesn't he?

The thought comes unbidden and lodges itself in my mind. He knows me. He knows me better than anyone. What if he's not running because he knows I wouldn't pick up the phone right now, wouldn't turn him in?

I feel numb. This can't be happening.

I shake my head and walk out of the room, away from the window, away from the phone. I step into the family room. Ella's curled up on the couch with a coloring book, crayons splayed on the cushions. I set Caleb down on the floor, next to his toys, and sink down onto the couch beside her. I feel her forehead, warmer now. She brushes my hand away and I wrap my arms around her.

"Stop, Mom." She half-heartedly pushes me away, then stops and acquiesces, crayon poised in midair.

I kiss the top of her head, the hair that smells like baby shampoo. Her words from earlier are echoing in my head. *Where's Daddy?* And then another phrase, one she never uttered but that I can imagine her saying nonetheless. *Why did Daddy go away?*

Caleb's entertaining himself on the floor, banging the lid of his shape sorter against the base, a steady rhythm. Chase has crawled over and is gnawing on one of his stacking cups. They're too young to even remember this, aren't they? The normalcy of our lives now. I watch Ella scribble, the thick crayons clasped tight in her fist, a look of fierce concentration on her face, and tears sting my eyelids. God, how I wish I could protect all of them from this.

I hear the back door open, Matt's and Luke's voices midconversation, something about Little League. Matt's going to coach this year. *Was* going to coach. I stand before the tears well any further.

"Hi," he says to me when he walks into the room. He looks hesitant, uncertain.

"I'll go bathe the twins," I say, avoiding his gaze. I scoop them up, one in each arm, turning my back to Matt. I bring them up to the bathroom, run the water, pour in the capful of bubbles, let the water fill while I undress them, peeling off clothes and diapers. I set Chase in the water, then Caleb, absentmindedly run the washcloth over their soft skin, dimpled thighs and bottoms, chubby cheeks, double chins. It seems like just yesterday they were tiny newborns, preemies, that we were bringing them to the doctor for weight checks. Where did the time go?

Matt's voice drifts up from the family room. A story, one I know I've read to the kids but can't place right now. I hear Ella giggle.

I lean back on my heels and watch the twins play. Chase is grabbing the edge of the tub, pulling himself up, laughing gleefully. Caleb's sitting quietly, mesmerized, marveling at the splash as his little hands hit the water again and again. We only bathe them when we're both home, when one of us can focus on the babies and one on the older kids. It'd be so much harder without Matt.

Everything would be so much harder.

I get the twins toweled off and in their pajamas, and I hear Matt in the next room getting Ella ready for bed.

"What about my bath?" she says.

"No bath tonight, princess," he says.

"But I want a bath."

When has she ever wanted a bath? "Tomorrow night," he says.

Tomorrow night. Will he be around tomorrow night? I try to picture bathing all the kids myself, somehow entertaining the twins while I wash Ella, getting them all into bed, alone. The thought seems overwhelming.

I put Caleb in one crib, Chase in the other, lay kisses on their cheeks, breathe in their sweet smell. I turn the night-light on and the overhead light off and step into Ella's room, the one that was going to be sunshine-themed. I had big plans for a mural, a painted ceiling fan, the works. Then work got busy. Now it's a yellow room. Bare yellow walls, yellow throw rug. That's as far as I got.

She's tucked into the twin-size bed, Matt perched beside her, holding a hardcover book angled so she can look at the pictures. It's the one about the princess fire-fighter, the one she's picked every night for the past week and a half.

She turns to look at me, her eyelids heavy. I give her a smile and stand in the doorway, watching them. Matt's doing the voices he always does, and Ella laughs, that little high-pitched giggle. Everything looks so normal, and it hurts to see it. She has no idea. No idea that everything's about to change.

Matt finishes the book, kisses her goodnight, and gives me a long look as he stands. I move over to her bedside and kneel down. I kiss her forehead, so warm against my lips. "Sleep tight, sweetheart."

Her little arms wrap around my neck, holding me close against her. "I love you, Mommy."

Mommy. I feel like I might melt, like the emotion I've barely been holding in check might come crashing down. "I love you, too, sweetie."

I turn off her light and step out into the hallway. Matt's there, near the doorway of Luke's room. "I gave him an extra half hour to read if he got tucked in early," he says quietly. "Figured we could use the time to talk."

I nod and walk past him into Luke's room, all blues and baseball and soccer. He's sitting up in bed, a stack of books beside him. He looks so grown-up right now. I kiss the top of his head and feel another pull in my chest. It's going to be hardest on him, isn't it? Of all the kids, it's going to be hardest on him.

I walk back down into the family room. The house has that eerie quiet after it goes so quickly from chaos to calm. Matt's in the kitchen, washing dishes in the sink. I start picking up, putting the scattered assortment of brightly colored plastic toys back into their bin, taking apart the wooden tracks of Ella's train set, piece by piece. We're alone now, just the two of us. We can talk.

Why does it matter? I have to turn him in, regardless of what he says. I know that, deep down. But there's a part of me that doesn't believe it. That believes there's a way out of this.

I look up at him, still at the sink, now drying a pan with a dish towel. I stop breaking down the train tracks and sit back on my heels. I realize I don't even know where to begin. "What kind of information do you give them?" I finally ask.

His hands still, and then he looks up. "Nothing of value. Atmospherics. If you're stressed at work, or happy. That kind of thing."

"You must give them more than that." I think back to what I might have said over the years that I shouldn't have, and my mind settles on my coworkers. There's a sinking feeling in my chest. "Oh God. Marta. Trey. You're the reason they were pitched, aren't you? *We* are the reason they were pitched."

His face registers surprise, then confusion. "No."

I'm frantically turning over what I've said to him. That Marta's always the first to suggest an office happy hour, those awkward ones where a dozen people sit in the conference room for a half hour in the afternoon, bags of chips, sometimes a plate of cookies, a few bottles of wine. That she usually brings two and they're always gone by the end of the day, even though half the office doesn't drink and she's the only one who ever refills her little plastic cup. And the bottle of whiskey in her bottom drawer—I've told him about that, too. The time I saw her splash some into her coffee.

And Trey. I distinctly remember a conversation, years ago. "He calls Sebastian his 'roommate,'" I said to Matt, using air quotes and rolling my eyes. "Why doesn't he just admit the truth? It's not like any of us would care."

"I told you those things in confidence," I whisper now, filled with an overwhelming sense of betrayal.

"Viv, I swear. I never breathed a word of it."

"They were pitched, Matt. I'm supposed to believe that's a *coincidence*?"

"Look, I don't know anything about that. But I promise you I've never said anything about them."

I stare at him. He seems sincere. But I don't know what to believe anymore. I shake my head, look down at the train tracks, continue pulling the pieces apart. I hear him go back to drying dishes, putting them away in the cabinets where they belong.

We're quiet for a few minutes, until he speaks again. "I'm telling you the truth, Viv. I haven't told them anything useful, and it doesn't seem to bother them. I think I'm considered a win already."

"Because you're married to me."

"Yeah." He looks embarrassed.

I toss the last of the train tracks into the bin and close the lid, then slide it over against the wall. That's our family room organization. Clear plastic bins of toys, stacked against a wall. "Are you loyal to . . . Russia?" The words sound so strange coming out of my mouth.

"I'm loyal to you."

I think of the American flag that hangs outside, the Fourth of July parades, the sparklers. Matt taking off his cap, hand over heart as he mouths the words to the

National Anthem at baseball games. The time I heard him telling Luke how lucky we are to live in the greatest country in the world. "Russia or America?"

"America. Of course America. You know me, Viv. You know what I believe in."

"Do I?"

"I was a kid. An orphan. I had no choice."

"You always have a choice."

"Not in Russia."

I'm quiet. "Your loyalty. It was to Russia once."

"Sure. At first I believed in what I was doing. I was Russian, and I was brainwashed. But living here . . . seeing the truth . . ."

I catch sight of a sippy cup wedged behind the toy kitchen and reach for it. "Why didn't you tell me?"

"How could I?"

"You've had ten years. Any single day in the past ten years. *Viv, there's something I need to tell you.* And you just say it."

He walks over, perches on the armrest of the couch. The dish towel's slung over his shoulder. "I've wanted to. God, Viv, you don't think I've wanted to? I've come close so many times. But then what? Then I see the look in your eyes, the one I'm seeing now. Betrayed, hurt beyond belief. I dreaded that. And I was terrified. What would you do? Take the kids and run? I couldn't lose you. I couldn't lose the kids. You and the kids"—his voice cracks—"are everything to me. Everything."

I say nothing. Finally he speaks again. "I love you, Vivian." I stare at him, that look on his face that seems so sincere, and in my mind it's ten years ago. A month after we'd met, a month of seeing each other practically every day. He was walking me home after dark; I can see us on the street outside my apartment, the trees on either side rustling in the breeze, the streetlights casting a soft glow. His arm was around my waist, our gait slow and in sync. He'd just laughed at something I said, something I've long since forgotten. "I love you, Viv," he said, and then he went quiet. Both of us did. The night was suddenly so still. I saw the color creep to his cheeks. He hadn't meant to say it. It had just slipped out, and that made it all the more tender, because it was unfiltered, and he must have really meant it. I thought sure he'd try to backtrack. *I love your jokes, Viv. I love spending time with you.* Something like that. But he didn't. He stopped, faced me, pulled me close. "I love you, Vivian. I really do."

I look down now. I'm holding the sippy cup so tightly my knuckles are white. I can barely choke out the next words. "How could you have brought kids into this?"

"Because I wanted a life with you. I wanted you to have everything you'd ever dreamed of."

"But you had to have known that one day—"

"No," he interrupts. His voice is firm. "I didn't. I truly believed that I could do this until you retired. Until I retired. And then I could be free from them."

I'm quiet. He's quiet. The whole house is unnervingly quiet.

"They'd have let me stay," he says softly. "It's happened before. I could've lived out the rest of my life and died and no one would've ever known."

Could've. Would've. The tense is jarring. He knows we can't just pretend this didn't happen, that I didn't learn about this. He knows I have to turn him in.

He gives me a weak smile. "If only you weren't so good at your job."

The words make my stomach turn. If I hadn't pushed for that algorithm, none of this would have happened. I bring the sippy cup into the kitchen, unscrew the top, put both pieces on the top rack of the dishwasher. He's watching me, silent. I close the dishwasher and lean on the counter.

He walks into the kitchen and stands behind me. Tentatively, like he's not sure what I'll do, how I'll react. I'm not sure, either. But I don't move. I let him take a step closer, put his hands on my shoulders, slide them down to my hips, until he's holding me close. My body softens into the familiar embrace, and when I squeeze my eyes shut, a single tear escapes from each one.

In my mind I'm back on that street outside my apartment. Leaning into his kiss, pressing against him, wanting more. Stumbling into the building, up the stairs. Feeling his touch, seeing the look in his eyes, the hunger that was there. And afterward, lying together on tangled sheets, intertwined. Waking up in his arms, watching as his eyes opened and he took in my presence; the slow smile that spread across his face. All of that was real. It had to be.

"What am I supposed to do now?" I say quietly. A rhetorical question, really. Voiced to my best friend, the one I've always turned to, relied on. My partner. My rock.

Or maybe it's a lifeline. *Get me out of this. Tell me what to do to make this all disappear.*

"There's only one thing you can do." He buries his head in the space between my neck and shoulder, and I feel the scratch of his stubble. A shiver runs through me. "Turn me in."

CHAPTER

5

THE WORDS DON'T SEEM REAL AT FIRST. HE'S SUPPOSED to be trying to talk me out of it. But instead there's just silence, a gaping hole where that conversation should have been. And I feel like I'm dangling over the edge of it, about to lose everything.

And then something changes in me. Like a switch, flipped. I swivel around to face him. He doesn't move back, stays close to me, close enough that I can breathe in his scent, feel his warmth. "There has to be another way," I say. He shouldn't be admitting defeat, throwing in the towel.

He moves away, and I feel a rush of cold air where he had been standing. He walks over to the cabinet, pulls out a wineglass, sets it down beside mine. I watch him, my mind trying to sort through what's happening. He pours wine into each glass, then hands me mine. "There's not."

"There's always—"

"There's not, Viv. Trust me. I've thought through

everything." He picks up his glass and takes a long sip. "I've had plenty of time to think about it. About what to do if this day ever came."

I stare down at my own glass. I shouldn't drink this. I need my head as clear as possible right now. But at the same time, the thought of drinking enough to make all of this disappear is strangely attractive.

"What else do you want to know?" he asks quietly. He's already moving on. That part of the conversation is done, in his mind. Turn him in. That's what I'm supposed to do. He doesn't have a plan. A way to get us out of this.

It's not done, in my mind. Not at all. I shake my head stubbornly, and then I consider his question. What else do I want to know? *I want to know if you're being completely honest with me. If I can trust you, one hundred percent. If we're really on the same team.* I look up and meet his eye. "Everything."

He nods, like he expected the answer. Swirls the wine around in his glass, then sets it down and leans back against the counter. "I have a handler. His name's Yury Yakov."

I keep my face impassive. "Tell me about him."

"He splits time between Russia and the U.S. He's the only other person I know involved in this. It's so heavily compartmented—"

"How do you communicate?"

"Dead drops."

"Where?"

"Northwest D.C. Our old neighborhood."

"Where *exactly*?"

"You know that bank on the corner with the domed roof? There's a little courtyard around the side, two benches. It's the one on the right, the one that faces the door. The drop spot is under the bench, on the right side."

That is awfully specific. And it isn't all information I already know. This is new. Valuable. "How often do you meet?"

"Whenever one of us signals."

"On average."

"Once every two or three months."

Every two or three months? I swallow past a lump in my throat. We'd always assumed handlers spent most of their time in Russia, meeting sleepers in the U.S. infrequently—every year or two—or in third countries. Yury has only a limited record of travel to the U.S., short trips. That means he's here under an assumed identity, doesn't it?

"How do you signal?" I ask.

"Chalk on the bench. Just like the movies." He gives a weak smile.

I could press the issue. I could find out if there's special chalk, where exactly the mark is made, what it looks like. And that would be enough information to lure Yury there, find him, arrest him.

Or, the CI analyst in me says, *he'd play me, give me instructions on how to signal that he'd been compromised. How to ensure Yury would disappear.* My throat tightens.

"What do you leave? What do you pick up?"

"Encrypted flash drives."

"How do you decrypt?"

"You know the storage area behind our stairs? There's a false floorboard. A laptop's inside."

The answers are coming fast, no signs of deception. I try to ignore the fact that the laptop is hidden in our home and think of what to ask next. "And you don't tell him anything I tell you?"

He shakes his head. "I swear, Viv, I don't."

"You've never mentioned Marta, or Trey?"

"Never."

I look down at my wine. I believe him. I do. But I don't know whether that makes sense. I look back up. "Tell me what you know about the program."

"You probably know more than I do, really. It's hierarchical, self-contained. I only know Yury. Beyond that, I have no idea."

I swirl the wine around in my glass and watch it cling to the sides. I picture myself at my desk, the intelligence gaps I have, the things I always wish I knew. Then I look back up. "How do you get in touch with Moscow? Like if something happened to Yury. Who would you contact? How?"

"I wouldn't. Not for a year. We're under strict instructions not to. For our own safety. SVR moles or whatever. I'm supposed to just hang tight, wait until someone steps into Yury's place and makes contact with me."

That's what I was afraid of. An answer—a program design—that makes finding handlers and ringleaders nearly impossible. But something he said is sticking in my head. Something new. *A year.*

"What happens after a year?"

"I get back in touch."

"How?"

"There's an email address. I'd go to another state, create a new account. . . . There's a whole list of protocols."

It makes sense, what he's saying. I always wondered what would happen if the replacement handler couldn't access the names of the five agents. Turns out the sleepers themselves would get back in touch.

"I'm sorry I don't know more. But I think it's intentional. So that if any one agent goes rogue, the program stays intact. . . ." He trails off, shrugs, a helpless look on his face.

Of course it's intentional. I know that, don't I? He gave me as much as I could possibly expect him to know. Without hesitation, without any sign of deception.

He drains the last of his wine and sets the glass down on the counter. "Anything else?"

I look at the defeat on his face, the look of a man who's powerless to help. Matt's never powerless. He's the one who can fix anything, solve any problem, *do* anything. I shake my head. "I don't know."

He gives me a long look, then casts his eyes to the floor, shrugs. "Then let's just get some sleep."

I follow him up to our bedroom, our footsteps heavier than usual on the stairs. I think of the laptop hidden in our storage area. An SVR laptop, in my home. One my husband uses to exchange secret messages with his Russian handlers.

In our room, Matt heads for the closet; I walk the other way, toward the bathroom. I close the bathroom door and stand silently, alone for the first time, then sink down to the floor and sit with my back against the door.

I'm drained. Exhausted. Overwhelmed. The tears should come. The emotion that's building inside me should be crashing down. But it's not. I just sit and blink into space, my mind numb.

Finally I make myself stand. I brush my teeth and wash my face, and I come out of the bathroom, ready to turn the cramped space over to Matt so he can get ready for the night. But when I come out, I don't see him. Not in the closet, not in our bed. Where is he? I walk down the hall, and then I see him. He's standing in the doorway of Luke's room. I see just his profile, but it's all I need to see. There are tears streaming down his cheeks.

It shocks me to the core. In the ten years I've known him, it's the first time I've seen him cry.

IN BED, WE LIE SILENTLY. I listen to Matt's breathing, even but fast, and I know he's awake. I blink again into the darkness, my mind struggling to craft thoughts into words. There has to be another way out. Turning him in can't be the only option.

I roll on my side, face him. There's enough light from the night-light in the hallway to see his face. "You could quit."

He turns his head toward me. "You know I can't do that."

"Why? Maybe you—"

"They'd probably kill me. Or at the least destroy me."

I watch his face carefully, the creases in his forehead, the eyes that look like they're processing the suggestion, sorting through the consequences.

He turns his head back so that he's looking up at the ceiling. "Matt Miller doesn't exist without the SVR. If they take away my identity, where would I go? How would I live?"

I roll to my back, look up at the ceiling, too. "Then we could go to the FBI." To Omar. Our friend, the man who wanted to allow sleepers to come out of the shadows and exchange information for immunity.

"And say what?"

"Tell them who you are. Give them information. Make a deal." Even as I say them, the words sound hollow. The Bureau rejected Omar's plan, swiftly and thoroughly. What's to say they'd agree?

"I don't have enough to give. I have nothing valuable to trade."

"The Agency, then. You could offer to be a double."

"Now? Look at the timing. Two decades of silence, and then I offer to work as a double now, when you're closing in on me? They'd never believe I'm sincere." He turns to face me. "Besides, I always said I'd never do that. If it were just me, fine. But I wouldn't put you and the kids in danger like that. It's too much of a risk."

My heart aches. "Then I'll quit. If you weren't married to a CIA officer—"

"They know you wouldn't. They know about our financial situation."

There's a strange feeling swirling around inside me, thinking of the Russians knowing the details of our lives, of our vulnerabilities. Of just how trapped we are. I try to ignore it, focus on the issue at hand. "Then I'll get myself fired."

"They'll see through it. And anyway, then what? What if they order me to leave you?"

Our bedroom door creaks the smallest bit, and I look up to see Ella standing there, framed in the light from the hallway, hugging her ratty stuffed dragon close to her chest. "Can I come sleep in your bed?" she asks, then sniffles. She's looking to Matt for an answer, but I'm the one who responds.

"Sure, sweetie." Of course she can. She's sick, isn't she? And I've been so preoccupied with Matt, I haven't paid her any attention, provided any comfort.

She climbs up, scoots in between us. Settles herself in, pulls the sheet up to her chin, adjusts it under the dragon's chin, too. And then the room is quiet again. I stare at the ceiling, alone with my fears. I know Matt is doing the same. How could either of us sleep right now?

I feel Ella's warmth beside me. I hear her breathing slow down, become softer. I look over at her, the little mouth open, the halo of baby-fine hair. She rustles in her sleep, sighs softly. I look away, back at the ceiling. I almost can't bring myself to say the words, but I have to. "What if we all go to Russia?" I whisper.

"I couldn't do that to you and the kids," he answers quietly. "You'd never see your parents again. None of you know Russian. The education there . . . the opportunities . . . and Caleb. The medical care, the surgeries . . . He wouldn't have the same life there."

We lapse back into silence. I feel tears stinging my eyes at the helplessness of it all. How is there no other solution? How is this our only option?

"They'll probably start an investigation," he finally

says. I roll back on my side so that I'm facing him again, looking at him over Ella, sandwiched between us. He turns to face me, too. "When you tell security. They'll watch my comms. I don't know how long. But we won't be able to breathe another word of this. Anywhere, anytime."

I picture our house bugged, a room full of agents listening to every word of what we say to the kids, to each other. All of it being transcribed, analysts like myself poring over every word. For how long? Weeks? Months, even?

"Never, ever admit that you told me," he goes on. "You need to be there for the kids."

My mind flashes back to those warning screens on Athena, the nondisclosure agreements I've signed. That was classified information. Highly classified, compartmented information. And I shared it.

"Promise me you won't admit it," he says, an urgency in his voice.

My throat feels unbearably tight. "I promise," I whisper.

I see the relief on his face. "And I'll never tell, either, Viv. I swear. I'd never do that to you."

MATT FALLS ASLEEP. I don't know how, because I can't. I watch the minutes pass in fluorescent green until I can't take it any longer. I go downstairs, the house dark, filled with a heavy silence that seems so lonely. I turn on the television, filling the room with a flickering bluish glow, tune to some mindless reality show, bikini-clad women and shirtless men, drinking, fighting. I finally realize I'm not catching a word and shut it off. The blackness returns.

I have to turn him in. We both know it. It's the only way. I try to picture myself doing it. Sitting down with security, or with Peter or Bert, and telling them what I found. It seems impossible. Traitorous. This is Matt, the love of my life. And then there's our kids. I try to imagine telling them Matt's gone away, that he's in jail, that he lied, wasn't who he said he was. And later, when they learn that I'm the reason he was sent away, that they grew up without a father.

I hear Matt's alarm at six-thirty. The shower turns on a minute later, like any other morning, like this was all a dream. I go upstairs and dress, my favorite pantsuit. I put on some makeup, run a comb through my hair. Matt comes out of the shower, a towel around his waist, and kisses the top of my head, like he does every morning. I smell his soap, watch him in the mirror as he moves on, over to the closet.

"Ella's burning up," he says.

I go to the bed, put my hand against her forehead. "Yeah, she is." Guilt runs through me; I hadn't even thought to check.

"I'll work from home. Can you drop the twins off on your way in?"

"Of course."

I watch him in the mirror and an unsettled feeling comes over me, like maybe this *was* all a dream. How can he act like everything's normal, when our lives are about to fall spectacularly apart?

The rest of the morning is our usual chaos. We get the twins and Luke dressed and fed, our tag team routine. I catch myself looking at him more than I should, like one of these times he'll be a different person. But he's not. He's Matt. The man I love.

I bring Ella down to the couch, get her settled under a blanket, her crayons and coloring book at her side. I kiss her goodbye, kiss Luke goodbye. Then I pick up Caleb and Matt picks up Chase, and wordlessly we get the twins into their car seats. When they're all strapped in, we stand awkwardly together in the driveway, just the two of us.

I'm going to do this, aren't I? There's no other choice. I wanted to come up with something, some way out. But there's no way out. I need to say something to him, but I can't find the words.

He smiles at me sadly, almost as if he can read my thoughts. "It's okay, Viv."

"I don't see another way," I say, my voice heavy with apology. "I thought about it all last night. . . ."

"I know."

"If it were just you and me, then going—*there*—would be an option. But the kids—and Caleb especially . . ."

"I know. It's okay, Viv. Really." He hesitates, and I can tell he wants to say something else. He opens his mouth, then closes it again.

"What is it?"

"It's just . . ." He trails off, starts wringing his hands. "Money'll be tight," he finally says. And then he lets out a choking sob, one that sends terror into me, because Matt doesn't lose control like this. I move toward him, wrap my arms around his waist, my cheek against his chest. I feel his arms encircle me, that embrace that's always felt so safe, so much like home. "God, I'm sorry, Viv. What have I done? What's this going to do to the kids?"

I don't know how to respond. Couldn't get my mouth to work, even if I did.

He pulls away and takes a deep breath. "I just wish none of this had happened." A single tear slides down one cheek. "Whatever you found, I wish I could make it disappear."

"So do I," I whisper. I watch the tear cut a path all the way to his chin. There's something else on my mind, something I need to say, but I don't know how to say it. Finally I force out the words. "You can go, you know." I can't help but think how strange, how sad, that it's come to this. Ten years, four kids, a life together. And now a goodbye in the driveway?

He looks at me, incredulous, then shakes his head sadly. "There's nothing for me back there."

"I'd understand."

He puts his hands on my shoulders. "My life is here." He looks so sincere when he says it.

"Still, if you change your mind . . . at least call a sitter. . . ."

He drops his arms, looks like a wounded animal. I'm not even sure why I said it. It's not like I really think he'd leave Ella alone.

I don't know what else to say to him. And even if I did, I don't know if I could get the words out without breaking down. So I look away, get into the car, turn the key in the ignition. It starts the first time. What are the odds of that? I throw it into reverse and watch him watch me as I pull away, down the driveway, away from the life I know, the one we built together, and only then do I start to cry.

A STEADY STREAM OF CARS passes through the checkpoints, the ones manned by armed officers. The color-coded parking lots are starting to fill; thousands work here at headquarters. I walk from one of the far lots to the office in a daze, numb. My footsteps feel heavy. Others trudge past me on either side of the wide concrete walkway. I look at the manicured landscaping off to my right, the plants, the colors, because it's better than thinking about what's next. It's better to pretend that none of this ever happened.

Warm air hits me as I walk through the automatic doors into the lobby. I focus my attention on the giant American flag hanging from the rafters of the atrium. Today it seems ominous, taunting. I'm about to betray the man I love most in the world. Because I have no choice. Because of that flag, my country, and the fact that it's not, in fact, his country, too.

The security officers are at the turnstiles, watching, observing, as always. Ron, the one I see here most mornings, the one who never smiles, even when I smile at him. Molly, the one who always looks bored. People are queued up, waiting to scan badges and enter codes. I join the line, removing hat and gloves, smoothing out my hair. Why do I feel nervous? Like I'm doing something wrong. It makes no sense. None at all.

I'm going to tell Peter first. I decided on the drive in. I need to practice getting the words out before I say them to security, because I still can't picture myself saying them. *I found my husband's picture.* . . . I don't know how I'll do it without breaking down.

I walk down the long hall to my vault—our locked suite of cubicles and offices, set behind a heavy vault door, like they all are. Another badge, another code. I walk past Patricia, the secretary, and past the offices of the managers, through the rows of cubicles, back to the one I call my own. The one I tried so hard to make *like* home. The crayon drawings; pictures of my kids, of Matt. My life, hung with pushpins.

I log on, another set of passwords, and start brewing a pot of coffee while I wait for system authentication. The computer's ready before the coffee; I open Athena. More passwords. Then I pour coffee into my mom mug, the one that Matt gave me last Mother's Day, the one with the picture of our kids. It's one of those rare ones where all four of them are looking at the camera, three of them actually smiling. Took us ten minutes to get that shot, me making ridiculous noises and Matt jumping up and down and waving his arms behind me, both of us looking like lunatics, I'm sure.

Athena loads, and I click through the warning screens, the ones I disregarded yesterday by telling Matt. His words run through my head, unbidden. *I'll never tell. I swear.* And he won't, will he? More of his words run through my head. *I'm loyal to you.* I believe that. I do.

I'm back in Yury's computer, same as yesterday. Same blue background, same bubbles, same icons lined up in four rows. My gaze settles on the last one, *Friends*. The vault is quiet. I glance around and no one's nearby. I double-click, and the folder opens to the list of five images. I click open the first. Same guy with the round glasses. Then the second, the redhead. My eyes linger on the next, the third, the one with Matt's picture, but I don't open it. Can't. I skip to the next, the fourth, a woman with pale skin and wispy blond hair. The fifth, a young guy with spiky hair. I close it, close the whole folder, and stare at the screen, the blue bubbles, the icon with the folder. *Friends*. All sleepers. How is this possible?

My gaze drifts to the top of the screen, right side. Two buttons. Active. Passive. There's highlighting around Passive, the only mode the analysts are permitted to use, the one that creates a mirror image of the target's screen, doesn't allow manipulation. But it's the Active button that draws my eyes, holds them in place.

I hear something behind me. I turn and see Peter standing there. I go shaky, even though there's no way he saw where my eyes landed, where my attention was focused. No way he knows the thoughts that are running through my head. He glances at my screen and I feel a rush of adrenaline. The folder's right there. But it's just a folder, and it was just a glance. His eyes are back on me. "How's your little girl?" he asks.

"Fever, but otherwise okay." I try to keep my voice as even as possible. "Matt's home with her today." Matt. I swallow down the lump in my throat.

"Tina came by yesterday," he says. "She wants to see you."

"Why?" I say quickly. Too quickly. Tina's the head of

the Counterintelligence Center. Fierce, no-nonsense. Tough-as-nails Tina.

There's a flash of confusion on Peter's face. "She knows we're in the laptop. Wants to know what we've found."

"But I haven't had time—"

"I told her that. Don't worry. I pushed the meeting to tomorrow morning. She just wants to know if there's anything that looks promising."

"But—"

"It's just ten minutes. Spend today digging around. I'm sure you'll come up with something."

Like pictures of five sleepers? One of whom is my husband? "Okay."

He hesitates. "Want a hand? I can take a look, too."

"No," I say, again too quickly, too forcefully. "No, don't worry about it. You've got a lot on your plate. I'll come up with something for her."

Peter nods, but there's an odd expression on his face. Uncertain. He hesitates. "Are you okay, Vivian?"

I blink at him, and I know what I have to say. I have to do this. I don't have a choice. "I need to talk with you about something. In private." There's a sick feeling in my stomach as I say it. But I have to get it over with, before I lose my nerve.

"Give me ten minutes. I'll ping you when I'm ready."

I nod and watch as he walks away, back toward his office. I just set this in motion. Ten minutes. In ten minutes my world will change. Everything will be different. Life as I know it will be over.

I turn back to the screen. The folder. *Friends.* And then I look away, because I have to. Over to my far wall, past the pictures of my family, because I can't look at them right now or I might break down. My gaze settles on a little chart, something that's been there for years, ignored. A handout from a training course on analytic rigor. I scan it now, for the first time in ages, something to take my mind off reality. *Consider second- and third-order implications. . . . Think about unintended consequences. . . .*

His words this morning, in the driveway, run through my head. *Money'll be tight.* We'll lose his salary. That much I've already considered. I'll have to pull the youngest three out of school for sure, probably hire a nanny, someone cut-rate, and I'll have to swallow my fear of a stranger watching my kids, driving them around.

For the first time, though, it dawns on me that I'll lose my job, too. There's no way Tina would agree to keep me on, to let me keep my security clearance, when I was married to a Russian spy. It's one thing to lose Matt's salary. How will we survive if we lose mine, too?

Oh God. We'll lose my health insurance. Caleb. How is Caleb possibly going to get the care he needs?

I picture Matt breaking down. *What's this going to do to the kids?* Suddenly the future appears before my eyes. The media spectacle that this is sure to become. My kids, no father, no money, ripped from everything they know. The notoriety that'll always follow them. The shame, the suspicion, because after all they're his flesh and blood. Sons and daughter of a traitor.

I'm frozen in fear. None of this should have happened. If I hadn't stumbled upon the photo, hadn't come up with that damn algorithm, fought my way into Yury's laptop, I wouldn't know about Matt. No one would. His words ring in my head. *If only you weren't so good at your job.*

My eyes shift back to the buttons at the top of the screen. Active. Passive. I can't do this, can I? But I'm moving the cursor there anyway, until the arrow's hovering over Active. I click, and the borders of the screen change from red to green. Guilt threatens to overwhelm me. I think of my first day on the job, raising my right hand, taking the oath.

. . . support and defend the Constitution of the United States against all enemies, foreign and domestic . . .

Matt's not an enemy, though. He's not a bad guy. He's a good person, a decent person, someone who was taken advantage of as a kid, trapped in circumstances beyond his control. He hasn't done anything wrong, brought any harm to our country. He wouldn't. I know he wouldn't.

I move the cursor to the folder. I right-click, guide the arrow down to the command Delete. And then I hover there, my hand trembling.

Time. I just need more time. Time to think, time to figure things out, time to come up with a solution. There has to be a solution, a way out of this. A way to go back to the way things were, before. I close my eyes, and I'm at the altar with Matt, looking into his eyes, saying my vows.

. . . in good times and in bad . . .

I promised to be true to him, all the days of my life. And then I hear his voice, last night. *I'll never tell, Viv. I swear. I'd never do that to you.* He wouldn't, would he? And here I am, about to do exactly that to him.

Images of our kids run through my mind. Each of their faces, so innocent, so happy. This would destroy them.

And then another memory from our wedding day, our first dance, the words Matt whispered in my ear, the ones that've never made sense, for all these years. There's a sudden clarity to them now.

I open my eyes, and they instantly find the word. Delete. Highlighted, the cursor still hovering over it. More words float through my head, and I don't even know if they're his, or mine, or if it matters. *I just wish none of this had happened.*

I wish I could make it disappear.

And then I click.

CHAPTER

6

THE FOLDER IS GONE.

I hold my breath and watch the screen, waiting for something else to happen. But it doesn't. The folder just vanished, like none of this ever happened. Exactly what I wanted, right?

My breathing starts again, quick little bursts of air. I guide the cursor up to the button at the top of the screen. Passive. I click, and the border turns red.

And the folder's still gone.

I continue to stare at the place where it should be, where it just was. Same blue bubbles in the background, one less icon in the last row. I hear a phone ring a few rows away. Typing from nearby keyboards; the strains of an anchor on a twenty-four-hour news channel, one of the televisions suspended from the ceiling.

Oh God, what did I just do? Panic courses through me. I deleted files from a target's computer. Switching to Active mode, stepping into operational territory—that alone would be enough to get me fired. What was I thinking?

My gaze drifts up to the top left corner, the familiar icon, the recycle symbol. It's in that bin, isn't it? I didn't get rid of it, not all the way. I double-click the icon, and there it is. *Friends*. The file.

I look at the buttons again. Active. Passive. I could restore it, pretend none of this ever happened. Or I could delete it altogether, follow through with what I started. Either way, I need to do something. It can't just sit there.

Delete it altogether. That's what I want to do, what I need to do. There's a reason I did it in the first place. Protecting Matt, my family. I glance behind me; no one there. Then I click the Active button, move the cursor, click Delete, switch back to Passive mode an instant later.

Gone. I stare at the empty bin and rack my brain, trying to remember what I know about deleting files. It's still there, somewhere. Data-recovery software could retrieve it. I'll need something to overwrite it. Something like—

There's a ding, and a small white box pops up in the center of my screen. I seize with fear. This is it, some sign that I've been caught, discovered. But it's Peter's face in the little box, words he typed: *Come on over.*

I go weak. It's just Peter. I forgot I even asked to meet with him. I close out the box and lock my computer, my hands shaking. Then I walk toward his office.

What am I going to say? I replay the last conversation in my mind. *I need to talk with you about something. In private.* Oh, this is bad. What on earth am I going to say?

His door is open a crack. I see him at his computer, his back to me. I give a quick rap on the door, and he swivels his chair around to face me. "Come on in."

I push the door open. His office is tiny—all of them

are—just his desk, modular and gray like mine, and a small round table, overloaded with stacks of papers. I sit in the chair beside it.

He crosses his legs at the ankles, peers at me over the top of his glasses. I can tell he's waiting for me to speak. My mouth feels dry. Shouldn't I have figured out what I was going to say before I came in here? I rack my brain. What do people tell their bosses in private?

"What's going on?" he finally asks.

I can taste the words I should say. The ones that were running through my head all morning. *I found a picture of my husband*. But it's too late for them now, even if I could force them out of my mouth.

I look at the maps that cover the walls. Big ones of Russia. Political maps, road maps, topography maps. My gaze settles on the largest one, the contours of the country. I zero in on the sliver of land between Ukraine and Kazakhstan. Volgograd.

"There's a family issue," I say. I can just barely make out the letters on the map. I don't know where I'm going with this. I don't have a plan.

He exhales softly. "Oh, Vivian." When I look over, his eyes are full of concern, sympathy. "I understand."

It takes a moment for what he's saying to register, and when it does, guilt washes over me. I look behind him to the framed pictures on his desk. All of the same woman. A yellowed picture of her in a white lace dress. A candid shot of her opening a present, puffy sweater, puffy hair, absolute delight on her face. A more recent one, she and Peter together, mountains in the background, both looking completely comfortable, at ease, happy.

I swallow and look back at Peter. "How is she? How's Katherine?"

He looks away. Katherine has breast cancer. Stage three, diagnosed last year. I still remember the day he told us all. A team meeting in the conference room. Stunned silence as we watched Peter, stoic Peter, break down and cry.

She got into a clinical trial soon after. Peter's never said much about it, but it seemed like she was fighting it. Then, a couple of weeks ago, he missed some work—completely out of character for him—and when he finally came back, pale and tired, he told us she was no longer in the trial. No tears this time, but the same silence. We knew what it meant. The treatment wasn't working. She was at the end of the road. It was only a matter of time.

"She's a fighter," he answers, but the look in his eyes says it's a battle she can't win. His jaw clenches tight. "And so's your little boy."

I have a moment of confusion, and then a flash of realization. He knows Caleb had a cardiologist appointment yesterday. He's assuming there's been a setback. I should correct him, but I don't. I look down at my lap and nod, a sick feeling in my stomach.

"If there's anything I can do . . . ," he says.

"Thanks."

An awkward pause, and then he speaks. "Go home, why don't you? Deal with this."

I look up. "I can't. I don't have the leave—"

"How many years did you spend working hours you didn't claim?"

I give him a half smile. "Many."

"Take the rest of the day."

I'm about to refuse, and then I hesitate. What am I worried about? Losing my job because of *this*? Failing my next polygraph over *this*? I feel some of the tension draining away from my body. This is what I need. Get away from here, clear my head, try to figure out what to do next. "Thanks, Peter."

"I'll pray for you," he says softly as I'm standing to leave. He gives me a long look. "For strength."

I walk back to my desk. Helen and Raf have their chairs rolled into the aisle near my cubicle, and they're deep in conversation. There's no way I could do anything about the file now. Not without them seeing.

Tomorrow. I can deal with it tomorrow.

I hesitate a moment, then log off the computer and gather my bag and jacket. I linger, watching the screen, waiting for it to go black. And as I do, my gaze drifts to the corner of my desk, the picture of Matt and me on our wedding day, and I'm overcome with a strange sensation, a feeling that we dodged a bullet but that somehow, inexplicably, I'm bleeding.

SIX MONTHS AFTER WE MET, I was finally going to see where Matt came from. Meet his parents, see the house where he grew up, his high school. Meet his childhood friends. I'd accumulated a week's worth of leave. Matt booked the tickets, or said he did, anyway. I was so excited to be going, I could barely contain myself.

He'd just met my parents; we'd all spent Christmas together in Charlottesville, and it went better than I could have hoped. My parents loved him. And I loved him even more, seeing him with them. I knew without a doubt I wanted to marry him. Engagement, though, still seemed like something far in the future. I hadn't even met his parents, and there was no way I'd get engaged to someone without meeting his parents. It just didn't seem right. I'd told him that, too. At least, I thought I had.

We were at the airport, a frigid day in January. I wore the outfit I'd spent hours agonizing over, pants and a cardigan, cute but conservative, picked to make a good impression on my hopefully future in-laws. We were in the winding security line, black rolling suitcases in tow. Matt was quiet. He looked nervous, and that made me nervous, because the last thing I wanted was him to be worried about me meeting his parents. To be having second thoughts about us.

When we neared the front of the line, it occurred to me that he still had my boarding pass, the one he'd printed off before we left. "Oh!" I said. "Can I have my boarding pass?"

He handed me a folded piece of paper, his eyes never leaving mine, his face studiously blank.

His look made me even more unsettled. "Thanks," I said. I finally broke his gaze, looked down at the pass to make sure he'd handed me mine and not his, since he did it without looking. I saw my name, Vivian Grey, and three letters, large and bold, that weren't supposed to be there. *HNL*.

Not the airport code for Seattle, that much I knew. I stared at the letters, trying to place them, trying to make sense of them.

"Honolulu," Matt said, and I felt his arms encircle my waist.

"What?" I spun around to face him.

He was grinning. "Well, Maui, actually. We have a connecting flight when we get there."

"Maui?"

He gave me a gentle nudge forward. I blinked, looked, and it was my turn at security. The TSA agent was giving me an annoyed look. I handed over the boarding pass and dug out my driver's license, fumbling, cheeks hot, utterly confused. He stamped the pass and I walked through, over to the conveyor belt, started taking off my shoes. Matt came up behind me and lifted my suitcase onto the belt, then his. Then I felt his arms around me again, his cheek coming to rest near mine.

"What do you think?" he said, his breath hot against my ear, and I could hear the smile in his voice.

What did I think? That I wanted to go to Seattle. I wanted to meet his parents, see where he came from. "But your family."

I walked through the metal detector. He did the same, and we stood beside each other again as my bag rolled to the end of the belt.

"I couldn't let you use all your leave on *Seattle*," he said.

What was I supposed to say? That I would have *preferred* Seattle? How ungrateful would that be? He'd just bought me a trip to Maui. *Maui*. And given up time with his family.

At the same time, didn't he know how important it was to me to meet his family? And that now we'd have to put off Seattle for months longer, until I'd built up more leave?

He lifted our luggage down to the floor. "I repacked your suitcase," he said. He pulled up the handle and spun it around toward me. "It's all warm-weather clothes now. Lots of swimsuits." He was smiling, then he pulled me close, until my hips were against his. "Of course, I'm hoping we'll be spending more time without them." His eyes were dancing.

"I don't know what to say," I finally said, my mind screaming, *Is it too late to change our tickets?*

The smile faded from his face, and his arms dropped to his side. "Oh," he said. Just that one syllable. And then I was overcome with guilt. Look at what he'd just done for me.

"It's just that . . . I was really looking forward to meeting your parents."

He looked absolutely crestfallen. "I'm sorry. I really am. I thought this . . . I just thought . . ." He gave his head a quick shake. "Let's go. Let's see if we can change the tickets—"

I grabbed his hand. "Wait." I didn't even know why I stopped him, what I was going to say. I just knew I hated the look on his face, hated the way I'd just made him feel.

"No, you're right. I shouldn't have done this. It's just that I wanted everything to be perfect when I asked you—" He stopped abruptly, and color rose to his cheeks.

Asked you to marry me. I could almost hear the words. I was certain that's what was coming next. I felt like my heart stopped. I stared at him, the look of panic on his face, cheeks redder than I'd ever seen them.

Oh my God, he was going to ask me to marry him. We were going to Hawaii because he'd planned the perfect proposal. A beach, an exotic location. There's nothing I would have wanted more. And now I'd gone and ruined it.

"Ask me," I said. The words came out of my mouth before I could think them through. But once they were out, they made sense. The trip would have been painfully awkward after this. The only way to salvage the trip was to change the whole tenor of it. Get rid of the elephant in the room.

"What?" he breathed.

"Ask me," I said with more confidence.

"Here?" He looked incredulous.

I was looking at the man I was going to marry, the one I loved with all my heart. What did it matter where we got engaged? I nodded.

The embarrassment left his face, was replaced with a half smile, a look of wonderment, of excitement, and I knew I'd made the right decision. This was salvageable after all.

He grabbed my other hand. "Vivian, I love you more than anything in the world. You make me happier than I ever thought possible, happier than I deserve."

Tears sprung to my eyes. This was my future, the man I was going to spend the rest of my life with.

"I want nothing more than to spend my life with you." Then he dropped one of my hands, reached into his pocket, pulled out a ring. Just a ring, no box; he must have placed it in the tray at the metal detector with his wallet and keys and I didn't even notice. He knelt down on one knee and held it out, his face so hopeful, so vulnerable. "Will you marry me?"

"Of course," I whispered, and I saw the relief and happiness etched on his face as he slid it onto my finger. Applause erupted around us from a crowd I didn't know had gathered. I laughed, giddy. Hugged Matt, kissed him, right there in the middle of the airport. Looked at the ring on my finger, the diamond sparkling under fluorescent lights. And didn't care a bit, in that moment, that I hadn't caught even a glimpse of his past. Because the future was all that mattered.

I PULL INTO THE GARAGE, my mind a jumbled mess. I did the right thing, didn't I? I mean, it was impulsive. And I need to do more tomorrow to clean it up, to get rid of the file permanently. But I was right to make this all disappear. To keep our lives intact.

Only, I have the overwhelming sense that I should have thought things through before I acted. That I need to think through the consequences now, at least. My mind is balking, though. It's like I know I can't handle what I'll learn.

I walk inside, and I see Matt through the kitchen doorway. He's looking in my direction, holding a dish towel, drying his hands. He looks calm, remarkably calm. Not like someone who thinks I just turned him in. Everything here looks normal. I can hear the TV in the family room, the show about the stuffed animals that come to life.

"You're home early," he says.

But then, we'd talked about keeping everything normal, hadn't we? For my protection. He's probably assuming someone's listening in right now, maybe even watching. I take off my jacket, hang it on the hook near the door. I drop my bag to the floor beside it. Then I take a step closer to him. "I couldn't do it," I say softly.

The dish towel goes still. It takes him a moment to speak. "What do you mean?"

"I couldn't do it. I couldn't turn you in."

He folds the towel and sets it down on the counter. "Viv, we've been through this. You have to."

I shake my head. "I don't. I got rid of it."

He's staring at me with an intensity that sends a chill through me. "Got rid of what?"

"The . . . thing . . . that connects you to all of this."

"What did you do?"

"I made it all disappear." Panic's creeping into my voice. I didn't, though. Not yet, anyway. *Can* I make it disappear?

His eyes are burning. "What did you do, Viv?"

What *did* I do? Oh God.

He runs a hand through his hair, then covers his mouth. "You were supposed to turn me in," he says quietly.

"I couldn't," I say in an equally hushed tone. And that's the truth, isn't it? I knew deep down it was the right thing to do. The *only* thing to do. But when it came time to actually do it, to set a ball rolling that I'd never be able to stop, that would crush us all, I couldn't do it.

He shakes his head. "Things like this, they don't just disappear." He takes a step closer to me. "It's going to come out eventually. They'll figure out what you did."

I feel like someone's grabbed hold of my heart. They can't find out. No one can ever find out.

"I needed you there for the kids," he says.

"I *did* this for the kids," I shoot back. How dare he act like I wasn't thinking about the kids. Our family was the only thing on my mind.

"And now what? What happens to the kids when we're *both* convicted of spying for Russia?"

I feel like all the air has left my lungs. I reach out a hand to the wall, steady myself. Spying for Russia. Espionage. Is that what I've done?

What *would* happen to the kids? Would they be sent to Russia? A country they don't know, a language they don't know, all their dreams destroyed?

The terror is all-consuming now, but I'm angry, furious at him at the same time, and it's this part of me that finds a voice. "If I turned you in, what would happen to the kids? What would happen to us?"

"It's better than—"

I take a step closer. "We'd lose your salary. I'd get fired, and we'd lose mine, too. We'd lose our health insurance. Our home."

He looks stricken, the color draining from his face. And I like it. I like seeing him this way, feeling as desperate, as hopeless as I do.

"They'd forever be known as the kids of a Russian spy. What would that do to them?"

He runs his hand through his hair again. He looks so unsure. So unlike the Matt I know, the one who's unflappable, who's unfailingly calm and collected.

"Don't you dare blame me for this," I add. I sound combative, *am* combative, but deep down I'm terrified. His words are ringing in my head. *I needed you there for the kids.* Needed, past tense. I didn't want to take away their father, but what if I've done something much worse?

Intentionally covering up evidence. Conspiracy, espionage—it would all be on the table. What if I go to jail for this?

"You're right," he says. I blink, focus on him. He's nodding. A look of confidence has returned to his face. Determination. Like he knows what to do. "This is my fault. I need to fix it."

It's exactly what I need to hear. *Yes, fix it. Get us out of this.* I can feel some of the tension start to drain from my shoulders. He's thrown out a lifeline, just when drowning feels inevitable. And I'm already reaching for it, already holding on.

He lowers his voice, leans forward, until his face is right in front of mine. "But in order to do that, I need you to tell me everything. Exactly what you found. And exactly how you made it disappear."

CHAPTER

7

I STARE AT HIM. HE'S ASKING ME TO SHARE CLASSIFIED information. To become the kind of person I've spent my career hunting down. He knows that. *He's manipulating you,* a voice in my head warns.

But he doesn't look like he's manipulating me. He looks so sincere. So desperate. He's trying to find a way to get us out of this. Something I don't know how to do right now. And it makes sense, really. I have to tell him what I know. How else can he do anything about it?

I've already crossed lines I never should have. Telling him I discovered his identity. Erasing the file. But this? Telling him exactly what I found, exactly what I *did*? I'd be disclosing information about Athena, one of the Agency's most sensitive programs. Information I'd sworn to protect. I swallow, my throat so tight I almost can't.

I need to think. I need to process whether this actually makes sense. I brush past him, wordless, into the family room, where Ella's sitting, tangled in a blanket, watching TV. I paste a smile on my face. "How are you, sweetie?"

She looks up and gives me a grin, one that morphs quickly into a faux-sick look. "Sick, Mommy."

Last week, I would have struggled not to laugh at her act. Now it chills me. Because it's a lie, isn't it? Something her father does so well.

I keep the smile pasted on my face. "I'm sorry you're not feeling well," I say. I watch her a moment longer, watch her attention turn back to the TV screen. I'm trying to marshal my thoughts into some semblance of order. Then I raise my head to meet Matt's eyes, speak to her even as I look at him. "Daddy and I are going to sit out front and talk."

"Okay," she murmurs, her attention on her show.

I walk out the front door, leaving it open. Matt follows, closes the door behind us. The cold air hits me like a slap. I should have grabbed my coat. I sit on the top of our front stoop and wrap my arms around my chest, huddle into a ball.

"Do you want a jacket?" Matt asks.

"No."

He sits down beside me, so close we're touching. I can feel his warmth, the pressure of his knee against mine. He's looking straight ahead. "I know it's a lot to ask. But I need to know more, if I'm going to fix this."

Manipulation. Is it, though? For whatever reason, our engagement day floats through my mind. That moment in the airport, the two of us. The crowd around us, dispersing, smiles on their faces. One on my own face, as well. Looking down at that ring, seeing it catch the light, so new, so clean, so perfect.

And then the realization. I got engaged without meeting his parents. Something that was so important to me. I'd told him that, hadn't I? I could feel the smile fading from my lips. Felt his arm around my shoulders, guiding me away, deeper into the airport, toward our gate. We were engaged, we were headed for Hawaii, just like he wanted.

But at the same time, he'd planned a perfect proposal for me. In *Hawaii*. And planned to surprise me with it. I looked up at him, saw the openness on his face, the happiness and excitement, and I smiled at him. I was being ridiculous. So he made one mistake. I wasn't even completely sure I'd mentioned it, that I wanted to meet his parents before we got engaged. Maybe I hadn't.

But the misgivings never quite went away. Through all the days on the beach, the hikes to waterfalls, the candlelit dinners, the thought was lodged in the back of my head. I'd gotten engaged in an airport, in front of a crowd of strangers, without ever having met his parents. That's not what I'd wanted, at all. *But you urged him to ask you, right then, right there,* I told myself.

And then it was our last morning there. We were out on the little balcony, sitting there with our mugs of coffee, watching the swaying palms, feeling the warm breeze.

"I know you wanted to meet my parents first," he said out of the blue.

I looked over in surprise. So I *had* said it. He *had* known.

"But I'm me, Viv. Regardless of who my parents are." He looked at me with such intensity I was taken aback. "The past is the past."

He's ashamed of his parents, I realized. *He's worried about what I'll think of them. What I'll think of him, after I meet them.* I looked down at the ring on my finger. *But still. What about what I wanted?*

"But what I did was wrong," he said. I looked back up at him, saw the sincerity in his eyes. The regret. So much regret. "I'm sorry."

I wanted the misgivings to dissipate. I really did. He'd made a mistake. He admitted it, apologized. But I could never quite get over it. That he knew I wanted to meet his parents first, went ahead and proposed anyway. It felt like manipulation.

But now, as I stare at the ring, the diamond that doesn't sparkle nearly as much anymore, on a hand that's so much older, it doesn't. It feels honest.

If those weren't his real parents, wasn't it more honest that I didn't meet them before we got engaged? They might have helped shape my opinion of him, my feelings toward him. Wouldn't that, in fact, have been the manipulation?

I turn toward him and scoot away, just enough so that I can face him comfortably, so that I can read his expression. It looks honest, open. The same look he had when he asked me to marry him. The same one I saw on our wedding day, all those years ago. I picture us before the priest, the old stone church in Charlottesville, the look on his face when he said his vows. That kind of sincerity can't be faked, can it? I swallow past the tightness in my throat.

I don't know. The truth is, I have no idea whether to believe him. But I need a hand. I need help. I've dug myself into a hole, and he's offered to help me climb out. His question won't stop running through my head. *What happens to the kids when we're* both *convicted of spying for Russia?* I can't let that happen. I have to believe him.

"We have access to Yury's computer," I say, and the words are harder to get out than I expected. With every syllable, I feel like I'm committing a crime. I *am* committing a crime. I'm disclosing classified information, violating the Espionage Act. Barely anyone in the Agency even knows about Athena's capabilities, it's so restricted. People go to jail for sharing information like this. "I was digging around, found a folder with five pictures." I glance over at him. "Yours was one of them."

He's staring straight ahead. Nods, ever so slightly. "Just my picture? Anything else about me?"

I shake my head. "Haven't come across anything else."

"Encrypted?"

"No."

He sits quietly for a moment, then turns to face me. "Tell me what you did."

"I erased it."

"How?"

"You know, clicked Delete. Deleted it."

"Then what?"

"Then deleted it from the recycle bin."

"And?" His voice has an edge.

I swallow. "Nothing else yet. I know I need to do more, overwrite the hard drive or whatever. But there were people nearby, and I couldn't."

I look away, out to the street. I hear an engine, a vehicle approaching. I watch the street, see it come into view, an orange van, that housecleaning service that so many of the neighbors use. It pulls to a stop in front of the Parkers' house. I watch as three women in orange vests get out of the van and gather cleaning supplies from the rear. When they're inside and the door closes behind them, quiet descends on the street once again.

"They have a record of you deleting it," Matt says. "There's no way they don't record user activity."

I watch my breath crystallize in the air, little clouds. I know that already, don't I? Didn't I click past screens warning me my actions are recorded? What was I thinking?

I wasn't. That's the problem. I just wanted it all to go away.

I look over at Matt. He's staring straight ahead, his brows knitted together, a look of deep concentration on his face. The silence around us is heavy. "Okay," he finally says. He places a hand on my knee, gives it a squeeze. He turns to face me, the creases in his forehead pronounced, his eyes clouded with worry. "I'll get you out of this."

He stands, walks back inside. I stay seated, shivering, his words reverberating in my skull. *I'll get you out of this.*

You.

Why didn't he say *us*?

I'M STILL ON THE front stoop a few minutes later when Matt returns, car keys in hand. He pauses above me. "I'll be back in a bit," he says.

"What are you going to do?"

"Don't worry about it."

He could be leaving. Getting on a plane back to Russia, leaving me to deal with the fallout. But he wouldn't do that, would he?

But what *is* he doing? And why didn't he do it to begin with?

"I deserve to know."

He starts walking past me, toward his car, parked in the driveway. "The less you know, Viv, the better."

I get to my feet. "What's that supposed to mean?"

He stops, turns to face me, speaks quietly. "Polygraph. Trial. It's just better if you don't know details."

I stare at him, and he stares back. The look on his face is troubled. Angry, even. And that makes me furious. "Why are *you* angry with *me* right now?"

He raises his hands, his car keys clanging together. "Because! If you'd just listened to me, we wouldn't be in this mess."

We glare at each other, the silence almost suffocating, then he shakes his head, like I'm a disappointment. I watch him go without another word. The emotions inside me are roiling, jumbled, making no sense at all.

WE CELEBRATED OUR FIRST anniversary in the Bahamas, five days of lying in the sun with an endless supply of tropical drinks, the occasional dip in the ocean to cool off, where we'd soon be wrapped around each other, finding lips that tasted like rum and sea salt.

Our last night there, we were at a beach bar, a little place in the sand with a thatched roof and string lights and fruity drinks. We sat on weathered barstools, close enough that our legs were touching, that his hand could rest on my thigh, just a little too high. I remember listening to the crash of the waves, breathing in the salt air, feeling warm all over.

"So . . . ," I said, running a finger over the little umbrella in my drink, tossing over the question that had been on my mind all night, the one that had been slowly forming in my head for weeks, months. I tried to come up with the best way to lead up to it, and when I couldn't, I just blurted it out. "When should we have a baby?"

He practically sputtered into his drink. Looked up at me, eyes wide, full of love, openness, excitement. Then something shifted, and they became more guarded. He looked away.

"Kids are a big step," he said, and even through my rum-induced haze, I was confused. He loved kids. We'd always planned to have some. Two probably, maybe three.

"We've been married a year," I said.

"We're still young."

I looked down at my drink, something pink, and stirred around the half-melted ice cubes with my straw. That wasn't the response I'd expected. Not at all. "What's going on?"

"I just think there's no rush, you know. Maybe we wait a few years, focus on our careers."

"Our careers?" Since when did he want us to focus on our careers?

"Yeah." He was avoiding my eyes. "I mean, take yours." He lowered his voice, leaned in closer, and this time he looked at me intently. "Africa. Is that really the part of the world you want to focus on?"

I looked away. I'd been perfectly happy with the African CI account. There was enough to keep me busy, to keep my days interesting. I felt like I was making a difference, albeit in a small way. And that's all I really wanted. Africa wasn't as high-profile as some of the other accounts, but that was fine with me. "Sure."

"I mean, wouldn't it be more interesting to work something like . . . Russia?"

I took a long sip of my drink through the straw. Sure, it'd be more interesting. More stress, too. Longer hours, for sure. And there were so many people working the account, how much impact would one person really have? "I guess."

"And maybe better for your career? For promotions and all that?"

When had he ever cared about promotions? And why did he think I did? If money was my goal, I wouldn't have chosen a career in government. The warm feeling inside me was starting to chill around the edges.

"I mean, it's up to you, of course, sweetheart. It's your job and all." He shrugged. "I just think you'd be happier if you were doing something more . . . important. You know?"

The words stung. It was the first time I'd ever felt like my job wasn't good enough for Matt. That *I* wasn't good enough.

His expression softened, and he placed a hand over mine, gave me an earnest look. Apologetic, like he knew he'd hurt my feelings. "It's just—well, that's what the best analysts focus on, right? Russia?"

Where was this coming from? I was so confused. Sure, it was a competitive account, the kind a lot of people wanted. But there was something to be said for working a low-profile account, too. Making sure nothing fell through the cracks, nothing was overlooked. Being able to see the impact I was making.

"You're the kind of person who always wants to be the best. That's what I love about you."

That's what he loved about me? The compliment felt like a slap.

"And it'd probably be harder to make that kind of move after we have kids," he went on. "So maybe you should get to a place you want to be, and *then* we should think about kids." He stirred his drink with his straw as he said it, still avoiding my eyes.

I drained the remnants of my drink, the sweetness gone, now nothing but bitterness. "Okay," I said as a chill ran through me.

AS SOON AS THE taillights of Matt's car disappear around the corner, I walk back into the house. I check on Ella, who's still in front of the TV, then head to the storage area behind the stairs. I need to see what's on that laptop.

It's a small space, crowded with stacks of blue plastic bins. I pull the chain to turn on the light and look down at the floor, the narrow section that's bare. Nothing seems out of the ordinary. I get down on my hands and knees, feel around, finally come across a floorboard that's raised slightly on one side. I run my hand over it, try to lift it, to no avail.

I glance around the room and spot a screwdriver on top of one of the plastic bins. I use it to pry up the floorboard, then peer inside. Something's catching the light. I reach in and pull out a small silver laptop.

I sit cross-legged and open the laptop, turn it on. It starts quickly, and I see a black screen with a single white bar, a blinking cursor. There's no text, but it's password-protected—that much is clear.

I try Matt's usual passwords, the ones he uses for everything, various compilations of our kids' names and birth dates. Then I try the password we use for our joint accounts. Nothing works. But why would it? A different set of words runs through my head. *Alexander Lenkov. Mikhail and Natalia. Volgograd.* I have no way of guessing what might have been on his mind when he came up with a password, if he's even the one who came up with it. This is futile.

Frustrated, I close the laptop and return the room to the way I found it. Then I head back to the family room to check on Ella. "You doing okay, sweetie?" I ask.

"Yeah," she murmurs. Doesn't take her eyes off the TV.

I linger for a moment, then walk upstairs to the master bedroom, pause in the doorway. I go over to Matt's nightstand first. Pull open the drawer, dig around. Crumpled receipts, spare change, some pictures Ella drew for him. Nothing remotely suspicious. I look under the bed, pull out a plastic container. It's full of his summer clothes: swimsuits, shorts, T-shirts. I close it and slide it back underneath.

I open the top drawer of his dresser. Move around the stack of boxers, the pile of socks, looking for anything that doesn't belong. Then I do the same with the next drawer, and the one after that. Nothing.

I head into the closet. Run a hand over the clothes hanging on his rack. Polos, button-downs, pants. I'm not even sure what I'm trying to find. Something that proves he's not the person I think he is. Or the absence of it; would that be enough to prove that he is?

There's an old duffel bag on the shelf above. I reach for it and pull it down to the carpet. I unzip it, rifle through. A collection of ties—he hasn't used those in years—and some old baseball caps. I check each zippered pocket. Empty.

I put the bag back on the shelf and pull down a stack of shoe boxes, kneel down on the carpet with them. The first is full of old bills. The second, receipts. The third, his dress shoes, shiny and black. I sit back on my heels, the open box in my lap. What am I doing? How has my life come to this?

I'm about to replace the lid of the box when something catches my eye. Something black, tucked into one of the shoes. I know what it is even before my fingers curl around it.

It's a gun.

I pull it out by the grip and look at it. The black metal slide, the wide trigger. A Glock. I move the slide, see brass inside.

It's loaded.

Matt has a loaded gun in our closet.

I hear Ella downstairs, calling for me. Hands shaking, I place the pistol back in the shoe, close the lid, stack the boxes back on the shelf. Give them one last look, then turn off the light and head downstairs.

MATT COMES HOME THREE hours later. Bustles in, removes his jacket, gives me a smile, apologetic and embarrassed. Then he comes over and wraps his arms around me. "I'm sorry," he says into my hair. He's still cold from the air outside. Cold hands, cold cheeks. A shiver runs through me. "I shouldn't have said all that. It's not fair for me to be upset with you. This is my fault."

I pull back and look at him. He looks like a stranger, feels like a stranger. All I can picture is that gun in our closet. "Did you do what you needed to do?"

He drops his hands, turns away, but not before I see the expression on his face. Tense. "Yeah."

"So . . . Are we okay?"

In my mind, I see the gun again. It's been hours now, and I still don't know what to make of it. Is it proof that he's not who I think he is? That he's dangerous? Or is it a way to protect us, his family, from the people who really *are* dangerous?

He's very still, his back to me. I see his shoulders rise and fall, like he's taken a deep breath and exhaled. "I hope so."

I GET TO MY desk the next morning and see the little red flashing light on my phone. Voicemail. I flip through the call history. Three calls from Omar, two yesterday and one this morning. I close my eyes. I knew this would come, didn't I? Or should have, at least. If I'd thought it through.

I pick up the phone, dial his number. I need to get this over with.

"Vivian," he says when he answers.

"Omar. Sorry I missed your calls. I left early yesterday, just got in this morning."

"No worries." There's a pause.

"Look, about Yury's computer." My nails are digging into my palm. "It's not looking very promising. I'm afraid there's nothing there." I hate this, lying to him. I picture the two of us, all those years ago, commiserating over the Bureau's rejection of his op plan. And all the times since, at O'Neill's and our offices and even our homes, sharing our frustrations about our inability to find anything worthwhile. Our conviction that the sleepers are a genuine threat, and we're powerless to stop it. A friendship cemented over a mutual feeling of futility. And now I finally have something, and I have no choice but to lie to him about it.

He's silent on the other end of the phone.

I close my eyes, like somehow it'll make the lies easier. "Obviously we need to wait for translation and exploitation. But so far I haven't found anything of interest." My voice sounds surprisingly confident.

Another pause. "Nothing?"

My nails dig in even harder. "There's always the chance there's something embedded in the files, steganography or something like that. But so far, nothing."

"You always find something."

Now it's my turn to pause. Disappointment I understand. But this is something more. This is unsettling. "Yeah."

"With the other four. You found something with each of them. Enough to warrant expedited translation."

"I know."

"But with this one, you didn't." It's a statement, not a question. And there's an unmistakable tone of skepticism in his voice. My heart's racing now.

"Well," I say, and fight to keep the tremor out of my voice. "Haven't come across anything yet."

"Hmm," he says. "That's not what Peter said."

I FEEL LIKE I'VE been punched in the gut, the wind knocked out of me. It's got to be the pictures. He found the pictures. Whatever Matt did, it wasn't enough. And then suddenly I'm aware of someone behind me. I turn, and it's Peter. Standing, silent, watching me. Listening.

"I didn't know he'd found anything," I say into the phone, my eyes on Peter the whole time, letting him hear what I'm saying. My mouth is very dry.

Peter nods. The expression on his face is impossible to decipher.

Omar's speaking, something about coming to headquarters, a meeting, but I don't hear the words. My mind is racing. Did Peter find Matt's picture? Impossible, because he'd have already gone to security. Did he see that I deleted the file? Again, security. He wouldn't be standing here talking to me.

"*Vivian?*"

I blink, try to focus on the conversation, Omar's voice in my ear.

"See you later?"

"Yeah," I murmur. "See you later." I hang up the phone and put my hands in my lap so Peter won't see them shaking. Then I turn to him, wait for him to say something, because I can't make my mouth work.

He takes a moment before responding. "You got on the phone before I could catch you. I went into Athena this morning, had a look around. Figured you could use a hand, someone to lighten the load."

Oh God. I should have figured he might do that.

"I found a file. It had been deleted."

My kids. I see each of their faces in my mind. Their smiles, looks of joy and innocence.

". . . called *Friends* . . ."

Luke's old enough to understand. How many times have we told him not to lie? Now he's going to know his father's whole life, his parents' marriage, all of it was a lie.

". . . five photos . . ."

And Ella. Ella worships Matt. He's her hero. What will this do to her?

". . . meeting at ten with the Bureau . . ."

Chase and Caleb. Too young to understand, too young to have memories of our family before this.

". . . Omar will be there . . ."

Omar. Omar knows Matt. I introduced the two, when Omar and I started spending so much time together. He's been to our house, we've been to his. Maybe Peter didn't recognize him. But Omar would. And in any case, if I'm in the room when they show his picture . . .

I need to pretend. Feign surprise.

"Vivian?"

I blink. Peter's looking at me with raised eyebrows.

"I'm sorry," I say. "What?"

"You'll be there? At the meeting?"

"Yeah. Yes, of course."

He hesitates a moment longer, a concerned look on his face, then leaves, back to his office. I stare at my screen, try to remember how I felt when I first saw Matt's picture, because I'm going to have to replicate it. Disbelief. Confusion. Fear.

Then my rationalization: He's being targeted.

I could ask to see the file now. Pretend to see it for the first time, in front of Peter. But better to let a bigger audience see my reaction, see me process these emotions.

If I can do it convincingly.

Not if. When. I need to do it convincingly. Because if I give them even the slightest indication I already knew, it won't take them long to figure out that it wasn't Yury who deleted the file.

That it was me.

PETER COMES BACK AT five minutes before ten. We walk down the hall together, to the suite that houses the CIC executive offices. "You okay, Vivian?" he asks as we walk, peering at me over his glasses.

"Fine," I say. In my mind, I'm already in the conference room, seeing Matt's picture.

"If you need more time off, more time with Caleb . . ."

I shake my head. Words won't come right now. I should have done what Matt said. I should have turned him in. He's going to be discovered anyway, and now I'm in trouble, too. Why didn't I listen?

We walk in, and the secretary ushers us into the conference room. I've been here a few times before, and each time it's as intimidating as the last. Darker than it needs to be, heavy gleaming wood table, expensive leather chairs. Four clocks on the wall—D.C., Moscow, Beijing, Tehran.

Omar's there at the table, along with two other Bureau guys in suits. His bosses, I think. He nods at me, but not with his usual grin. Just a nod, doesn't take his eyes off me.

I sit down on the other side of the table and wait. Peter goes to the computer, logs on, and I see the large screen on the wall come to life. I watch him navigate to Athena, launch the program, and then I stare at the clock, the one that shows the local time. I watch the second hand tick around, focus on that, because I know if I think of Matt, of the kids, I'll fall apart. Everything will fall apart, and I'll never get through this. And I have to get through this.

Tina strides in moments later, followed by Nick, the chief of CIC Russia, and two assistants, each in a black suit. She gives curt nods around the room and takes her seat at the head of the table. There's an unpleasant look on her face. Unpleasant and intimidating. "So we're inside laptop number five," she says. "More luck than the first four, I hope?" Her eyes scan the room and land on Peter.

He clears his throat. "Yes, ma'am." He gestures up at the screen, the Athena home page. He double-clicks on the icon with Yury's name, and moments later I see the mirror image of Yury's laptop, the blue bubbles, so familiar at this point. My eyes go to the last row of icons, the place where the folder should be and isn't.

Peter's talking, but I'm not hearing the words. I'm focusing on how I'll feign surprise, trying to keep my face impassive, because I know Omar's watching me. I watch as the screen morphs into strings of characters: the data recovery program at work. Moments later the folder reappears. *Friends.*

This is it. Life as I know it is over.

I try to push my kids' faces from my mind. Breathe through my nose, in and out.

He double-clicks, and I see the list of five images. He moves the cursor up to the top, changes the view from text to large icons. At once, five faces appear on the screen. I'm dimly aware of round glasses on the first, bright orange hair on the second. But my eyes focus on the third. On Matt.

Only it's not Matt anymore.

CHAPTER

8

IT'S SOMEONE WHO LOOKS LIKE MATT. AT LEAST A LITTLE. Dark hair, dark eyes, straight smile. And it definitely looks like the picture of Matt that had been in this very place, with this very file name. Same tilt of the head, same distance from the camera, same background. But the features are unmistakably different. It's a completely different person. Not my husband at all.

I blink. Once, twice. Disbelief courses through me. Then it morphs, slowly, into a wave of relief. An overwhelming, utterly exhilarating wave of relief. Matt did it. He fixed this, just like he said he would. I don't know how he did it, but his picture is gone. Our family is still intact.

We're safe.

I finally pull my eyes away from the picture, shift them left, to the first and second pictures, the man in the round glasses, the woman with the orange hair. My breath catches in my throat. The man has sharper features than yesterday, a squarer chin. The woman has higher cheekbones, a broader forehead. These are different people, too.

I look right, to the last two images, the pale woman and the man with the spiky hair, even though I already know what I'll see. Similar features, similar camera angles, but not the same people as the day before.

Oh God.

Matt was one thing. But four other sleepers?

My chest feels tight, a crushing pressure inside. And I don't know why, either. I deleted the other four pictures when I deleted Matt's. I was willing to hide them to protect my husband. So why does it bother me now, seeing the pictures replaced? How is this any different?

I hear voices through the fog in my head. A conversation, Tina and Peter. Whether these could really be sleepers. I blink again, try to focus.

"But the file isn't encrypted," Tina says.

"True, and all our intelligence indicates it should be," Peter replies. "But it was deleted."

Tina cocks her head, frowning. "Some sort of mistake on Yury's part?"

Peter nods. "Could be. The file was accidentally loaded, or the encryption failed, or something along those lines, and Yury's response was to delete it."

"Not realizing it would still be there," Tina adds.

"Exactly."

"And that we'd find it."

He nods again.

She raises an index finger to her lips, bright red polish catching the light. Taps once, twice. Then she looks over at the Bureau contingent, the three agents sitting in a row, dark suits, hands clasped in front of them. "Thoughts?"

The one in the center clears his throat and speaks.

"Seems reasonable to approach this as a lead to Russian sleepers."

"Agreed."

"We'll do what we can to identify the individuals, ma'am."

Tina offers a curt nod.

There's a throbbing in my head. These aren't sleepers. They might not even be real people. Digitally altered compositions of individuals, leads the Bureau will be chasing in vain.

And ultimately I'm responsible. I disclosed classified information. I did it to protect my family, sure. But now we've lost our insight into the identities of four other Russian agents. I grip the armrest of my chair, suddenly light-headed. What have I done?

There's more conversation. I try hard to focus, hear Yury's name.

". . . in Moscow," Peter says.

"Do we know where in Moscow?" Tina asks.

"We don't. We'll certainly devote extra resources in the coming days to determining his whereabouts."

"The computer? Do we have any location information?"

"No. He hasn't used it to connect to the Internet."

He's here, my mind screams. In the U.S., in our own metro area. On false papers. Stopping by a Northwest D.C. bank courtyard every few months, or whenever my husband signals. I clench my jaw shut, and when I look up, I see Omar watching me. Unblinking, unsmiling. The rest of the conversation fades away until all I can hear is the blood pounding in my ears.

I'M IN THE HALLWAY after the meeting, attempting a hasty retreat back to my desk, when Omar catches up to me, half-jogging to do so. He falls into step beside me. My heart's racing. I don't know what to say to him, what he's going to say to me, how I can possibly answer his questions.

"You okay, Vivian?"

I glance over and he looks concerned, or maybe fake-concerned. My mouth is suddenly very dry. "Yeah. Just got a lot on my mind right now."

A few more steps, still in sync, and then we're at the elevator. I push the button, watch it light up, hope the elevator arrives quickly. "Family stuff?" he asks. The way he says it, the studiously blank look on his face, makes me think of an interrogation, one of those early innocuous questions designed to build rapport—or maybe entrap.

I look away, to the closed elevator doors. "Yeah. Ella's been sick, Caleb's had some medical appointments. . . ." I trail off, wondering irrationally if I'm somehow jinxing their health with these lies. Karma and all that.

Out of the corner of my eye, I see him look straight ahead, too. "I'm sorry to hear that." Then he glances over at me. "We're friends, remember. If you ever need help with anything . . ."

I give a quick nod, look up at the numbers above the elevator doors. I watch them light up in sequence, but slow, much too slow. What did that mean? If I ever need help with anything? We stand side by side and wait.

Finally there's a ding, and then the doors open. I walk in, and Omar follows. I press the button for my floor, and then I glance over at him. I should say something, make some conversation. We can't have a silent elevator ride. That wouldn't be normal. I'm trying to think of what to say when he speaks. "There's a mole, you know."

"What?"

He's eyeing me. "A mole. In CIC."

Why's he telling me this? Is it me they suspect? I struggle to keep my face impassive. "I didn't know that."

He nods. "The Bureau's investigating one."

It can't be me, though, can it? What's the appropriate response here? "That's crazy."

"It is."

He goes quiet and I have no idea what to say next. In the silence, I feel certain he can hear my heartbeat.

"Look, I vouched for you," he says, speaking quickly and softly. "I said you're my friend, that there's no way you'd do this. That you shouldn't be a priority in the investigation."

I feel the motion come to a stop. I'm not breathing. I'm absolutely frozen. The elevator doors open.

"But something's going on. I can see it." He lowers his voice. "And they're going to investigate you eventually."

I force myself to look at him. There's concern on his face, and sympathy, and for some reason that feels almost more unsettling than pure suspicion. He puts a hand out on one side, tripping the sensors, holding the doors open for me. I step out of the elevator, expecting him to follow. When he doesn't, I turn back. His eyes are boring into me. "If you're in trouble," he says, removing his hand, allowing the doors to begin sliding closed, "you know where to find me."

THE REST OF THE DAY is a blur. Our bay of cubicles is abuzz, chatter about the five pictures, how best to track down Yury, strategy sessions about how to get to *his* handler, the elusive ringleader. And I want nothing more than for it to all just disappear. To have time alone with my thoughts, time to process everything that just happened.

The conversation with Omar, for one thing. Why did he warn me there's a mole? And why did he act like he suspects I've been compromised? If he thinks I'm the double, why is he standing between me and an investigation?

None of it makes sense.

And then there's Matt and the pictures. I don't know how he did it. He wouldn't have access to Yury's computer himself, right? It seems more likely he talked to Yury. But Matt wouldn't betray me that way, would he? He promised he'd never tell.

A heaviness is settling down around me. A darkness. All five of those pictures changed. If the goal was to protect our family, the only one that needed to change was his. Changing all five did more than protect our family. It protected the sleeper program.

I look at the picture on the corner of my desk, the one from our wedding. I stare into Matt's eyes until they look almost taunting. *Are you trying to do what's best for us?* I think. *Or for them?*

I FOUND OUT I was pregnant two months to the day after I made the jump to working Russia CI. I remember sitting on the edge of the bathtub, staring at the little stick, the blue line that was slowly darkening, comparing it to the picture on the box, disbelief and excitement coursing through me in waves.

I'd had all these cute ideas about how to break the news to Matt, things I'd heard about, read about online, mentally filed away over the years. But seeing that line, knowing there was a baby in there, *our* baby, I couldn't wait. I practically burst out of the bathroom. He was in the closet, buttoning his shirt. I hesitated for a moment in front of him, then held up the stick, a big smile on my face.

His hands went still. He looked at the stick, then at my face, his eyes growing wide. "Really?" he said. And when I nodded, he broke into the biggest smile, one I knew I'd never forget. I'd had a niggling fear, ever since the Bahamas, that maybe he didn't want kids as much as I'd thought, as much as I wanted them. But that smile made any lingering doubt disappear. It was pure joy. He was the happiest I'd ever seen him.

"We're going to have a baby," he breathed, and I could hear the same wonderment I was feeling. I nodded, and he came toward me, wrapped his arms around me, kissed me like I was suddenly something fragile, and I felt my heart swelling like a balloon, threatening to float right out of my chest.

I spent the day at work in a happy stupor, caught myself staring at my computer screen for hours on end, the same page, not really seeing anything. When no one was looking, I opened the online employee handbook, navigated to the section on maternity leave, then the one about leaves of absence. Hit the Print button, tucked the sheets into my bag.

I left work early, had a nice dinner at home with Matt, one he cooked. He must have asked a half-dozen times how I felt and if I needed anything. After I changed into some sweats, I pulled out the handbook pages, brought them over to the couch where Matt was sitting, flipping through shows on the DVR. He paused and looked over at them, then at me. There was an expression on his face I couldn't quite read.

He settled on a show, one of those cooking competitions, and I watched with him, curled up beside him, my head on his chest. When it was almost over, when the contestants were all lined up in front of the judges' table, he paused it.

"We need a house," he said.

"What?" I'd heard what he said, but it was so out of the blue, I felt like I needed to hear it again for it to make sense.

"A house. We can't raise a kid *here*." He gestured around us, the main floor of our townhouse. I looked around. Living room, kitchen, dining room—I could see every inch in one glance. Never had it seemed so small to me before.

But at the same time, we weren't tied down. We didn't have the weight of a mortgage. We lived close to the city. I'd never felt the urge to buy. I didn't think he had, either. "Well, the first few years—" I started to say.

"We need space. A yard. A real neighborhood."

He looked so adamant, so *worried*. And those would all be good things to have, eventually. I shrugged. "No harm in looking, I guess."

By the following week, we had a realtor, a mousy man

with patchy gray hair that I stared at from the backseat of his sedan during all those long drives around the D.C. area. We started out close to the city, within our price range. The houses were small. Fixer-uppers, for the most part. I could tell from the look on Matt's face as we walked through that he hated them. Hated them all. *That stairway wouldn't be safe for kids,* he said. *We need more space. No room for a swing set.* It was always something.

So we went farther from the city, where houses got bigger, but not necessarily better. Or better, but not bigger. Then we upped our price range. I thought that brought us some viable options. Frustratingly out-of-date, perhaps, but livable. Cramped, but we could make do. In the suburbs, but it's not like either of us commuted on public transportation.

In each one, though, Matt found something unacceptable. A landing that would be dangerous for toddlers. Backing to a creek—what if the kids fall in? I'd never seen him so picky about anything. "We're not going to find anything perfect," I said.

"I just want what's best for the baby. For any other kids we have, too," he said. And he gave me a look: *Isn't that what you want, too?*

If the realtor hadn't been so passive—and if he didn't stand to make such a hefty sum whenever we *did* make a decision—I swear he would have left us. But still we looked. Raised our budget once more, looked even farther out, counties that were half-suburban, half-rural. The "ex-urbs," our realtor explained.

Matt started to look more interested. He liked the big colonials, the big yards, the neighborhoods full of kids on bikes. I cringed at the prices, the distance from the city. "Just think how great this would be for the kids," he said, and how could I argue with that?

Then we found one. Great layout, updated, on a cul-de-sac, backed to trees. I could tell by the look on his face Matt thought it was perfect. I liked it, too. I could see us raising a family there. And even though I wouldn't admit it, I was so, so done with the search. I wanted to be home, reading baby books. We decided that night that we'd put in an offer.

The next morning, I walked downstairs, and Matt had his laptop open. I could tell from his face that something was wrong. He looked like he hadn't slept. "It's the schools," he explained. "They're horrible." I walked around and looked. He had the ratings up on the screen. He was right; they were.

"We need good schools," he said.

He turned back to his screen. Minimized that window, and another appeared. A house. A small one, rather unimpressive, the kind we'd been looking at during the beginning of our search. "It's in Bethesda," Matt said. "The schools are all tens." There was excitement in his voice, the kind I'd last heard when we'd walked into the perfect colonial. "This is our house, Viv."

"It's small. You hated the small houses."

"I know." He shrugged. "So we'll be a little cramped. We won't have the biggest yard. I won't get everything I want. But the schools are awesome. It'd be worth it, for the kids."

I took a closer look at the screen. "Did you see the price?"

"Yeah, it's not that much more than the last one. The one we were ready to buy."

I could feel my heart doing flip-flops. Not that much more? It was nearly fifty grand more. And the last house was already way above our budget, and our budget had already increased way beyond what I thought we could afford. There was no way we could afford this house.

"We can afford it," he said, reading my mind. He opened up another screen, a spreadsheet. "See?"

It was a budget. He'd budgeted everything.

"I'm due for a raise soon. You're going to get step increases every year, promotions eventually. We can make this work."

My breathing was almost jagged. "It only works if I stay at my job."

There was an awkward silence. "You want to quit?"

"Well, no. Not quit. Maybe a leave of absence . . ." It's something we'd never talked about, I guess. I just assumed I'd stay home for a while. And I assumed it was something he wanted, too. Both our mothers stayed home while we were young. We didn't have any family nearby. We weren't going to put our baby in day care, were we?

"You're not the stay-at-home type, are you?" he asked.

The stay-at-home type? What was that supposed to mean? "I'm not talking about staying home *for good*." It was like that day at the beach all over again, that feeling that I wasn't good enough, that he thought he'd married someone better. "Just for a while."

"But you love your job."

I didn't love it, not anymore. Not since I moved to the Russia account. I didn't like the stress, the long hours, the feeling that no matter how hard I worked, I wasn't actually accomplishing anything. And I knew I'd like it even less with a baby in the mix. "I love the idea of making a difference. But ever since I started working Russia—"

"You've got the best job in the Agency, don't you? The one everybody wants?"

I hesitated. "It's a good account, yeah."

"And you'd leave it to stay home with a baby all day?"

I stared at him. "*Our* baby. And yeah, maybe I would. I don't know."

He shook his head, and more awkward silence filled the room. "If you're not working, how would we save for college? How would we travel with the kids, do anything like that?" he finally asked.

For the first time since getting that positive test, I started to feel nauseous. Before I could reply, he spoke again. "Viv, the schools are all tens. *Tens.* How awesome would that be?" He reached out, placed a hand on my abdomen, gave me a meaningful look. "I just want to do what's best for our baby." And in the silence that followed hung the unspoken question: *Don't you?*

Of course I did. How was I already feeling like I wasn't a good enough mother? I looked back at the screen. The house was back up. The house that already felt like a weight, and we hadn't even seen it yet. When I spoke, my voice was strangled. "Let's go take a look."

I GET HOME LATER than usual that night, and I see them all at the kitchen table as soon as I walk in, the remnants of spaghetti and meatballs in bright plastic bowls and on high-chair trays. "Mommy!" Ella yells, at the same time Luke calls out, "Hi, Mom." The twins are shirtless, their faces covered in spaghetti sauce, little bits of pasta clinging to odd spots—foreheads, shoulders, hair. Matt gives me a smile, like everything's normal, like none of this ever happened, then gets up and heads to the stove, starts to scoop out some dinner onto a plate for me.

I leave my jacket and bag by the door and walk into the kitchen, a smiled pasted on my face. I kiss the top of Ella's head, then Luke's. Wave at the twins, on either end of the table. Chase gives me a toothy grin back and bangs his tray, sending droplets of sauce flying. I pull out my chair and sit down at the same time Matt sets the plate of spaghetti in front of me. He sits across from me, and I look at him, feeling my expression harden. "Thanks," I say.

"Everything okay?" he asks carefully.

I avoid the question, turn to Ella instead. "How are you feeling, sweetie?"

"Better."

"Good."

I glance up at Matt briefly. He's watching me. I turn my attention to Luke. "How was your day at school?"

"Fine."

I try to think of something else to ask him. Something specific. About a test or show-and-tell or something like that, but I don't know what to ask. So instead I just take a bite of lukewarm spaghetti, studiously avoiding Matt's eyes.

"Is everything okay?" he asks again.

I chew slowly. "I thought it wasn't going to be. But lo and behold, everything is *just fine*." I don't take my eyes off him.

He understands. I can see it. "I'm glad to hear that," he says.

There's an awkward pause. Finally Ella breaks the silence. "Daddy, I'm all done," she says. We both look at her.

"Wait till Mommy's done, too, sweetheart," Matt says.

I shake my head. "Don't worry about it."

He hesitates, and I give him a look. *Let her go. Let them all go, so we can talk.*

"Okay," he says to me, and then to Ella: "Bring your bowl to the sink, please."

"Can I be excused, too, Dad?" Luke asks.

"Sure, buddy."

Luke and Ella both leave the table. Matt gets some wet paper towels, starts wiping off Chase's face, his hands. I take a few more bites, watching as he cleans Chase, lifts him out of the chair, puts him down on the floor. He glances at me briefly before turning his attention to Caleb's face. Finally I set down my fork. No appetite; no point in eating any more.

"How did you do it?" I ask.

"Switch the images?"

"Yeah."

He's focused on Caleb's hands now, wiping between chubby little fingers. "I told you I'd get you out of it."

"But how did you *do* it?"

He doesn't answer, doesn't look at me, just keeps wiping Caleb's hands.

I grit my teeth. "Can you please answer my question?"

He lifts Caleb out of the seat, sits back down with him on his lap. Caleb sticks his fingers into his mouth, starts sucking on them.

"I told you it's better if you don't know details."

"Don't give me that. Was it *you*? Or did you tell someone?"

He starts bouncing Caleb on one knee. "I told Yury."

A jolt runs through me, a rush of betrayal. "You said you wouldn't tell."

There's a flash of confusion on his face. "What?"

"You promised you'd never tell."

He blinks, and then there's a look of recognition. "No, Viv, I promised I'd never tell the *authorities*."

I stare at him. Caleb's squirming, straining to get out of Matt's lap.

"I had to tell Yury. I had no choice," he says. Caleb lets out a wail; he's squirming harder now. "I'll be right back," Matt murmurs, and leaves the room with Caleb on his hip.

I look down at my hands, my wedding ring. Is this what it feels like to be cheated on? I thought, when I married Matt, I would be lucky enough to never experience that feeling. I couldn't, in a million years, picture him ever betraying me. I place my right hand over my left, and the ring is gone from my sight.

He comes back a moment later, alone. Sits back down. I listen to the sounds from the other room. Luke and Ella playing Go Fish. I lower my voice, lean forward. "So now the Russians know I disclosed classified information to you."

"*Yury* knows."

I shake my head. "How could you do that?"

"If I could have fixed it myself, I would have. But I didn't have a way to do that. The only way was to go to Yury."

"And change *all five* pictures?"

He leans back in his chair, looks at me. "What are you saying?"

I don't answer him. What am I supposed to say? That I'm not sure if he's really loyal to me?

"None of this would have happened if you'd just turned me in." He's looking at me like *he's* the one who's been betrayed.

But he's right. And I can feel some of the anger inside me starting to morph into guilt. He did tell me to turn him in. He didn't go to Yury right away. Those pictures didn't change the first day.

If he was worried more about the program than about me, he'd have done something that very first day.

"So everything's okay now?" I finally say. I try to push the faces of the other four sleepers from my mind, the fact that they're going to remain hidden, because of me. *You deleted the file, Viv. You deleted the pictures first.* "We're safe?"

He looks away, and I know before he speaks that we're not. "Well, not exactly."

Not exactly. I force myself to think. "Because they'll still be able to tell I deleted the file?" I picture security interrogating me, telling me they discovered I erased it. I can say it was an accident. I had no idea I did it. It might be a stretch, and it might put me under some suspicion, albeit temporarily. But it's not like they'll find Matt's picture on there.

"Yeah," he says. "But not just that. Athena keeps a log of user activity."

How does he know the name Athena? I'm sure I've never mentioned it.

"So there's a record of exactly what you saw on Yury's computer, Viv. In theory, someone could go in and essentially watch you navigate around Yury's computer, see the files you opened."

"They could see me open your picture."

"Yeah."

"So your photo still exists on the server?"

"Yes."

That means the other four pictures exist, too. It wouldn't be too late to get the real photos into the hands of the FBI. I still have a chance to come clean, to let the Agency know about the other four sleepers, and Matt, too. To do the right thing.

No harm done, right? Maybe they'd be able to excuse the fact that I deleted the file. An impulsive act by a frightened wife.

Except not really. Because there's only one explanation for those five pictures changing. I told the Russians details about a highly classified program. I committed treason. That very fact would land me in prison. Fear turns the blood running through my veins to ice.

I think of Omar, the way he's looked at me the past couple of days. *There's a mole in CIC.* If I'm the one they suspect, all they need to confirm their suspicions is sitting right on that server.

"There's a way out of this," Matt says. "A way to erase it." He looks troubled, reticent.

"How?" My voice is barely a whisper.

He reaches into his pocket, pulls out a flash drive. A small rectangle, black plastic. He holds it up. "There's a program on here. It'll erase your activity history for the past two days."

I stare at it. That would wipe out any evidence of me finding Matt's picture. They'd have nothing to use to convict me. To take me away from my kids.

"Yours and everyone else's," he adds. "It'll set the servers back two days."

I look up at him. *Set the servers back two days.* Two days of lost work, for the entire Agency, all those people, all that work.

But it's not much, in the scheme of things, is it?

It would keep my family together. It would erase Matt's picture, once and for all. It would erase the four other sleepers' pictures, too, but there's not a question in my mind I want the Russians to use it. I don't even have to think about it. I'd let those other four sleepers escape detection in exchange for keeping my family together. I know it's wrong. And I feel like a snake just for thinking it. But this is my kids we're talking about.

"So, what?" I ask. "They'll just load it on?"

"Well, that's the thing." He looks at me. "*You* would load it on."

CHAPTER

9

HE SETS THE FLASH DRIVE DOWN ON THE TABLE AND I look at it like it's something that might detonate. "There's nothing I can do with that. The computers are modified. I don't have a port—"

"There's one in the Restricted Access room."

I stare at him. Have I ever mentioned the Restricted Access room? I certainly haven't said anything about the computers in there. But he's right, isn't he? There's a computer set aside for uploading data from the field. "Well, it doesn't matter. That computer's password-protected. I don't have the credentials—"

"You don't have to. The program runs on its own. It just needs to be plugged in."

The magnitude of what he's asking stuns me. "You're asking me to load something onto the Agency's computer network."

"It'll erase the evidence that you deleted the file."

It'll erase the pictures, too. All five of them. I look away. Then I say the words at the forefront of my mind, even though I know I shouldn't. "You're a Russian agent, asking me to load a program onto a CIA network."

"I'm your husband, trying to keep you out of jail."

"By asking me to do something that could get me locked up for the rest of my life."

He reaches across the table, places a hand on mine. "If they discover what you did, you're going away for a really long time as it is."

I hear Ella in the other room. "That's not fair!" she's yelling. *You're right,* I think, staring at the flash drive. *It's not fair. None of this is fair.*

"Daddy!" she screeches. "Luke cheated!"

"I did not!" Luke shouts.

I'm still staring at the flash drive. I can feel Matt's eyes on me. Neither of us is getting up to go in there, to referee. The kids continue arguing, but quieter now. When their conversation returns to normal, I pull my hand out from under Matt's and clasp them together. "What's on it, for real? Something that's going to let the Russians into our systems?"

He shakes his head. "No. Absolutely not. I swear to you, it's just a program that will reset the servers to their state two days ago."

"How do you know?"

"I checked. I ran diagnostics on it. That's all it is."

And why should I believe you? I don't say the words, but I don't have to. I'm sure he can read it all over my face.

"If you don't do this, you're going to jail." His expression looks completely open, honest. And scared, too. "This is a way out."

I look back down at the flash drive, willing it to disappear, wishing this all could just disappear. I have a sense that I'm spiraling down deeper and deeper, and I'm powerless to stop it. Is this really something I could do?

I raise my head, give him a long look. His words are echoing in my head. *I ran diagnostics on it.* "Let me see."

Confusion clouds his features. "What?"

"You said you ran diagnostics on it. Let me see."

He recoils, like he's been slapped. "You don't believe me."

"I want to see it for myself."

We stare at each other, unblinking, until he finally speaks. "Fine." He stands, leaves the room, and I get up to follow. He goes to the storage area behind the stairs. Turns on the light, reaches for the screwdriver, the same one I used. I watch as he pries open the floorboard, removes the laptop. He turns around, gives me a long look, one I can't read, then brushes past me, back to the table.

He opens the laptop and sits down in front of it; I stand behind him, watching the screen. The white bar appears, the cursor flashes. I look down at the keyboard, follow his fingers as they strike the keys, slowly and deliberately. A pattern I recognize, one of his usual passwords, the kids' birthdays. He taps a few extra keys at the end, and it takes a moment for realization to dawn. It's our anniversary date. He was thinking about us, after all.

"You're not going to understand any of this, are you?" he asks, without turning around.

And I'm grateful his back's to me, because he's right. I'm not a tech person; the details won't be clear. But it's not about that. It's about how he acts right now, what he shows me. I'll understand enough to know whether he really ran diagnostics on it, or whether that was a lie. And maybe that's enough. "I know more than you think I do."

He opens a program, types a command, and text starts to roll down the screen. "A log of user activity," he murmurs. He points to a line: today's date. Then another, a time stamp from a few hours earlier.

He scrolls down the screen, gestures to a section of text. "The contents of the drive," he says. I scan the text, much of it indecipherable, but bits and pieces make sense, align with what Matt said. Nothing suggests it's anything more.

And most important, the date and time stamp. The fact that he had something to show me. He ran diagnostics on the drive, just like he said.

He wasn't lying.

He turns in his chair and looks up at me. There's hurt on his face, and it sends guilt washing over me. "Do you believe me now?"

I walk around to the other side of the table, sit in the chair across from him. I hesitate before speaking. "They're good, you know. Agency people. What if they trace this back to me?"

"They won't," he says quietly.

"How can you be sure?"

"Think of the things I told you. The things the Russians know." He reaches over the table, puts his hands over mine. "They're good, too."

I DON'T SLEEP THAT night, again. Instead I wander the house, my heart aching. I watch the kids sleep, the rise and fall of their chests, the faces that look even younger in slumber. I pad through the halls, looking at each photo on the walls, all those fleeting moments, the happy smiles. The artwork hanging on the fridge with magnets. The toys, lying idle in the darkness, waiting. I just want this all to continue. Normal life.

But the fact of the matter is, I could go to jail. It's pretty much a certainty now, if they find out what I did. Disclosing compartmented information, jeopardizing Agency operations. And oh how much I'll miss if that happens. Emotion wells up inside me just thinking about it. Caleb's first steps, his first words. Ella losing her first tooth, the excitement of the Tooth Fairy. Dance recitals, T-ball, learning to ride bikes. Most of all, all those little moments. Cuddling them when they've had a nightmare, or when they're sick. Hearing *I love you, Mommy,* and what they learned at school, what they're excited about, scared about.

Sure, this will mean the Bureau won't catch sleepers it otherwise might have. But in the scheme of things, how much does it matter? There were literally dozens of sleepers at my wedding. This problem is so much bigger than we realized. Five is a drop in the bucket.

I'm sitting on the couch in the predawn darkness when Matt comes downstairs. He turns on the kitchen light, blinks as his eyes adjust. He walks to the coffee maker, presses the button. I watch him in silence. Finally he notices me, stops and stares. I hold his gaze. Then, slowly, I lift up my hand, flash drive between thumb and forefinger. "Tell me what I need to know."

I'M GOING TO DO THIS. The enormity of it is almost over-powering. I watch in a daze as he wipes down the flash drive with a little cleaning cloth, the kind he uses to clear smudges from his sunglasses. *For the fingerprints,* he says. He places it into the false bottom of a double-walled travel coffee mug. Shiny, metallic, something I've never seen before. Where was this? Where does he keep these things?

How have I been so blind?

"All you do is plug it in," he says, handing me the mug. I take it from him. I can see my reflection in it, distorted. It's me, but it looks like someone else. "There's a USB port in the front of the computer terminal."

"Okay." I continue to stare at the reflection in the tumbler, this image of me that isn't really me.

"Plug it in, wait at least five minutes, no more than ten, then remove it. In ten, the servers start resetting. If the drive's still connected when the reset's complete, they'll be able to trace it back to the computer."

Five minutes? I have to sit there for five minutes, with the drive attached? What if someone sees? "I'll wait till after hours, then."

He shakes his head. "Can't. The computer has to be logged on."

"Logged on?" His words fill me with fear. That means business hours. Peter's the one with the credentials; he usually logs on to that computer in the morning, locks it for the day, then logs off again before he leaves. This seems like such a risk, what he's asking me to do. "What if someone sees me do it?"

"That can't happen," he says, and I can see the fear on his face, the first little tremor of uncertainty I've seen since he showed me the flash drive. "Don't let that happen."

THE TUMBLER SITS IN the cup holder beside me as I drive to the office. I grip it tightly on the trek in from the parking lot, even tighter as I enter the lobby and see the American flag hanging from the rafters. Every ounce of my concentration is dedicated to looking calm, impassive.

I pass three signs on the way in—I never noticed there were so many—with the list of prohibited items. A long list, anything and everything electronic. Even if the flash drive were blank, bringing it in would still be prohibited. And it's not like I can say I didn't know.

I wait in line for the turnstiles. Off to the right there's a woman about my age pulled aside for a spot check; Ron's going through her bag. On the left, an older man's being wanded, another spot check. I avert my gaze. I can feel beads of sweat pricking my forehead, my upper lip. When it's my turn, I hold my badge over the reader, enter my code on the touch pad. The turnstiles unlock, allow me to pass.

The sensors sound, a low-pitched beep, and two officers I don't recognize look in my direction. My heart is galloping away, so loud I'm sure the people around me must be able to hear it. I paste on a confused look, just for a split second, then smile, hold up the mug in their direction. *Here, it's just this. Don't worry, it's not electronics.* These sensors, the ones that can detect electronic devices, are notoriously fickle.

One of the officers walks over. He takes a wand, runs it up and down me, over my bag. It beeps only at the tumbler. With a bored look, he waves me in.

I give him a smile, a nod. I continue down the hall, even pace, even gait. When I'm out of his sight, I wipe the dampness from my brow with the back of a trembling hand.

I badge into the vault, enter my code. The heavy door unlatches, and I push it open. I see Patricia right away. I offer her a smile as I pass. A "Good morning," just like any other day. Then I walk back to my cubicle and log on. Normal routine, normal greetings, everything's normal.

I sit at my desk and stare at the door. RESTRICTED ACCESS, large red letters. The readers beside it: one that scans badges; the other, fingerprints. There's a program open on my screen, but I'm not looking at it. Not running my searches, not opening my emails. Just staring at the door.

A few minutes after nine, Peter walks over. I watch as he holds his badge to one of the readers, enters a code, then touches his finger to the other, holds it there. He enters, shuts the heavy door behind him. Minutes later, the door opens again, and he leaves.

I turn my gaze to the tumbler, sitting in front of me on the desk. The computer's logged on; I could do it anytime. I need to do it. I reach for the tumbler, close my fingers around it. It's almost hard to stand up from my chair, make my legs walk toward the door.

I badge in, hold my finger to the reader. The lock disengages, and I pull open the heavy door. Inside it's dark; I flip on the light switch. It's a small space, smaller even than Peter's office. Two computers, side by side on a table, screens angled away from each other. A third, set against the opposite wall. It's this one that draws my attention. I see the USB drive on the front.

I sit down at one of the other two computers, set the tumbler down in front of me. Log on; if anyone else comes in, I need to look like I'm working. I pull up the most compartmented piece of information I have access to, one that only a handful of people in the whole Agency can see. Something so sensitive that I'd have no choice but to ask any newcomer to leave, to come back when I'm finished. Then I take a soft breath, unscrew the bottom of the tumbler. Once open, I see the flash drive. I pull my sleeve over my hand, shake the drive out into it, screw the bottom back on.

I'm still for a moment, listening, but all is quiet.

And then I'm out of the chair, over to the third computer. With my sleeve covering my fingertips, I insert the drive, quickly and easily. The end of it flickers orange almost immediately. I'm back in my chair mere seconds later.

Shaking. I've never been so terrified in all my life.

Everything's still quiet. I look at the clock at the bottom of my screen. Five minutes. That's all I need. I just need to be alone in here for five minutes, remove the drive, stick it back into the tumbler, and this is all over and done with. Like it never happened.

I glance back at the drive, the end of it glowing orange. What's it doing right now? Worming its way into the servers, I guess. Getting ready to erase everything from the past two days. That's it, though, right? God, I hope that's it.

A minute passes, and it feels like an eternity. I'm doing the fractions in my head. One-fifth of the way there. Twenty percent.

And then there's a beep outside the door, a badge being held to the reader. I go still, then turn toward the door. Be calm. I *must* be calm. Four minutes. I just need four more minutes.

The door opens, and it's Peter again. Oh God, it's Peter. Fear is clutching my insides. He's read into everything I am. I have no excuse for keeping him out, do I? He's going to sit down at that computer next to me, and how can I possibly get to the other computer, remove that drive?

"Hi, Vivian," he says. Pleasant, normal. I hope he can't see how panicked I am. How utterly terrified.

"Hey." I fight to keep my voice calm.

He walks in, sits at the terminal beside me, starts typing his passwords. I'm so incredibly conscious of the flash drive in the computer behind us. There's no reason he'd use that computer, right? But what if he notices it?

I look at the clock. It's been three minutes now. Sixty percent. Two more, and—

"Vivian?" Peter says.

"Yeah?" I turn to him.

"Could you excuse me for a few minutes? I need to check a new piece of intel. Eagle Justice."

A compartment I don't have. He's doing exactly what I was planning to do, kick out anyone without the right clearances. I look back at the clock. Still three minutes. I swear time isn't moving the way it should. "Could you just give me a few more minutes to finish up? I'm almost done."

"Wish I could, but I need to take a look at this before the morning management meeting. Nick's orders."

No. No, this can't be happening. What am I supposed to do? What in the world am I supposed to do right now?

"Vivian?"

"Right. Sure. Let me just log off."

"If you could just lock it for now . . . I really need to look at this quickly."

I hesitate. My brain's failing me right now, not coming up with a single thing to do, besides just acquiesce. "Okay." I lock my screen, Control-Alt-Delete. I stand, and as I'm opening the door to leave, my eyes drift to the flash drive, still attached, the end of it still glowing orange.

I walk back to my desk, sit down in a daze. My eyes find the clock—five minutes—and then settle on the door. My mind seems paralyzed, unable to come up with anything to do. I think back to Matt's words this morning. *Five minutes . . . no more than ten . . . the servers start resetting.*

Six minutes now, and still the door is closed. What if Peter sees it?

Seven minutes. I sit, terrified, fear coursing through me.

Eight minutes now. Could I lure him away? I have no idea how. Just wait? He has to finish up soon, doesn't he?

Nine minutes. I'm frozen, unable to move. I force myself to push back from my chair, stand. I'll say I forgot something. The tumbler. Then I'll knock it over, toward the computer, pull out the drive when I'm down on the floor to pick it up—

A flash in front of me draws my attention. A change in color, in contrast. My screen goes black, just for an instant. I spin around, look down the row of cubicles, see other screens go black, too. In succession, one after another. A swift flicker, running through the vault like an electrical current. Normal screens return. People are looking around, murmuring. *What's going on?*

Oh God.

I bolt for the Restricted Access door. Hold up my badge, press my finger to the reader. Matt's instructions are running through my head. *If the drive's still connected when the reset's complete, they'll be able to trace it back to the computer. . . .*

The door opens just as the lock disengages, just as I start to push, and I almost lose my balance, practically fall into Peter.

"Vivian," he says, startled. He pushes up his glasses on the bridge of his nose.

"Cup. I forgot my cup," I say quickly. Too quickly. He shoots me a quizzical look, one that's tinged with suspicion. But it doesn't matter right now, nothing matters but getting to that flash drive, pulling it out. I move out of his way, wait for him to pass, every fraction of a second that he doesn't feeling like torture.

Finally he steps out of the room and I enter, shut the door behind me. I'm on the floor an instant later, yanking out the flash drive, then finding my way to the tumbler, unscrewing the bottom, placing the drive back in, screwing the bottom back on.

And then I collapse in the chair, utterly and completely spent. My whole body is shaking. I can't catch my breath.

The terror stays, even after the shaking stops. And I don't know why. It should go away. I have the flash drive. I'm safe, right? There's no way the reset was complete.

And yet I'm filled with a strange sensation that I'm not safe, even if this works exactly the way it should.

IT DOESN'T TAKE LONG for the room full of analysts to determine that all work from the past two days has been erased. Everyone's commiserating over lost documents, PowerPoint slides. Word quickly spreads that the outage is system-wide. Conspiracy theories abound, everything from foreign intelligence services to hackers to disgruntled IT employees.

Peter's walking from cubicle to cubicle, checking to see if all his analysts' accounts were similarly affected; I hear the quiet conversations, hear him approaching. When he gets to my cubicle, he stands for a long moment, just watching me, silent. His face is expressionless, but somehow it still sends fear flowing through me.

"Same, Vivian?" he asks. "Two days of work?"

"Looks that way."

He nods, still expressionless, and moves on.

I watch his back, and the fear morphs into a powerful wave of nausea. Suddenly I'm certain I'm going to be sick. I need to leave, need to get out of here.

I push back from my desk, hurry down the aisle, through the rows of cubicles, out the vault door. Hand on the wall for balance, I make my way to the ladies' room. I push inside, hurry past the double bank of sinks, the double row of mirrors, down to the row of stalls. Close myself in the farthest one. Lock the door, then spin around to vomit in the toilet.

When it's over, I wipe the back of my hand against my mouth. My legs are trembling; my whole body, weak. I stand, breathe deeply, try to calm my nerves. This worked, it has to have worked. And I have to calm down, get through the rest of the day.

I finally force myself to leave the safety of the stall back up to the row of sinks. Stand in front of the nearest one, wash my hands. There's someone else at the far end of the row, a girl who looks fresh out of college. She gives me a small smile in the mirror. I return it, then glance at my own reflection. Dark circles under my eyes. Pale skin. I look awful. I look like a traitor.

I avert my eyes, pull off a section of scratchy brown paper towel, dry my hands. I need to calm down. I need to *look* calm. I'm surrounded by CI analysts, for God's sake.

Deep breaths. Deep breaths, Viv.

I let myself back into the vault, wind my way through to the back, try to tune out the conversations, the nervous chatter about the outage. My teammates are gathered in the aisle; I join them, hovering near my cubicle. They're talking, but I'm barely paying attention, catching snippets here and there, nodding at the right time, making the right exclamations; I hope so, anyway. I can't keep my eyes off the tumbler, or the clock. Can't wait to get out of here and go home. To hand the flash drive back to Matt, get rid of the evidence, be done with this.

"Who do you think it was?" Marta asks, half-joking, her voice piercing through the fog in my mind. "The Russians? Chinese?"

She's looking around at all of us, but it's Peter who answers. "If the Russians had a chance to get into our systems, they'd do more than erase our work for the past two days." His eyes are on Marta, not me, but the expression on his face is enough to send a chill through me, nonetheless. "If it's the Russians, this isn't all. Not by a long shot."

I'M ON MY WAY HOME, and the tumbler's back in the cup holder beside me. Some of the tension is dissipating, draining away from my shoulders, but it's done nothing to loosen the knot in the pit of my stomach. What have I done?

My hands tighten on the steering wheel. A storm of emotions is swirling around inside me. Relief, uncertainty, regret.

Maybe it'll work. Maybe it'll keep me out of jail. But won't I always live in fear of being caught? I'll get to watch my kids grow up, but won't everything be tainted? Every sweet moment just a little less sweet?

Should I have taken my chances with punishment?

I have a vague sense that I should have thought this through more than I did. That I acted impulsively, even if I thought I didn't.

I pull up to the house. Matt's car is out front, like it always is. It's dusk, and the interior of the house glows bright. The curtains in the kitchen are open, and I see them there, all five of them, around the dinner table.

So I'll never be one hundred percent comfortable, one hundred percent happy. My kids can be. And isn't that what being a parent is all about?

I turn off the ignition, get out of the car, walk down to the mailbox. There's the usual stack of envelopes and ads. And on top, a thin manila envelope, curved to fit in the narrow box, wedged in. I pull everything out, my eyes on the envelope. No postage, no return address, just my first name, black marker, block letters. *VIVIAN*.

My whole body goes cold. I stare at the envelope, immobile, and then I force my legs to move, to bring me to the front stoop. I sit down, set the rest of the mail beside me, hold just the envelope in my hands. I turn it over, slide a finger under the seal.

I already know what it is. There's only one possibility, really.

I pull out the contents—a slim stack of papers, three or four, nothing more. My stomach is in a knot. There, on top, is a screenshot. My computer. Classification bars at the top and bottom, my employee ID number. Athena is open, and inside it, the image of Yury's laptop. A file, open. *Friends*.

I lift the first sheet so that I can see the next one. Same classification bars, same employee ID number, same file. Only this time, one of the images is open, and a close-up headshot fills the screen.

I'm looking, once again, at the face of my husband.

CHAPTER
10

I CAN'T BREATHE. I ERASED THIS. I DID EXACTLY AS MATT said, took that risk, inserted that flash drive. Yet here it is, in front of me. On my lap. Evidence that could get me locked away. That someone brought *here*, to my house.

I lift the page to see the next one, and the one after that. Computer syntax, strings of characters I don't fully understand. And I don't need to. It's a record of my activity, my searches. Proof that I saw Matt's picture. That I deleted the file.

I hear the door open behind me. "Viv?" Matt says.

I don't look up. Can't make myself do it. It's like suddenly any shred of energy I had is gone. There's a pause, and I can picture him behind me, hovering in the doorway, looking down at me, at the papers, catching a glimpse. Will it shock him the way it shocked me?

I feel him come closer, and then he's there next to me on the stoop, sitting down beside me. I still haven't looked at him. I can't.

He reaches for the papers, and I let him. He looks

through them, flipping the pages quietly. Not a word. Then he slides them back into the envelope.

More silence. I focus on breathing, watch each puff of air form, then disappear. I don't even know what to ask him. How to process the jumble of thoughts in my mind into something coherent. So instead, I wait for him to speak, to answer my unspoken questions.

"It's insurance," he finally says.

Insurance. It's not, though. It's something more than that. Much more than that.

"A warning," he goes on. Then, more quietly, "They want to make sure you don't tell."

I turn toward him. His cheeks are flushed, his nose red from the cold. He's not wearing a jacket. "It's blackmail," I say, my voice cracking.

He holds my gaze momentarily, and I desperately try to read his expression. Troubled? I don't know. He looks away. "Yeah, it's blackmail."

I look down the street, the sidewalk where we push the twins' stroller, where Luke learned to ride a bike. "They were here," I say. "They know where we live."

"They always have."

The words feel like a blow. Of course they have. Suddenly nothing seems safe. "The kids . . . ," I manage to choke out.

Out of the corner of my eye I see him shake his head, an adamant shake. "There's no danger to the kids."

"How do you know?" My voice is a whisper.

"I work for them. In their mind, the kids are . . . *theirs.*"

I know the words are supposed to reassure me, but they leave me even more terrified. I wrap my arms around myself and turn back to the street. There's a car coming our way, engine rumbling, headlights swinging into view. The Nguyens' car. Their garage door opens, and the car pulls up the driveway, into its spot. The garage door closes behind it, before the engine's even off.

"What I did today . . . ," I say, and then lose my words. I try again. "It was supposed to erase this."

"I know."

"Why didn't you tell me they'd have this?"

"I didn't know." His forehead has those wavy lines; his brows are knitted together. "I swear, Viv. I didn't. They must have access to the program somehow. Or someone who can tap into the search records."

Another set of headlights. A car I don't recognize. It drives past, continues on its way. I watch until the tail-lights disappear.

"It's not like they're going to do anything with it," he says. "It would blow my cover."

There's a thought beginning to crystallize, something that makes sense of all this. I try to let my mind process it.

"They're not going to just throw away twenty-two years . . . ," he says.

My mind is still processing the thought, forming it into words. Three of them. Three words that explain everything. I voice them, slowly, one syllable at a time.

"They own me."

How could I be so naive? I'm a CI analyst, for God's sake. I know how these intel services work, the aggressive ones. They get you to do something, and then they own you. They blackmail you into doing more. More, and more, and more. There's no way out.

"It's not like that," he says.

"Of course it is!"

"They own *me*. You're my wife. They wouldn't do that to you."

"Really?" I look pointedly at the envelope. *Because that's not what this looks like.*

Something crosses his face—uncertainty?—and then just as quickly vanishes. He turns away from me, faces the street. We're both quiet. Those three words are almost overpowering now, reverberating in my brain, taunting me. *They own me.*

"They'll ask me to do something," I finally say.

He shakes his head, but not adamantly, not like he means it. Probably because deep down, he knows it, too. *They own me.*

"It's only a matter of time," I say. "They'll ask me to do something, and then what am I supposed to do?"

"We'll figure it out," he says, but the promise sounds hollow. "We're in this together."

Are we? I think. I watch a streetlight flicker, then burn out.

Have we ever been?

SOMETHING CHANGED IN ME the day Luke was born. I was completely unprepared for the overwhelming, crushing, all-consuming love I felt for this tiny person. This need to protect him, to be there for him.

The first month of his life was bliss. Exhausting, sure. But wonderful. The second and third, not so much. Every day I woke up knowing I was one day closer to going back to work. To leaving him in the care of someone who wasn't his parent, someone who couldn't possibly love him the same way I did, for all those hours, those oh-so-long days. And for what? I didn't feel like I was making a difference. Not anymore.

I wished I still worked on Africa. But that position was gone, filled by someone else, and this was the next best thing, wasn't it? When the day finally came, I was as ready as I could be. We were sending Luke to the best day care center in the area, the one with the longest list of accreditations, a flawless reputation. I had a freezer full of pumped breast milk. Bottles, carefully labeled. A sheet for the crib, diapers and wipes, all the essentials, packed and ready to go. And I had a new outfit picked out for myself, silk blouse and pants, something that made those last few pounds of baby weight all but disappear, something I hoped would give me the extra confidence I needed to tackle one of the most difficult days of my life.

As it turned out, I wasn't ready at all. Nothing could have prepared me for the feeling of handing Luke off to a woman I didn't know. Turning back at the door, seeing him watching me, alert, almost confused, his eyes glued on me, the question that was in them: *Where are you going? Why are you leaving me?*

I broke down the moment the door to the infant room closed. Cried the whole way to work, arrived with red puffy eyes and tearstains on my silk blouse, felt like I was missing a limb. Three times that morning someone came by, welcomed me back, asked about Luke. And each time, I started crying. Word must have finally gotten around, because colleagues studiously avoided me the rest of the day, which was just fine with me.

When I came home that evening, Luke was asleep in his crib. He hadn't napped at day care, so bedtime came early. I'd missed it. I'd missed an entire day with him. A day I'd never get back. How could I possibly handle this five times a week? Seeing him for just an hour a day? I broke down again in Matt's arms. "I can't do this," I said and wept.

He held me, stroked my hair. I waited for him to agree. I waited for him to say that it was my choice. That if I wanted to stay home with Luke, we'd make it work. If I wanted a new job, we'd survive the pay cut. We'd sell the house, we'd move out of the area, we'd do without trips and savings and meals out. We'd do whatever it took.

When he spoke, his voice was strained. "It'll get easier, honey."

I stilled. Then I looked up at him. I wanted him to see my face, to see how serious I was. He knew me. He'd understand. "Matt, I really can't do this."

I could see in his eyes my own pain. I buried my head back against his shoulder and felt myself begin to relax. He understood. I knew he would. He stroked my hair again, quietly.

A few moments later, he spoke. "Stick with it," he said, words that cut through me like a knife. "It'll get easier."

DAYS PASS, THEN WEEKS. I've gone to work each day, this job that's now a lie. If there's been any saving grace, it's that there's no sign they've traced anything back to the Restricted Access computer. The flash drive doesn't seem to have done any major damage, aside from those two lost days; I've paid attention to all the rumors floating around, read the reports I've been able to lay my hands on. And I haven't heard anything else from the Russians, Matt's people, beyond that envelope.

The Agency was focused on Yury at first. Trying to track him down, in Moscow. And the Bureau was wrapped up in trying to identify the five people in those pictures—until a week or so ago, when an analyst stumbled upon the same five photos in the possession of a known recruiter. With details. The Bureau tracked down the five people, interviewed them, determined they had no connections to Yury and were probably just individuals the Russians hoped to recruit. Yury quickly faded from the Bureau's agenda—just another low-level recruiter—and the Agency's soon after.

I breathed a sigh of relief. The less focus on him, the better. Plus, after the Bureau determined Yury wasn't involved in the sleeper program, Omar's suspicions seemed to subside, at least a bit. I've talked to him a handful of times since then; our conversations have gradually become friendlier, more normal. I still suspect he doesn't fully trust me, but things are improving.

And Peter. Peter hasn't been around much. Katherine's health took a turn for the worse, Bert told us in one of our morning meetings, on the third day Peter was absent. The room went silent. Helen started to cry, and the rest of us got a bit teary, as well. Days later, Katherine was gone. Peter came back to work eventually, but ever since he's looked empty. Broken. The last thing that's on his mind is me.

Matt and I have been walking on eggshells around each other. I blame him for this. Not just the fact that he lied to me for years, got us into this. But that he went to Yury. Told the Russians everything. Sold me out.

Home no longer seems safe. I had our locks changed, installed extra dead bolts. I leave the blinds drawn. I powered off the tablet, the laptop, the wireless speakers, put everything into a box in the garage. When we're all together, the kids and Matt and me, I turn off my cell, remove the battery. And I make Matt do the same. He looks at me like I'm paranoid, crazy, like it's all pointless, but I don't care. I don't know who's watching, who's listening. But I have to assume someone is.

One day, not long after the envelope arrived, I left work early, went to a cellphone store in the mall across town. Made sure no one was following me, paid cash for a prepaid cell, a burner phone that I keep hidden away. I didn't tell Matt, and wasn't even sure why I did it. Just seemed like something I should have.

The kids are my only salvation. I find myself just sitting and watching them, soaking in every little moment. Housework, cooking, cleaning—none of that matters right now. I've let Matt pick up the pieces, keep our lives together, while I just sit and watch. He owes me that.

And he knows it. He's brought me fresh flowers every week. Kept the house spotless, meals always at the ready, laundry cleaned and folded. Taken whichever baby's the fussiest, refereed all the kids' arguments, done all the chauffeuring to playdates and after-school activities.

Like somehow these things can make up for the lies that nearly undid us, that still very well might.

IT'S A FRIDAY, FIVE weeks after I found the picture, after our lives changed. The days are longer now, the temperature higher. The trees are green again. The grass, lush. Spring has sprung, at last, and I'm finally starting to feel like it's a new season for us, too. A fresh start.

I left work a couple of hours early so we could take the kids to the county fair. We parked in a big pasture, long lines of minivans and SUVs ushered into place by volunteers in orange vests. Trekked in, Matt pushing the double stroller through the field, me holding the older kids' hands. Ella practically skipped along, she was so excited. Chattered away, the whole time.

We spent the evening watching the kids on rides: the spinning cups, the wavy slides, the mini roller coaster in the shape of a dragon. The delight on their faces made the overpriced sheets of tickets worth every penny. We snapped cellphone camera pictures. Split a funnel cake between the six of us and laughed at the twins' faces, spattered with powdered sugar.

We're standing in front of the train now, the little cars that circle the tracks. The last ride of the night. All four kids are on it—Luke and Caleb in one car, Ella and Chase in another. And all four are smiling. I think my heart might actually burst.

Matt reaches for my hand, a gesture so familiar and yet so foreign. For weeks I've pulled away from his touch. But I don't today. I let his fingers encircle mine, feel the warmth and softness of his skin. And then, like that, reality comes crashing down. I think of the Russians, the lie. The flash drive and the looming threat of prison. All of the things that have consumed my mind for weeks—but that for the past couple of blissful hours, I actually haven't thought about.

My instinct is to pull away. But I don't. I hold on.

He smiles at me and pulls me close, and for a moment it's just the two of us, like it used to be. I feel the tension I didn't know I still carried start to fade away. Maybe it's time to forgive. Time to move on, embrace this life, stop living in fear. He might have been right; the envelope was just a warning. One I didn't need, because it's not like I'd ever turn him in. And now that I know the truth, maybe they'll be done with us. We can find a way to leave all this behind.

The train comes to a halt back at the start. I walk over and pick up Caleb. The other three scramble off themselves, Chase toddling along behind the older two. We get the twins strapped into the stroller and walk back to the car, through the pasture. Ella's holding tight to a balloon and Luke's wearing a plastic fire hat, the one he insisted he was too old for but accepted nonetheless. The twins are quiet in the stroller, bumping across the uneven field. By the time we reach the minivan, both of them are asleep.

I pick up Chase and Matt takes Caleb, and we transfer them carefully, delicately, into the van. We shush Ella and Luke with smiles, try to quiet their lingering excitement. I watch Luke fasten his seatbelt, then give it a check myself. "Nice work, buddy," I say. I glance over at Matt on the other side, getting Ella strapped in, making sure her balloon is tucked safely inside. Then I open the front passenger-side door.

And I see it.

A manila envelope, my name in block letters, black permanent marker. Sitting on my seat. Just like the one in my mailbox.

I'm frozen in place. Staring, just staring. There's a throbbing in my head, in my ears. I can't hear anything but the throbbing. The kids' voices are gone; all sound is gone except that pounding.

Move, my brain tells me. *Pick it up.* And I do. I pick up the envelope, slide inside the car. I'm vaguely aware of voices behind me, of Matt opening the driver's-side door, getting into the car. But I don't turn. I'm staring at the envelope in my lap. Out of the corner of my eye I see him pause, go motionless. And I know he sees it, too.

I force myself to lift my head and make eye contact with him. We exchange a long look, one heavy with unspoken thoughts.

There are voices from the backseat. Ella, asking why we're not moving. Luke, asking what's going on.

"All right, all right," Matt says, his tone purposefully light, but I can hear it's not all right. "On our way, on our way." He turns the key in the ignition, puts the car into reverse. I'm staring at the envelope again. Knowing I need to open it, see what's inside.

Who put it here? Yury? Someone else? How did they get into our locked car? They must have followed us. Are they watching us right now?

I turn the envelope over and slide my finger under the seal. I lift the flap, peer inside. There's a flash drive.

Black, just like the one Matt gave me, the one I brought to work. I shake it out into my hand. A small piece of paper falls with it. A note, those familiar block letters.

JUST LIKE LAST TIME.

CHAPTER
11

I STARE AT THE FLASH DRIVE, AT THE NOTE. I SHOULD feel like my world is falling apart. I should be thinking, *Now? Just when I'm finally letting myself enjoy life again?* Instead, a strange sense of calm comes over me. Deep down, I knew this was coming. Ever since I got that first envelope in the mailbox. I may not have known exactly what form it would take, but I always knew the other shoe would drop eventually. Having it actually happen, finally, gives me some measure of peace. Like knowing the bad news is better than knowing nothing at all.

Matt's staring straight ahead, eyes on the road. His face looks pale, ghostly white almost, but I don't know whether it's just the moonlight. The tense jaw, though— that's because of this. "You saw?" I say. My voice sounds strangled.

I see his throat working. "Yes."

"I knew they'd do this," I say in a hushed tone.

He glances into the rearview mirror at the kids, then over at me. "We'll figure this out."

I look away, out the window, watch the streetlights until they're nothing more than blurs. Matt's quiet, the kids are quiet, the only sound is the engine of the car, the noise from the road. I close my eyes. This is it. This is what I was waiting for. I feel almost justified, proved right, but there's no satisfaction in it. None at all. Just emptiness. And that feeling, once again, that everything I love, everything that's most important to me in the world, is about to be ripped away.

By the time we get home, Ella's asleep, too. We get all four kids into bed, a thankfully quick process tonight. After I kiss Luke good night, I grab the baby monitor and walk out the back door. I don't wait for Matt. I sit in one of the chairs on the back deck and stare out at the yard, through the darkness, glancing every so often at the monitor, the grainy black-and-white picture that shifts between the rooms where the kids sleep. The air smells sweet; the fragrance of flowers from the neighbor's garden wafts over. The cicadas are humming their tune. It's a peaceful quiet, interrupted only when the back door creaks open. I don't turn around.

Matt comes over and sits down in the chair beside me. He doesn't talk right away, just sits in silence with me. "I'm sorry," he says. "I didn't think this would happen."

"I did."

Out of the corner of my eye, I can see him nod. "I know."

We lapse back into silence.

"I could try to talk to Yury," Matt finally ventures.

"And say what?"

There's a beat of silence that follows, and I know he has no idea. "Try to talk him out of it?"

I laugh, and it sounds cruel. There's no point in even responding, the statement is so ludicrous.

"It's not like they can release anything. Not without burning me," he says, almost defensively.

"Do they care if they burn you?" I ask harshly. "I mean, really. If they're not going to get anything from me, what's the point in keeping you around?"

He moves around a piece of mulch with his toe, doesn't answer.

I blink into the darkness, let the silence settle over us, heavy and thick. "What's on it?" I say.

"I can check," comes his reply. There's a pause, and then his chair scrapes the deck as he pushes back, stands up. He walks inside without another word. I don't turn around, don't look at him, don't watch him go. I just sit and stare at the outline of the trees in the dark, alone with my thoughts.

I GOT PREGNANT FOR the second time when Luke was two. I didn't tell Matt right away this time. I kept the news to myself all day, my own little secret. I stopped on the way home from work and picked up a shirt for Luke. BIG BROTHER, it said. That night I bathed him, got him into pajamas. The fleece pants with dinosaurs, but instead of the top, I put him in the T-shirt.

"Go show Daddy your new shirt," I whispered to him. And I watched as he ran into the family room, jutted out his chest.

Matt glanced at it; then I saw his face change. His eyes swung up to my face, and I saw in them that same unbridled joy I'd seen when I showed him the first pregnancy test, three years before. "We're pregnant?" he said, looking like a kid on Christmas morning.

"We're pregnant," I said, grinning back.

Weeks passed. Clothes got tighter, bump got bigger. I finally put away my regular pants, pulled out the stretchy maternity ones. We had an ultrasound, saw the little peanut. Found out it was a girl, spent evenings looking through baby name books, tossing suggestions back and forth. Luke liked to give my belly kisses, wrap his little arms over it, say *I love you, little sister*. The very first kick I felt was against his hand.

Life was good.

"I'm going to take some time off when the baby's born," I told Matt one night as we lay in bed. It was something I'd been tossing over in my own mind for months, and I'd finally worked up the nerve to say it. "Two in day care is almost my whole salary. . . ."

He was silent. I looked over, could barely see his face in the dark. "For how long?"

"A year or two."

"Will your job still be there at the end?"

I shrugged. "I'm not sure." There were rumors of impending budget cuts, the kind that would make hiring—and rehiring—nearly impossible.

He went quiet again. "Is this really what you want, honey? You've worked so hard to get to where you are."

"I'm sure." I wasn't, not totally, but it seemed like the right thing to say.

"Okay," he said firmly. "If that's what you want."

So we made a new budget, one that relied just on Matt's salary. *Didn't* put the baby on the waiting list at day care. I made plans to request a leave of absence, figured out exactly what I'd say.

Then, as I should have figured, the other shoe dropped. "They're downsizing," Matt said one night over dinner. "Laying people off." I could see the concern etched in the tightness of his lips.

I felt like my heart stopped, just for an instant. My fork was suspended in midair. "Is your job safe?"

He pushed mashed potatoes around his plate. Didn't look at me. "I think so."

Each night after that, he'd have more news. This person was laid off. This person might be laid off; that's what everyone's saying. And each night, I felt a little more hopeless. We didn't talk about it, but I knew. I couldn't leave, not yet. My job was secure. We'd have two children. We needed at least one salary.

So I waited. And waited. The baby, and my bump, continued to grow. We registered her at day care, just in case. Soon I was waddling into work, waddling to the ladies' room every hour, waddling to human resources to schedule my maternity leave. To set my return date, three months after she was due.

That was the day it all became real. That I wasn't leaving. That life, once again, wasn't turning out the way I'd planned. I told Matt that night at dinner. "I scheduled my return date today," I said. Matter-of-fact. Part of me hoped he'd argue. But I knew he wouldn't.

"It's just temporary," he said. "Once the layoffs end . . ."

"I know," I said, even if I didn't. There was a permanence to it all. I'd be putting another baby into day care. I wouldn't have that time at home, after all. Not with the baby, not with Luke.

"I'm sorry, sweetheart," he said. And he looked it, too.

I shrugged, then put my fork down. My appetite was gone. "It's not like I have a choice."

THE DOOR OPENS, and Matt steps back outside. I've lost track of time. Has it been an hour? Two? Nothing seems real right now. The moon is high in the sky, a sliver of light. The cicadas have quieted, the breeze has stilled. He sits down beside me. I watch him, wait for him to speak. He doesn't, just twists his wedding band around his finger.

"How bad is it?" I finally say.

He keeps twisting the ring, around and around. Looks like he wants to say something, but doesn't.

"What would it do?" My voice is flat.

He takes a soft breath. "Give them access. Let them into whatever programs are on the network."

"Classified programs."

"Yes."

It's what I assumed. What I'd do, if I were in their shoes. I nod. I feel numb, like this isn't real. "So I'd be giving them classified information," I say quietly.

He hesitates. "More or less."

"And they could do whatever they want."

"Until your tech people spot the intrusion and kick them out."

I try to think of the first thing they'd do with access. Learn whatever they could about our assets, about the information they're providing. Track them down in Russia. Imprison them, or worse.

Resetting the servers was one thing. But this? This could get people killed.

A breeze blows through, makes me shiver. I wrap my arms around myself, listen to the leaves rustle. How can I do this? How can I live with myself, if I do this?

"Your tech people," Matt says. "They're good. They'll probably catch this quickly."

"Your people are good, too. You said so yourself." I squeeze my arms tighter across myself. Warmth, protection, whatever. "What if they're better?"

He looks down at his hands, doesn't respond. It dawns on me that I called the Russians his people. And that he didn't correct me.

I stare out into the darkness. How did I get to this point? This point where I'm sitting here, seriously considering doing something so awful, so traitorous, that I'm not sure I could live with myself if I did.

Because I was weak. Because I didn't stand up in the beginning and do the right thing. I got in deeper and deeper, and each time I did, it was harder to crawl out, so I didn't even try. I just buried myself further.

Another breeze blows through, harder this time. I hear a branch snap off one of the trees, a quiet thud as it hits the ground below.

It's what I've done with my life, too, isn't it? There were so many times I should have stood up for myself, done what I knew deep down was right. Not bought the house. Insisted on taking time off after Luke was born, then Ella. Life would have been so different if I had.

I feel a raindrop against my skin, then another, like cold pinpricks. It won't end with this. If I do this, I'm just digging myself in deeper.

"I can't do it," I whisper.

More raindrops, falling faster now. I hear them hit the deck, feel them soak my clothes. I can't be responsible for this. Putting lives in jeopardy. And then I speak again, louder this time, resolute, like I can convince myself. "I'm not going to do it."

CHAPTER

12

"NOT GOING TO DO IT?" MATT SAYS. EVEN IN THE DARKNESS, I can see the surprise on his face. It morphs, before my eyes, into something else. Frustration, I think. "You can't just . . . not do it."

"Maybe I can." I stand up and walk back into the house, as much to escape him as to escape the rain. I sound more confident than I feel. The fact of the matter is, I have no idea if I can. Or *how* I can. Refuse Yury's order, but stay out of jail. Stay with my kids. But I don't want him telling me I can't.

He follows, closes the door behind us, shutting out the sound of the rain. "They'll get you sent away."

I say nothing, head for the stairs, up into our bedroom. *Not if I fight back,* I think. But I don't say it out loud. I know what it would be met with. A scoff. Like it's impossible. Like I don't have a choice.

Well, maybe I do. Maybe I *can* fight.

Maybe I'm stronger than he thinks.

WE WERE IN THE MIDDLE of an argument the day Luke almost died. I can't remember exactly what it was about— something frivolous, organic fruit maybe, the fact that the grocery bill was too high. We were in the garage. I'd unstrapped Luke, lifted him out of the car and set him down, grabbed a shopping bag from the trunk. Matt was lifting the infant car seat out of the car, Ella tucked safely inside, fast asleep. Neither of us noticed that Luke had wheeled his new bike out of the garage, out to the top of the driveway. That he'd climbed on, angled the handlebars toward the street.

I heard it before I saw it, the bike moving toward the street. Training wheels against concrete. I spun toward the sound. There he was, holding on tight, bike picking up speed. And something else, too—a car coming down the street toward our house.

I swear time stopped, for just an instant. I saw it in slow motion, the careening bike, the moving car, both on the same path, the collision that was sure to occur. Luke. My Luke, my heart, my life. I'd never get there in time. The bike was moving too fast. I'd never be able to stop him.

So I screamed. A bloodcurdling cry, a sound so loud, so animal, that to this day I can't believe it came from me. And I started running toward him with a speed I didn't know I had. The sound startled Luke enough that he jerked toward it, twisted his head around toward me, the handlebars turning with him, just enough to unbalance the bike, to send it toppling. He fell to the ground at the bottom of the driveway, hard, the bike landing on top of him, the car whizzing past a fraction of a second later.

And then I was there, scooping him up, kissing his face, his tears, the scrape on his knee. I looked up and Matt was standing over us. He bent down, too, hugged Luke, who was still sobbing over his scraped knee, unaware of just how close he'd come to getting killed. Hugged me, too, because I was still holding on to Luke, wouldn't let him go. I could see the infant car seat on the garage floor, Ella still sleeping peacefully inside.

"Oh my God," Matt breathed. "That was close."

I couldn't speak. I felt like I could barely move, couldn't function. All I could do was clutch Luke, like I'd never let him go. If that car had hit him, I would have wanted to die, too. I couldn't have gone on after losing him. I honestly couldn't.

"I saw it, the bike, the car," Matt said, his voice muffled by the way we were huddled together. "I saw what was going to happen. Saw there was nothing we could do."

I squeezed Luke even harder. My mind worked to process what Matt said. He saw it about to happen. He saw it, and he did nothing. And I can't fault him; it's not like I thought things through before I screamed. It was instinct.

I had that instinct, the one that saved his life. And I didn't even know it.

I SLEEP THAT NIGHT, soundly, and I awake filled with a sense of resolve. Conviction that this is the right thing to do. But also conviction, just as strong, that I'm not letting them take me away from my kids. I'm not letting them send me to jail.

I'm brushing my teeth when Matt walks into the bathroom. "Morning," he says. He catches my eye in the mirror. He looks rested, more so than he should, with all this stress.

I lean down and spit into the sink. "Morning." Beside me, he reaches for his toothbrush, squeezes toothpaste from the tube. Then he starts brushing, too—vigorously. I watch him in the mirror, and he watches me. He spits, and then turns to me, toothbrush suspended in the air.

"So what now?"

I pause, briefly, then continue brushing, biding my time. What now? I wish I had an answer for that. The fact that I don't chips away at the edges of my resolve. Finally I lean over and spit. "I don't know," I say, and then turn the water on to rinse my brush. Shift my gaze down. His look is making me uncomfortable.

"I'm telling you, sweetheart, you can't just ignore what they say."

I set my toothbrush back on the counter, then I walk past him, out of the bathroom, into my closet. I grab a blouse from the rack, then a pair of pants. He's right. Yury knows everything I've done. Disclosing classified information. Deleting the file. Inserting the flash drive. And he has proof. Evidence to convict me. I know that, and he knows that.

The question is, what's he going to do with it?

"I have time," I say, again with more confidence than I feel. But I do, right? Yury's not going to burn Matt right away. Lose me. He's going to try to convince me to follow his orders. That means I have time.

"Time for what?"

I look down at the buttons, line them up, start to fasten them. "To figure out a plan." To convince him to leave me alone. I just have no idea how to go about doing that.

Matt comes and stands in the doorway of the closet. His hair's sticking up in the back, like it does when he's just woken up, before he showers. It'd be cute, if not for the expression on his face. Exasperated. "There is no plan, Viv."

I look back down at the buttons. There has to be a way. Yury has information I don't want getting out there. What if I had information *he* didn't want getting out? "What about a compromise?"

"A compromise?"

"Like, silence in exchange for silence."

Matt shakes his head, looks incredulous. "What could you possibly have to trade?"

There's only one thing I could come up with that would be valuable enough. I straighten the edges of my blouse, then look up at him. "The name of the ringleader."

ONCE THE IDEA LODGES in my head, I latch on. It feels right, like it's the only way out of this mess. And so I go to work, day after day, stay chained to my desk long into each night, searching for the ringleader.

I come up with another algorithm, same idea as the last one, but tweaked slightly. It casts a wider net, hopefully traps anyone who might hold the critical role, overseeing handlers like Yury, receiving orders directly from the SVR.

I run it, cross-reference it against anyone who's ever had contact with Yury, or with Yury's contacts, or even with his contacts' contacts. And I come up with a long list of potential candidates, far too long. I need a way to winnow it down, but until I think of one, until I can figure one out, I research. I build profiles on anyone who might possibly be the ringleader. Pictures, bio data, operational leads.

I've caught Peter watching me a few times, looking confused. *Why now?* he asked once. *I just need to find this guy,* I answered.

I've barely seen the kids in days; I come home long after they're in bed. Sometimes after Matt is, too. He hates it, me working these hours. He hasn't come right out and said it, but I know he thinks this is a futile task. That I should just do what Yury said. But I can't. I won't.

I finally print the research, hundreds of pages of material. I flip through it, look at one angry face after another. One of these guys is the ringleader. And once I figure out who it is, once I can convince Yury that I'm on the brink of exposing the whole network, I can buy his silence.

Trouble is, there's too much information. With a mounting feeling of despair, I continue flipping through the pages. I need some way to narrow it down further, but that's going to take time. And how much time do I have, really? When will Yury expect me to complete the task? When will I get his next envelope? I feel overwhelmed. Frustrated. Afraid. A compromise is my only hope, though, isn't it?

I stick the papers into a file. It's thick and bulging. I place a hand on top of it, sit quietly at my desk. I need something, a way out. Finally I place the file into one of my desk drawers, lock it, and gather my things.

I go home that night more dejected than usual. I expect a dark house, quiet. But there's a light on in the family room. Matt's there, awake, on the couch. The TV is off. His hands are clasped in front of him, and one of his legs is bouncing up and down, a nervous habit of his. I walk over warily.

"What's going on?" I ask.

"Yury's willing to make a deal."

I stop. "What?"

"He's willing to make a deal." The leg's bouncing faster now.

I force myself to keep moving forward, to walk into the room, take a seat on the couch. "You talked to him?"

"Yeah."

I don't know whether to press that point or keep going. I leave it for now. "What kind of deal?"

He's wringing his hands now, and the leg's still bouncing.

"Matt?"

He takes a shuddering breath. "It's the last thing they'll ask you to do."

I stare at him. He's gone suddenly still.

"You do this, Viv, they destroy those screenshots. The whole file. There'd be no proof of what you did."

"The last thing," I say, a statement, not a question.

"Yeah."

I'm silent for several moments. "Betray my country."

"Go back to normal life."

I raise my eyebrows. "Normal?"

He leans forward, toward me. "This is enough to let me retire. Viv, we could be done with them after this."

I exhale slowly. *Be done with them.* That's all I want. I want them to go away. I want a normal life. I want none of this to exist. When I speak, my voice is barely above a whisper. "They really agreed to that?"

"Yeah." I can see the excitement on his face, the feeling that he's found a solution, figured this out for us. "We'd have earned it, after that."

We'd have earned it. A shudder runs through me. *But at what cost?*

And besides, what's to say they'd honor the deal? I know how these people work. I've spent years studying them. They'd come back with something else. Maybe not tomorrow, maybe not this year. But someday they would. It wouldn't be over. And then they'd *really* have leverage.

He's looking at me expectantly, waiting for me to respond. Waiting for me to agree, to ask what to do next.

"No," I say. "The answer's still no."

CHAPTER 13

THE BLACK SEDAN IDLES OUTSIDE THE SCHOOL, PARALLEL-parked on a quiet, tree-lined street. Its engine hums softly, barely audible over the rumble of the nearby buses, the happy shrieks and chatter from the arriving children.

"That's him," Yury says. He takes one hand off the steering wheel, points out the passenger-side window. There's a circular drive there, a line of yellow buses. A low white fence separates school from community.

His passenger, Anatoly, looks down at the arm that's reaching across his chest, then out the window in the direction of the extended finger. He raises a pair of binoculars to his eyes.

"The one in the blue shirt," Yury says. "Red backpack."

Anatoly focuses the binoculars until the boy becomes clear. He's standing on the sidewalk, just past the doors of the bus. Bright blue T-shirt and jeans, a backpack that looks almost comically large. He's laughing at something his friend said; the gap where he's missing a tooth is visible.

"A miniature Alexander," he murmurs.

The boy's speaking now, talking animatedly. His friend's listening, laughing.

"He's here every morning?" Anatoly asks. He looks at the fence closest to the buses, a stone's throw from where the boy stands.

"Every morning."

Anatoly lowers the binoculars into his lap. Then, unsmiling, unblinking, he continues to watch the boy.

CHAPTER
14

AT WORK THE NEXT DAY, AND THE ONE AFTER THAT, MATT'S words keep floating through my head. *This is enough to let me retire.*

Viv, we could be done with them after this.

Each time, I try to push away the words, the thought. It's what I want, to be done with them. But how could I do it, the thing they're asking me to do? Load that program. Be responsible for the Russians learning our secrets, bringing harm to our assets. I can't. I just can't.

And so I work. I type names into my search bar, one after the other. Read everything I can find on each of these guys. Search for something, anything, that suggests one of them might be the ringleader. Or something that lets me eliminate them from the list, winnow the file.

But by the end of the week, I've barely made a dent in it, barely crossed off any names, haven't come up with a single person I think might be the ringleader.

It's hopeless.

I drag myself home that night, once again after the kids are in bed. Matt's there, waiting up. He's on the couch, a show on TV—one of those home repair ones. When I walk in, he aims the remote at it, and the picture disappears.

"Hi," I say, coming into the room, hovering near the TV.

"Hi."

"Kids all okay?"

"Yeah." He seems off. I can't put my finger on it, but something's wrong. He's not himself.

"What's going on?" I ask.

"Don't worry about it."

I open my mouth to speak, to argue the point, but I catch myself, close it again. "Fine." I have enough to worry about, and I'm exhausted. *Fine.*

We look at each other for a few awkward moments, then he gets to his feet, picks up the baby monitor from the counter, heads for the stairs. He pauses at the first step, turns back to me. "Have you thought any more about just doing it?"

"Inserting the drive?"

"Yeah."

I watch him closely. He's definitely off. Something's bothering him. "I can't do it. I know you think I should, but I just can't."

He gives me a long look, his forehead creased. "Okay." And there's something about the way he says it, so resigned, so *final,* I catch myself staring after him, long after he's out of my sight.

THE NEXT DAY AT work is as futile as the ones before, and tonight I don't stay late. I come home early in the evening, and when I walk in, the house is quiet.

It's almost dinnertime. Luke and Ella should be arguing, Chase and Caleb screeching, banging. Matt should be in the kitchen, cooking, refereeing, somehow juggling it all.

Instead, it's quiet. A feeling of dread begins to settle over me. Something isn't right.

"Hello?" I say into the void.

"Hi, Mom," I hear. I walk farther in, and I see Luke at the kitchen table, his homework in front of him. I look around and don't see Matt anywhere. Or the other kids.

"Hi, honey. Where's Dad?"

"He's not here." Luke doesn't look up. His eyes are on the paper in front of him, a pencil poised above.

"Where is he?" Panic's taking hold. Luke's seven. He can't be here alone. And where are the other kids?

"I don't know."

Panic feels like full-blown terror now. "Did he pick you up at the bus stop?"

"No."

I can barely breathe. "Is this the first time he hasn't been there to pick you up?"

"Yeah."

My pulse is hammering. I search my bag for my cellphone, pull it out, find Matt on speed dial. As it rings, I glance at my watch. School closes in nineteen minutes. Are the kids still there? The call goes straight to voicemail; I end it.

"Okay, honey," I say, trying to keep the panic out of my voice. "Let's go pick up your sister and brothers from school."

In the car, I try Matt's cell again. Still it goes to voice-mail. *Where is he?* I'm flying by other cars on the road, my foot like lead on the pedal. Are the kids still there? I don't even know why I'm thinking that, but I am. Please, God, let them be there.

I can't wait until I get there to find out. I pick up the phone again, tap another entry on my speed dial. School. The secretary picks up on the first ring. "It's Vivian Miller," I tell her. "I can't reach my husband, and I'm just wondering if he's picked up our kids." There's a silent prayer running through my head, on repeat. *Please, God, let them be there.*

"Let me check," she says. I hear the shuffle of papers, and I know she's checking the clipboards at the front, the ones we use to sign the kids in and out. "Doesn't look like it," she says.

My eyes flutter shut, relief coursing through me, along with a new kind of fear. "Thank you," I say to her. "I'm on my way."

The kids are there. Thank God the kids are there, although I'll feel a thousand times better when I can lay eyes on them. But why are they still there? The place is about to close. Matt knows the rules. And he also had no way of knowing I'd be home in time to get them. If the recent past was any indication, he should have assumed I wouldn't have.

There's a terror running through me like electricity. Luke, alone at the bus stop, alone at home. The other kids, left at school far beyond their usual pickup time.

Matt's gone.

Oh God. Matt's gone.

"Mom!" Luke's voice from the backseat startles me. I glance in the rearview mirror. He's looking at me with wide eyes. "It's a green light!"

I blink at him, then look ahead. Green light, turning yellow. Someone behind me blasts their horn. I slam my foot down on the gas and accelerate through the light.

I think about the last words we spoke to each other last night. Me, saying I still wouldn't do what they want. The way he said *Okay,* the look on his face. Did he realize, finally, that he couldn't talk me into loading the program, and there was no longer any point in sticking around? But that would mean he left the kids on their own, didn't care what happened to them. That's not Matt.

We pull up to school, bouncing over the curb. I pull into a spot, barely between the lines, press down too hard on the brakes, sending my purse sliding from passenger seat to floor. I grab the keys out of the ignition, hurry Luke out, rush up to the front door. Out of the corner of my eye I see the clock—two minutes late, strike two and a fine, five dollars per minute per child—but I don't care. I see the three of them as soon as I step inside, up by the front desk, waiting with the director.

Relief floods through me, and I don't know why. I don't know why I'm so relieved to see them. Did I think the Russians might hurt them? It's not like I thought Matt would take them or anything, did I? I don't know. I can't make sense of the jumble of thoughts in my mind right now, and I don't care.

I wrap my arms around them, bring them all in close to me, not even caring how crazy I must look to the director, the family hug in the lobby that probably just cost us another minute, another fifteen dollars. All I care about right now is that they're here, with me.

And I am never, ever letting them go.

IT TOOK US FAR longer than it should have to make a will. We should have done it before Luke was born, really. But it wasn't until we already had two kids that we trekked into D.C., to the law firm high in that building on K Street, and sat down with a lawyer.

The will itself was easy, barely took any time at all. We named my parents executors of our estate, if anything should happen to both of us. Guardians of the kids. It wasn't an ideal situation, but neither of us has any siblings. There weren't any friends we'd trust enough, any other relatives.

I brought it up on the drive home from the lawyer's office, the fact that they'd have the kids if anything happened to us both. "I don't know how they'd do with Luke's tantrums," I said with a smile, turning around to look at him in the backseat, fast asleep. "We better make sure one of us is always around."

Matt kept his eyes on the road, didn't look over. The smile faded from my lips as I watched him. "Are you okay?" I asked.

The muscles in his jaw clenched. His hands tightened on the steering wheel.

"Matt?"

He shot a quick glance my way. "Yeah, yeah. Fine."

"What's on your mind?" I pressed. He was acting strange. Was it the will? My parents being the guardians?

He hesitated. "Just thinking about, you know, what if something happens to me?"

"Huh?"

"Like, just me. What if I'm not around anymore?"

I gave a little laugh, a nervous one.

He looked over, and his eyes were intense. "I mean it."

I turned away, looked out the windshield, watched cars pass us on the left. The truth was, I hadn't ever really considered it. The kids, sure. From the very beginning, when they were newborns, leaning over the crib to make sure they were still breathing. When they started solids and would gag on their food. The ever-present fear, irrational as it was, that I'd drop them. Their lives always seemed so tenuous, so fragile. I never thought about losing Matt, though. He was my rock, the constant presence in my life, the person who would always be there.

I thought about it now. I thought about getting a call, a trooper telling me he'd died in a car crash. Or standing in front of a surgeon, hearing he'd had a heart attack, that they did everything they could. The gaping hole that would be in my life, the incompleteness. And I answered honestly. "God, I don't know. I don't think I could go on."

And then the fact that I said it, the fact that I *thought* it, shook me, made me feel like I no longer knew myself. What happened to the girl who'd traveled through four continents on her own, who'd worked two jobs in grad school to afford a place without roommates? How, in a handful of years, had I become so intertwined with someone else that I couldn't imagine being alone?

"You'd have to," he said quietly. "For the kids."

"Yeah, I know. I just mean . . ." I looked over at him. He was staring straight ahead, his jaw muscles working. I lost my train of thought, went quiet, looked back out the windshield.

"If anything happens to me, Viv, do whatever it takes to take care of the kids."

I glanced over at him, saw the creases in his forehead, the worry etched on his face. Did he not believe I'd be able to take care of our kids without him? Did he really think that little of me? "Of course I would," I said, defensive.

"Whatever it takes. You'd need to forget about me and just do it."

I had no idea what to think, why he was saying all this, *thinking* all this. No idea how to respond. I just wanted the conversation to be over.

He looked at me, took his eyes off the road for an uncomfortably long stretch. "Promise me, Viv. Promise me you'd do anything for the kids."

I gripped the handle on the door, squeezed it tight. Why did I have to promise that? Of course I would. In that moment, I felt less than mediocre, completely inadequate. When I spoke, my voice was scarcely a whisper. "I promise."

I GET THE FOUR kids home, heat up dinner in the microwave, get them all to the table. They haven't stopped asking about him. *Where's Dad? When's Daddy coming home?* And I have no idea how to answer the question, except honestly. *I don't know. Hopefully soon.*

Luke barely touches his dinner. Ella's quiet. And it's not like I should be surprised. He's their rock. The one they count on to be there.

My presence is unpredictable. His isn't.

I get them bathed and into pajamas, all of them. The whole time, I'm waiting for him to walk in the door. Waiting for my phone to ring. I keep looking at it, like maybe a text came through and I didn't hear it, even though I checked the volume a half-dozen times. I refresh my email, even though I don't think he's written me an email in years.

He has to get in touch somehow, doesn't he? He can't just disappear.

I finally get them into bed, then I go downstairs, alone. I wash the dishes myself. Dry them. The house is hushed around me, an overpowering lonely kind of quiet. I pick up the toys, put them back in their bins. It feels like I'm suspended in time, like I'm just waiting for him to come through the door, hug me, and apologize for being so late. It's like I'm aware of the possibility that he might not, that he might be gone, but I can't process it, can't believe it.

I think back to that awkward car ride, years before. The conversation. *What if something happens to me? What if I'm not around anymore?* Was it a red flag? His way of warning me that one day he'd disappear?

I shake my head. It doesn't make sense. Not the way he left. He wouldn't leave the kids like that.

My gut tells me something happened to him. That he's in danger. But what am I supposed to do about it? I can't go to the authorities. I have no idea how to find him, and I can't tell anyone. I don't even know for sure he's in trouble.

Fear and hopelessness swirl inside me.

I think back to the panic I felt on the way to day care. Panic about the kids. If I thought Matt was in trouble, that something had happened to him, shouldn't I have felt that same panic about him? Shouldn't I be feeling it now?

Maybe I'm wrong. Maybe deep down I think he left. Maybe I'm even glad he did.

And then a thought strikes me. Something so obvious, I don't know why I didn't think of it before. I start moving toward our bedroom. I find my way to the closet, pull down the shoe box from the shelf, the one with the dress shoes. Sink down to the carpet with it in my lap. I'm almost afraid to open it. Afraid of what I might find, even though I already know.

I lift the lid, see the shoes. They're empty.

The gun is gone.

This isn't real, can't be. I continue to stare at the empty space, like the gun might reappear. *He left.* The words are reverberating in my head. I raise my fingers to my temples as if they can somehow silence the thought. He didn't. He wouldn't. There has to be another explanation.

Finally, I reach into my back pocket, pull out my phone, scroll to a number on speed dial.

"Mom?" I say when I hear her voice.

"Honey, what's wrong?"

How she knows something's wrong from that one syllable astounds me. I swallow. "Can you and Dad come stay for a bit? I could use a hand with the kids."

"Of course. Is everything okay?"

My eyes are filling. I can't get words to form.

"Honey? Where's Matt?"

I'm trying hard to keep it together, trying to find my voice at the same time. "Gone."

"For how long?"

A choking cry escapes my lips. "I don't know."

"Oh, honey," my mom says, her voice pained. And I can't hold it in any longer. I cry silently in the dark, lonely house, until tears cloud my vision.

CHAPTER
15

THE NIGHT PASSES WITHOUT ANY WORD FROM MATT, AND by morning I've stopped spending every moment expecting it. I still don't know if he left or something happened. And I don't know why I'm not more desperate, why I feel like none of this is real.

The four kids are around the kitchen table, bowls of cereal in front of the older two, scattered O's and smashed blueberries on the twins' trays. I'm at the counter, making Luke's lunch—another of those things Matt usually does—and nursing my second cup of coffee; another sleepless night. There's a knock at the door, a few quick raps. Ella gasps. "Daddy?" she squeals.

"Dad wouldn't knock," Luke tells her, and the smile fades from her lips.

I open the door and Mom bustles in, in a wave of perfume, bulging shopping bags in each arm, full of what I'm not sure. Presents for the kids, probably. My dad follows close behind, hesitant, more awkward than usual.

I didn't tell the kids they were coming. Wasn't sure when they'd arrive. But here they are, and the kids are thrilled, Ella especially. "Grandma and Grandpa are *here*?" she screeches when she sees them.

My mom heads straight for the kitchen table, drops the bags to the floor beside it, wraps her arms around Ella, then Luke, then plants kisses on the twins' faces. I see lipstick marks where her lips hit their cheeks.

"Mommy, why are they here?" Ella says, turning to me.

"They're going to help out while Daddy's gone," I say. I make eye contact ever so briefly with my mom as I spread jam on bread, then quickly avert my gaze. My dad's hovering over near the coffee maker, like he doesn't know what to do with himself.

"How long are they going to be here?" Ella presses. "How long is Daddy going to be gone?"

The room goes quiet. My parents are suddenly very still. I can feel their eyes on me. Everyone's eyes are on me, waiting for an answer. And all I can do is look at the sandwich in front of me, because I can't for the life of me remember if Luke likes it cut into triangles or rectangles. My mom jumps in. "Presents! I've got presents."

She reaches down into the bags, and the kids begin clamoring for whatever treats are inside. I exhale slowly, and when I look up, my dad's still watching me. He gives me a half smile, uncomfortable, then looks away.

When the kids have their gifts—stuffed animals, markers and coloring books, great big tubes of finger paint—and finish their breakfast, I get Ella's backpack ready, help her find something for show-and-tell—it's the letter *W* today, and we settle on her princess wand, the one with the sparkles. I give hugs and kisses to Luke and the twins, pour another cup of coffee into my travel mug.

Then I remind my parents of the time Luke's bus arrives, the corner where it stops. "Are you sure you're okay watching the twins?" I ask. They offered to watch Ella, too, but two kids all day seemed far more manageable than three; I told them not to worry, that Ella could go to school, like usual.

"Of course," my mom says.

I hesitate, car keys in hand. "Thank you," I say. "For being here." I can feel myself fighting back tears, and I look down, because I'm terrified if I keep looking at my mom, the floodgates will burst open. The next words are a mere whisper. "I wouldn't be able to do this alone."

"Nonsense." My mom reaches over and gives my hand a squeeze. "Of course you would."

ELLA WASN'T EVEN ONE when I got pregnant for the third time. It was an accident, really. We hadn't talked about when—or even whether—we'd have a third, and we certainly hadn't been trying. But I'd packed up my maternity clothes in a plastic tote, just as I'd packed up all the newborn ones. I hadn't gotten rid of anything, and Matt hadn't suggested it. They'd just gone into the basement, into the storage area, along with the infant bathtub and the baby swing and everything else. So I guess we both assumed we'd have another, eventually. Just not this soon. Definitely not this soon.

I left work early that day and picked up a shirt for Ella on the way home. It was actually hard to find one that small, but I did. A little pink shirt with purple writing. BIG SISTER. I put Luke in his BIG BROTHER shirt, the one that still fit from the last time. When Matt called to say he was on his way home, my heart started fluttering. I knew he'd be thrilled. A little scared, a little over-whelmed, like me, but thrilled.

When I heard the key in the lock, I gathered the kids, made sure they were both facing him—Ella in my arms, Luke at my side. He walked in, greeted them enthusiasti-cally, like always, bent to kiss me. Then I saw his eyes take in the shirts, Luke's first, then Ella's. His face froze, his entire body froze. I waited for the smile, the joy that had been all over his face with the first two. But it didn't happen. "You're pregnant?" was all he said. It was almost accusatory.

You're pregnant. The words cut through me. With the other two pregnancies, he'd said *We're pregnant* so much it had grated on me. I'd even lashed out a couple of times, reminded him that *I* was the one with the morning sick-ness, with the heartburn, the aching back. But now I wished like anything that he'd say those words again. That we'd be in this together.

"Yeah," I said, trying to brush it off. *He's in shock. He's worried. Give him a minute, let him adjust, let him get excited.*

"You're pregnant," he said, still no smile. And then an emotionless "Wow."

The bleeding started that night. I remember seeing the blood on my underwear, the terror of it. Brown at first, red when the cramping started. Calling the doctor, because that's what you do, right? The sad voice that spoke back. *There's nothing you can do.* Then the sta-tistics. One in four. Like that somehow made it easier. I remember huddling in a ball on the cold tile of the bathroom. Not taking anything to ease the pain, because I wanted to feel it. I owed her that, at least.

Her. She was a girl. I could feel it. I could see her little face, an existence that would never be.

I couldn't bring myself to go wake Matt and tell him. Not after the way he'd reacted to the news. Picturing his face, his words—he wouldn't feel the same level of absolute heartbreak I was feeling. I was sure of that. I needed to do this myself. Lose my baby, mourn my baby. The most painful, heart-wrenching experience of my life, and I wanted to do it alone.

I'm sorry, I whispered to her as the cramping intensified, as the pain became almost unbearable, as tears dripped down my face. I didn't even know what for. Matt's reaction, I guess. In that very brief existence, shouldn't she have known nothing but love? Excitement? Joy? *I'm so sorry.*

And then the pain, which I thought couldn't possibly get any worse, did. I was doubled over, immobilized, sweating, clenching my teeth to keep from screaming. I knew I was going to die, it was that bad. Blood was everywhere, so much blood. No one told me this would be like childbirth, that it would be *that* bad. And then I couldn't hold it in any longer. Just when I was about to scream, Matt was there on the floor beside me, wrapping his arms around me, almost like he could somehow sense my pain.

"It's okay, it's okay," he murmured, and the words were wrong, so wrong, because it wasn't okay, none of this was okay. He rocked with me, back and forth on the floor. And then all the emotion inside me came rushing out and deep sobs racked my body, ones I couldn't control, because I didn't want him to be here, because I'd lost the baby, because life wasn't fair.

"Why didn't you wake me?" he asked. My head was buried against his chest. I could hear his heartbeat, the vibration of his words when he spoke, louder almost than the words themselves.

I pulled away, looked up at him, whispered the truth. "Because you didn't want her."

He recoiled, his eyes widening. I could see the pain in them, and then guilt ripped through me like a flood tide. This was his baby, too. Of course he wanted her. Could I have said anything worse?

"Why would you say that?" he asked, his voice barely a whisper.

I looked down at the floor, the grout between the tiles, and the silence hung heavy around us.

"I was scared," he admitted. "I didn't react the right way." I looked up at him, but the hurt in his eyes was more than I could handle, so I leaned back against his chest, the shirt that was now cold from my tears. I felt his hesitation, then his arms wrapped around me, and for the first time all night, I felt like it *was* going to be okay.

"I'm sorry," he murmured, and in that moment I knew I was wrong. I never should have assumed the worst. I never should have done this alone. "I love you, Viv."

"I love you, too."

MOM CALLS IN THE LATE AFTERNOON to let me know she picked up Ella from school, that my dad walked Luke home from the bus stop, that somehow Luke is missing his backpack, but everyone is home, safe and sound. I breathe a sigh of relief. *I don't care about the backpack,* I finally tell her, exasperated, after she mentions it for the third time. *We can get him another.* I care that the kids are safe. I didn't even realize I was waiting for her call, waiting to make sure the pickups went smoothly.

I spend the day working feverishly. Typing names in search bars, combing through records, trying desperately to find the ringleader, to make some progress, to be in control. It's futile. Another fruitless day of searching.

Another wasted day.

I leave work after eight hours exactly. Dusk is beginning to settle by the time I reach my street. I pull into the driveway, let the car idle for a moment while I look at the house. Lights are on inside, the curtains sheer enough to see the shapes of my parents, of my kids.

And then something catches my eye. A figure on the porch. Sitting in one of the chairs, settled into the shadows.

Yury.

Even without seeing his features, I know it's him. Almost like a sixth sense.

My heart does a backflip. What's he doing here? *Here,* my home, just a few feet from my kids. What does he want? Without thinking, I pull the keys from the ignition, reach over for my bag, never taking my eyes off him. I get out of the car and walk up to the porch.

He sits very still, watches me. He looks bigger in person. Meaner. He's in jeans and a black shirt, the top two buttons undone, a gold chain around his neck, some sort of pendant. Black boots, the combat kind. I come to a stop in front of him, my mind willing the door to stay closed, for the kids to stay tucked away inside.

"What are you doing here?" I say.

"Come sit down, Vivian." He speaks with an accent, but not as thick as I would have expected. He motions to the chair beside him. *My* chair.

"What do you want?"

"To talk." He pauses, watching me, waiting for me to sit, but I don't. Then he gives a half shrug and stands. He reaches back into his rear pocket, pulls out a box of cigarettes. There's something solid at his hip; I can see the outline through his shirt.

A holster, probably. My heart's racing now.

He taps the box against his hand, once, twice. He eyes me appraisingly. "I'll be quick, because I know your kids are waiting for you."

A shiver runs through me at the mention of the kids, and my eyes drift back to his hip.

He opens the box, pulls out a cigarette, closes it again. There's nothing quick about what he's doing, nothing at all. "I'm going to need you to go ahead and take care of that flash drive."

I have the fleeting thought that he shouldn't be lighting up here. That I don't want the cigarette smell lingering on the porch, anywhere near the kids. Like *that's* what I should be concerned about right now.

He puts the cigarette between his lips, reaches into his front pocket for a lighter. The edge of his shirt lifts just enough that I see black plastic at his hip. Definitely a holster. "You do that, and we both get what we want." The cigarette dips and bobs as he speaks.

"Both?"

He clicks the lighter once, twice, and a flame appears. He holds it to the tip of the cigarette until it glows orange. Then he looks at me, shrugs. "Sure. I get the program loaded, you get to go back to your life. You get to be with your kids."

Kids. Not husband and kids. "What about Matt?" The words come out before I can censor them, think through them.

"Matt?" A brief look of confusion crosses his face. Then he laughs, pulls the cigarette from his mouth. "Ah, Alexander." He shakes his head, smiling. "You really are quite naive, aren't you? But then, that's what Alexander counted on, wasn't it?"

There's a sick feeling rising in me. He takes a drag of the cigarette, blows out a puff of smoke. "Isn't he the one who got you into all this? Betrayed you?"

"He wouldn't betray me."

"He already did." Another laugh. "He's been telling us everything you tell him. For *years*."

I shake my head. *Impossible.*

"Your coworkers? What were their names? Marta? Trey?"

I feel like my lungs constrict. Matt denied doing that. He swore. And I would have sworn he was telling the truth.

The smile leaves Yury's face, vanishes, leaves behind a cold expression. His eyes narrow, and he pulls the cigarette out of his mouth. "Let's cut the crap. Talk intelligence professional to intelligence professional. Don't you want this to end?"

He's waiting for an answer. "Yes," I say.

"You know you have no choice."

"I have a choice."

His lips curl into a half smile. "Prison? Is that really what you'd choose?"

My heart is beating fast.

"If you refuse to cooperate, what reason do I have not to share those search results with the authorities?"

"Matt," I whisper, but even as I say it, I know it's not a reason.

He laughs, then takes another deep drag of the cigarette. "Your husband is long gone, Vivian," he says, the words coming out in a stream of smoke, the kind that seeps into everything.

"I don't believe it," I whisper, even though I don't know what I believe anymore.

He stares at me, an expression I can't read. Then he taps ash off the end of the cigarette. "He wanted us to take care of you, though."

I hold his gaze, hold my breath, wait for him to continue.

"We'll pay. Enough for you to provide for your children, for a long time to come."

I stare at him, watch him take another drag, blow smoke from his nose slowly, looking out at the street. Then he drops the cigarette onto the porch, grinds it out with the heel of his boot. Gives me a pointed look. "You're all your kids have left. Never forget that."

AFTER THE MISCARRIAGE, there was no question I wanted another child. I ached for the one I'd lost. The little girl whose face still came to me in my dreams. Every time I saw a pregnant woman, I compared her belly to where mine should be, and my heart hurt. I wanted to be the one in pants with elastic waistbands, the one with the puffy ankles. I wanted to be turning the guest room into a nursery, folding the impossibly tiny newborn clothes.

And most of all, I wanted a baby. I knew I'd never have *her*, the one I lost, but I wanted another. An infant to cuddle, to nurse, to love, to protect. I wanted another chance.

We could afford two in day care, but not three. Matt was quick to point that out, and I couldn't get his reaction to the last pregnancy out of my mind. So even though I wanted nothing more than to be pregnant, we waited until Luke was in kindergarten to try again.

And this time, when the little line turned blue, I was terrified. That I'd lose this baby, too. That Matt would have the same reaction as last time. So I kept the news to myself, first for a day, then for two. I waited for the bleeding to begin. And when it didn't, I decided I needed to tell him.

I didn't plan any sort of announcement. The BIG SISTER shirt was a painful memory. When the kids were asleep, when we were alone, curled up together on the couch for TV before bed, I held up the test strip and waited.

He looked at it, then at me. "We're pregnant," he whispered, and a grin slowly spread across his face. Then he wrapped me in a hug, so tight I almost worried about the little one inside me.

A few weeks later, we had our first ob-gyn appointment. I'd been counting down the days, desperate for this reassurance that everything was okay, terrified every time I went to the bathroom that I'd see blood. As I sat in the chair, beside the ultrasound machine, there was another fear filling my mind. That there'd be no heartbeat. That something would be wrong.

Dr. Brown began the ultrasound. Matt reached for my hand, and I gripped it hard as I watched the screen, panic setting in. Waited for the fuzz to come into focus as she adjusted the wand, searching for just the right spot, the right view. Desperate to see movement, the flutter of a beating heart. And then there it was, a little white blob, heart beating away.

And beside it, a second one.

I stared at the screen, knowing exactly what I was seeing. Then I peeled my eyes away, over to Matt. He could see it, too. His face paled, and he shot me a smile, but it was strained.

He may have been scared, nervous, whatever, but I was beyond thrilled. Twins. Not just one baby to cuddle, but two. Almost like I was getting a second chance with the baby I'd lost a year earlier.

On the car ride home, we were quiet, each of us alone with our thoughts, until finally Matt spoke. "How are we going to do this?"

I wasn't sure if he meant raising four kids, or dealing with two babies waking through the night, or finances, or whatever. But I answered the question I thought was on his mind. The one that was on my mind. "I'll stay home."

Matt was gripping the steering wheel so tight I could see the skin stretch over his knuckles.

"At least for a while—"

"But won't you miss it?"

I looked out the windshield. "I might." I stopped myself before I said more. I knew I'd miss it. I'd miss the promise of making a difference. Of seeing if that new methodology I'd developed would actually lead us to anyone involved in the sleeper program. "I'd miss the kids more, though."

"But eventually—"

"Eventually I can go back." I hoped I could, anyway. When the kids would all be in school, when time didn't feel like it was slipping through my fingers before I could catch it. When I could really focus on the job, give it the attention it deserved, and not feel like I was doing a mediocre job at everything in my life.

"Can you, though?" He glanced over.

I was quiet. The truth was, there was no guarantee I could return. Those long-rumored budget cuts had come to pass, and hiring was at a standstill. If I left, it might be for good.

"Health insurance is going to be a problem," he said. "We've been lucky with yours." He shook his head. "My coverage is terrible. Premiums are through the roof."

I looked away from him, out the window. The words

were true; Matt's job had some real benefits, but good health insurance had never been one of them. "We're healthy," I said. I didn't want roadblocks right now.

"It's just with twins, sometimes there are complications. . . ."

A car whizzed by in the next lane, much too fast. I didn't respond.

"And getting used to one salary's going to be an adjustment."

There was a sick feeling in my stomach, a pressure in my chest, enough that I felt a flash of panic for the babies. I couldn't be stressed like that. I needed to calm down. I took a deep breath, then another.

"The babies won't be babies forever, you know," he said.

"I know," I said, my voice a whisper. Everything outside was a blur. What if I wasn't just taking a break from climbing the career ladder? What if I could never get back on the ladder at all? My job was part of my identity. Was I ready to let it go?

I wanted both. Time with the kids, and a rewarding career. But it didn't seem possible.

A few moments later, his hand reached for mine. "I just don't know how it's going to work," he said quietly. "I just want us to be okay."

I WATCH YURY WALK AWAY, to a car parked across the street, a black four-door sedan. D.C. plates—red, white, and blue. I read the tag and repeat it under my breath, once, twice. Watch him pull away from the curb, off down my street, until his taillights disappear. Dig into my bag, pull out a pen and a scrap of paper, scribble down the plate number.

Then I collapse. I sink to the ground and wrap my arms around my knees. I'm shaking uncontrollably. Is this really happening?

The only reason I'm in this whole mess is because I wanted to protect Matt, keep him there for the kids, keep our lives as normal as possible. And now he's gone.

He lied to me about Marta and Trey. He told Yury about them; of course he did. How could I have been so gullible? And why didn't he just tell me the truth? I can't get his face out of my mind, the way he looked when he swore to me he never told. Not a glimmer of deception. I really have no way of telling what's a lie and what's not, do I?

And the kids. Oh God, the kids. *You're all your kids have left.* Yury's right, isn't he? What would happen to them if I went to jail?

I hear the door opening behind me, that creak that needs to be fixed. "Vivian?" My mom's voice. And then footsteps, coming closer, the smell of her perfume as she kneels down next to me. "Oh, honey," she murmurs.

She wraps her arms around me, in a way she hasn't since I was small. I bury my head in her softness, like I'm a child again.

"Vivian, honey, what's the matter? Is it Matt? Did you hear from him?"

I feel like I'm drowning. I shake my head, still buried in her arms. She's stroking my hair. I can feel the love radiating out from her. The overwhelming sense that she wants to fix this, to take away this pain. That she'd do anything for me.

I pull away slowly and look at her. Somehow, in the dark, the way the light from the front door is falling on her face, the way her features are contorted in concern, she looks older. How many years do she and my dad have left, in good health? Not enough to care for my four kids. To raise them.

And seeing me sent to prison, I can't even imagine what it would do to them.

"You will, honey. I'm sure you will." But the uncertainty is etched on her face. I know the look. The self-doubt. The realization that maybe Matt isn't who she thought he was, because the man she thought he was wouldn't just disappear. And I don't want to see it. I don't want the doubt, or the lies that are somehow supposed to make me feel better.

She moves from kneeling to sitting, scoots close to me. We sit in silence. One of her hands is on my back, rubbing gentle circles, the same way I do with my own kids. I hear the cicadas. A car door opening, closing again.

"What happened?" she asks quietly, finally voicing the question that I know has been at the forefront of her mind since I first called. "Why is Matt gone?"

I stare straight ahead, the Kellers' house, the blue shutters, blinds drawn, lighting peeking through a few of the windows.

"If you don't want to talk about it, that's fine," she says.

I do want to talk about it. I have an overwhelming urge to just start babbling, to spill everything, to share the secrets. But it wouldn't be fair to put that burden on my mom. No, I can't do that. This is my burden, alone, to bear.

But I have to tell her something. "There were some things in his past," I say carefully. "Things he never told me about."

Out of the corner of my eye I see her nod, like it's what she expected to hear, or at least like it's not surprising. I picture her and my dad sitting around the night I called, trying to come up with explanations for what happened. I fight the urge to laugh. *Oh, Mom, it's nothing like you thought.*

"Before you met?" she asks.

I nod.

It takes her a moment to respond, like she's gathering her thoughts. "We've all made mistakes," she says.

"The mistake was not telling me the truth," I say quietly. Because it's true. It wasn't a single moment of weakness that brought us to this point, was it? It was ten years of lying.

I see her nod again. She's still rubbing my back, endless circles. One of the windows in the Kellers' house goes dark. "Sometimes," she begins haltingly, "we think that shielding the truth will protect those we love the most."

I stare at the dark window, the little rectangle, now black. That's what I did, isn't it? Tried to protect my family. I picture myself in front of my computer at work, cursor hovering over the Delete button.

"I don't know the details, of course," she adds. "But the Matt I know is a good person."

I nod, tears stinging my eyes, trying my best to hold them in. The Matt I know, too, is a good person. One who wouldn't just disappear.

But what if the Matt we both knew didn't really exist at all?

WHEN THE KIDS ARE all in bed and Mom and Dad have slipped into the makeshift guest room, the little nook with the pull-out couch, I sit alone in the family room, the silence heavy around me.

Yury came to my home. This isn't over. They're not going to leave me alone like they left Marta alone, and Trey.

I did something illegal. And they have proof that could send me to prison.

They own me.

Yury's warning is reverberating in my skull. *You're all your kids have left.* It's true. Matt's gone. I can't keep waiting for him to come back, to swoop in and save the day. I need to do it myself.

I need to fight.

I need to stay out of jail.

As long as Yury has proof of what I did, remaining free seems impossible. *As long as Yury has proof.* The thought hits me like a blow. What if he didn't have it anymore?

The CIA has nothing on me. It's only the Russians. Only Yury.

He must have a copy of what he left in my mailbox. Those printouts that prove I saw Matt's picture. That's what he's using to blackmail me. What if I find his copy and destroy it? He'd have no leverage. Sure, he could still tell the authorities everything, but it'd be his word against mine.

That's it. That's the solution, the way I stay out of jail, stay with my kids. I destroy the evidence.

And that means I need to find him.

Adrenaline's coursing through me. I stand up, head into the hallway. Dig into my work bag, find the scrap of paper with Yury's license plate number.

Then I go up to the closet in the twins' room, pull a plastic bin down from the highest shelf. Clothes they've outgrown. I dig around, find the burner phone. I head back into the family room, find Omar's number, remove the battery from my cell, and place the call on the pre-paid line.

"It's Vivian," I say when he answers. "I need a favor."

"Shoot."

"I need you to run a plate for me."

"Okay." For the first time, he hesitates. "Can you tell me why?"

"There was a car on my street today." Truth, so far. "Just sitting there. Seemed suspicious. It's probably nothing, but thought I'd check it out." The lie comes more easily than I expected.

"Yeah, of course. One sec."

I hear shuffling in the background, and I picture him opening up his laptop, navigating to a Bureau database, something that pulls in registry information from every-where, all the data that's out there. The plate will give me a name and address. Whatever alias Yury's using in the U.S., if I'm lucky. And if not his actual address, then at least a lead. Something to run down.

"Ready," Omar says. I read him the plate number and hear the click of keys on his keyboard. There's a long pause, followed by more typing. Then he reads the number back to me, asks if I'm sure that's it. I double-check the scrap of paper, tell him I'm sure.

"Hmm," he says. "That's weird."

I hold my breath, wait for him to go on.

"I've never seen this before."

My heart's thumping so loud I can hear it. "What?"

"There's no record that the plate exists."

THE NEXT MORNING, I'm pulling a coffee mug from the cabinet when I catch sight of the tumbler. Shiny metal, just sitting there on the shelf. I freeze.

That license plate was my only lead to Yury. I have no idea how to find him, how to destroy the evidence that could land me behind bars.

Slowly, I reach for the tumbler. I take it down from the shelf, place it on the counter.

I could do it. I could bring that flash drive in to work, put it in the computer. Just like last time. And then this would all be over. Matt said so; Yury said so.

We'll pay. Enough for you to provide for your children, for a long time to come. Yury's promise runs through my mind. That was a big part of the reason I didn't turn Matt in to begin with—the fear that I couldn't provide for the kids, on my own, if he were gone. Now he's gone. And Yury just offered me a way to do it.

And then Matt's words, from so long ago, that day in the car. *If anything happens to me, do whatever it takes to take care of the kids.*

Whatever it takes.

"Vivian?"

I turn, and it's my mom. I didn't even hear her come into the kitchen. She's watching me, a look of concern on her face. "Are you okay?"

I look back at the tumbler, see my reflection in it, that distorted image. That's not who I am, is it? I'm different than that. I'm stronger.

I turn away from it, back to my mom. "I'm okay."

I SIT AT MY DESK, a mug of coffee in front of me, bits of grounds floating on top. I stare at my screen, open to an intelligence report, something random, so if anyone glances over it looks like I'm reading, when I'm actually not. I try desperately to get my mind to focus.

I have to find that evidence. I have to destroy it. But I have no idea how.

Omar checked more databases, still came up empty on the plate. *Vivian, what's going on?* he asked. *I must have written down the wrong number,* came my reply. But I knew I hadn't, and the fact that there's no record of the plate terrifies me.

I think fleetingly of taking the kids and running, but it's not an option. The Russians are good. They'd find us.

I need to stay here and fight.

LATE THAT NIGHT, after the kids and my parents are asleep, I'm alone in the family room, mindless television for company, to avoid the heavy silence that descends on the house when it's off. A dating show, dozens of women competing for a single man, all of them madly in love, even though not one of them can really, truly know who he is.

My phone begins to vibrate, dancing ever so slightly on the couch cushion beside me. *Matt*, I think, because that's the whole reason I keep it on now. But the screen says UNKNOWN instead of displaying a number. *Not Matt.* It continues to vibrate, a nagging buzz. I mute the TV, then reach for it and answer, holding it to my ear carefully, like it's something dangerous. "Hello?"

"Vivian," he says, the distinctive voice, the Russian accent. My stomach twists into a knot. "Another day, and *still* you haven't completed the task." The tone is friendly, conversational. Unnerving, really, since the words are threatening, accusatory.

"There wasn't an opportunity today," I lie, because in this moment, stalling seems to be my only option.

"Ah," he says, one thick syllable that somehow lets me know he doesn't believe me. "Well. I'm going to patch you through to someone who"—he pauses, as if searching for the right words—"might convince you to find the opportunity."

There's a click on the line, then another. Some sort of shuffling. I wait, tense, and then I hear it. Matt's voice. "Viv, it's me."

My fingers tighten around the phone. "Matt? Where are you?"

A pause. "Moscow."

Moscow. Impossible. Moscow means he left. Left the kids alone that day, without a parent. I hadn't realized until this moment that I didn't truly believe it. That I was still holding on to hope that he'd make his way back to us, that he hadn't really left.

"Look, you need to do this."

I'm numb. Speechless. *Moscow.* This doesn't feel real.

"Think about the kids."

Think about the kids. How dare he say that? "Did you?" I ask, my voice hardening. I picture Luke, alone at the kitchen table, the day Matt disappeared. The younger three, waiting by the front desk at school.

There's no response. I think I can hear him breathing, or is it Yury's breath, I'm not sure. And in the silence, I picture us on the dance floor at our wedding, those words he spoke in my ear. I give my head a shake. I don't know what to believe anymore.

"They'll pay you," he says. "It's enough that you can leave your job."

"What?" I breathe.

"Spend more time with the kids. Just like you've always wanted."

This isn't how I wanted it. Not at all. "I wanted *us,*" I whisper. "You and me. Our family."

There's another pause. "I did, too." His voice is heavy. I can picture the look on his face, the creases in his forehead.

My eyes are filling, my vision blurring.

"Please, Vivian," he says, and the urgency, the desperation, in his voice sends a rush of fear through me. "Do it for our kids."

CHAPTER

18

I'M STILL HOLDING THE PHONE TO MY EAR LONG AFTER the line goes dead. Finally I set it down, back on the couch cushion beside me, and I stare at it. The last words he spoke are ringing in my head, the way he said them, the fear in his voice. Something isn't right.

I should just do what they say. The promises are stacking up: It's the last thing I'd have to do. I'd be paid well. I could provide for my kids. Be there for them. All I'd have to do is stick that flash drive into that port, the same thing I'd already done once before.

But I can't. I can't be responsible for bringing harm to our assets, to my country. And I can't trust that they're sincere, that they won't task me with something else, whenever the opportunity arises.

I'm supposed to feel like I have no choice. Like I'm alone, and I'm not strong enough to do this on my own.

But they're wrong. I do have a choice.

And when it comes to my kids, I'm stronger than they think.

I WAS EXACTLY TWENTY weeks pregnant when I got the call. On my cell, as I was driving home from work. A local number; the OB's office, probably. I'd had another ultrasound that morning—the anatomy scan, the one I'd looked forward to for weeks.

A long string of fuzzy black-and-white photos lay on the seat beside me. Faces that finally looked distinct, arms and legs and the tiniest fingers and toes. The sonographer caught one of them smiling, another sucking a thumb. I couldn't wait to show Matt.

And the envelope. Plain, white, the word *genders* scrawled on the front. Sealed, because I didn't trust myself not to peek. We'd open it together when I got home, Matt and the kids and me.

"Hello?" I said.

"Ms. Miller?" I heard, and it was a voice I didn't recognize. Not the receptionist, the one who called for routine matters like this, to say that everything looked good. My hands tightened on the wheel. I had a vague sense that I should pull over. That whatever this was, I wasn't going to want to hear it. I'd almost started to believe that everything was going to be okay, too.

"Yes?" I managed to say.

"This is Dr. Johnson, from pediatric cardiology."

Pediatric cardiology. I felt like a weight settled down around me, unbearably heavy. They'd run a fetal echo-cardiogram today, after the ultrasound. *Don't worry,* the nurse had whispered as she led me across the hall. *Sometimes with twins they just want to get a closer look.* And I believed her. I believed I shouldn't worry. I believed that the sonographers were just standoffish, that they weren't allowed to tell me anything, that everything was okay.

"One of the fetuses showed no anomalies." Dr. Johnson's voice was heavy.

One of the fetuses. There was a dull thought pounding at the edges of my brain. *That means the other did.*

"Okay." My voice was barely above a whisper.

"Ms. Miller, there's no easy way to say this. The other has a critical congenital heart defect."

I don't remember pulling over, but the next thing I knew, I was in the emergency lane, hazards flashing, cars whizzing by on my left. I felt like I'd been punched in the gut.

She was going on and on, and little snippets were connecting, reaching my brain. "*. . . pulmonary valve . . . cyanosis, trouble breathing . . . surgery immediately . . . that said, there are options . . . if you decide . . . two male fetuses . . . selective termination . . .*"

Two male fetuses. That's what stuck, what lodged in my mind. It was two boys. There would be no huddling around the envelope, no excited yelps from Luke and Ella. But there wouldn't have been, anyway. What did gender matter when there was news like this?

"*Ms. Miller?* Are you still there?"

"Mm-hmm." My mind was racing. Would he have the same life as the other kids? Would he run, would he play sports? Would he even survive?

"I know this is difficult news to receive. Especially over the phone. I'd like to schedule an appointment as soon as possible. You can come in, we can talk about options. . . ."

Options. I looked down at the pictures beside me, the smile on one baby's face, the thumb in the mouth of the other. I closed my eyes and saw them wiggling around on the ultrasound screen. Heard the sound of one heartbeat, *thub-thub-thub-thub,* and the other, *thub-thub-thub.* Then I laid a hand on my belly and felt it shift, the two of them in there, jockeying for space.

There weren't options. This was my baby.

"Ms. Miller?"

"I'm keeping him."

There was a pause, brief but long enough that I could hear the judgment in it. "Well, in that case, it would be good to sit down and discuss what to expect. . . ."

I hated her. I hated this woman. I knew, with absolute certainty, that every appointment I had from here on out, I'd make sure it was *not* with her. He was my son. He was going to reach his full potential. I'd keep him safe, I'd give him strength. Whatever it took, I'd do it.

Her voice drifted through my thoughts. *". . . a series of surgeries in the future . . . potential for delayed development . . ."*

I felt like I'd been punched again. Surgeries. Therapy. All of that would take money. A stable paycheck, one that would keep growing. It would take good health insurance, the kind I got from my job. Not the kind we'd have to pay out of pocket for, that would bankrupt us, that wouldn't provide the same level of care.

The plan to stay home with the babies evaporated, just like that.

But whatever it took, I'd do it. This was my son.

I'M STILL STARING AT the phone on the couch cushion beside me. A plan is starting to take shape in my mind.

It could work, or it could blow up spectacularly in my face. But right now I don't have another option. I need to find Yury. And I finally have another lead.

I remove the battery from my cell, then find the burner phone. I dial, hold it to my ear, hear Omar pick up.

"I need to talk to you," I say quietly. "In private."

Two heartbeats before I hear him say, "Okay."

"How about the Reflecting Pool? Tomorrow morning at nine?"

"That works."

I pause. "Just you and me, okay?"

My eyes drift to a photo on the mantel, Matt and me at our wedding. I hear Omar's breathing.

"Okay," he says.

I ARRIVE BEFORE HE DOES, sit on a bench near the center of the pool. The park is quiet; the trees, still. The air is cool, but holds the promise of warmth. Tourists mill around up near the Lincoln Memorial, little specks of color, but this section of the park is deserted, except for the occasional jogger.

There are three ducks in the water, a little straight line, ripples cascading around them. How nice it would be if I were here with the kids, if they were throwing little chunks of bread into the water, watching the ducks swim over and gobble them up.

I don't see Omar until he's there beside me. He sits down on the opposite end of the bench, doesn't look at me right away, and for a moment I feel like I'm in a movie, like none of this is real. Then he looks over. "Hi."

"Hi." I meet his eyes briefly. There's some suspicion there, but not like there was months ago, when we first broke into Yury's computer. I look away, back to the water. One of the ducks has trailed off, turned himself in the opposite direction.

"What's going on, Vivian? Why are we meeting out here?"

I twist my engagement ring around my finger. Once, twice, a third time. I don't want to do this. "I need your help."

He's silent. I've spooked him. This will never work.

I swallow. "I need you to trace a call. Tell me everything you can about the number."

There's a beat of hesitation. "Okay."

I clear my throat. This is a risk. I don't know if this is the right thing to do. But I do know it's the only idea I've had, the only way I might be able to track down Yury. And he's the only one I can turn to. "It was to my phone, last night. Unknown number. Patched through from Russia."

His mouth opens into a little circle, then quickly closes. "I can talk to my boss—"

"No. You can't tell anyone."

His expression darkens. He raises an eyebrow. I can read the question on his face, even without him saying a word.

I can feel pinpricks of sweat on my brow. "You know how you said there's a mole in CIC? Well, there's a mole in your department, too. The Agency's investigating one."

I fight to keep my expression open, honest. Omar knows how to look for lies. I can't give him any of the signs.

He looks away, shifts in his seat, visibly unsettled.

"You're the only one I trust. We need to keep this between the two of us."

He's staring straight ahead, out into the pool. I look that way, too. The ducks are back in their straight line, far from us now, moving fast.

"What you're asking me to do—trace a call to your cellphone, not document it—it's illegal."

"I need help. I don't know where else to turn."

He shakes his head. "You gotta tell me more."

"I know." I realize I'm twisting my engagement ring around my finger again. It feels wrong, what I'm about to do. I can hear Matt in my head, those words from so long ago. *Whatever it takes. You'd need to forget about me and just do it.*

"It's the sleeper cell. I think I'm close to breaking in."

"What?" he breathes.

"Someone's wrapped up in it." I hesitate. "Someone who's important to me."

"Who?" His eyes are searching mine.

I give my head a shake. "I need to be sure first. I'm not ready to talk about it. Not yet." *Not until I've destroyed anything they can use to blackmail me.*

There's a jogger approaching on the path, bright pink shorts and headphones in her ears. We watch her pass, her footsteps pounding the dirt in front of us, then trailing off in the distance. Finally I turn back to him. "I'll tell you everything, I promise. Just let me get to the bottom of it first."

He runs a hand through his hair, and when he lifts his arm, I can see the bottom of his holster under the edge of his shirt. I stare at it.

"I can't let you do this on your own," he says.

I pull my eyes back to his face and give him my sincerest look, try to channel all of my desperation into it. "Please."

"I won't tell anyone. Just you and me, Viv. We can—"

"No." I pause. "Look, we're friends. That's why I came to you. You said that if I ever needed help . . ."

He runs a hand through his hair again. Gives me a long look, hard and worried at the same time. He'll do it, right? He has to do it.

He looks hesitant. *Too* hesitant, like he's going to say no. I need something else. Something he'd care enough about to bend the rules for me. I think back to the conversation in the elevator, months ago. *There's a mole in CIC.*

If you're in trouble, you know where to find me.

My throat feels tight. "You were right about the mole. In CIC." I need to promise him something. I need to buy time. "I'll learn more if you trace this number for me."

"The number's connected to the mole? *And* the sleeper cell?"

I nod. His eyes search mine, and I can see the excitement, the hunger. I've dangled a carrot in front of him, and he wants it. He wants it enough to do anything, right now.

"Just give me a little time," I say.

Finally he exhales. "I'll see what I can do."

HE'S GOING TO LOOK into the number on his own. I know he will; there's not a question in my mind. I've started a ball rolling, started a timer that's going to give me the smallest of windows to get to Yury before the Bureau closes in. I just need to get to that evidence before they do.

Maybe it was the wrong thing to do, going to Omar. But I'm in an impossible situation. That call is the only real lead I have. I need to exploit it.

Back in the office, I stare at the phone, waiting for it to ring. I catch myself doing it, force myself back to the folder of potential ringleaders, the one that's growing ever so slightly more slim, but only just barely. Every time I hear a phone, I jump, but it's never mine. I try to imagine what Omar's doing, pray he's not telling his superiors, that they're not calling mine, because someone would make me talk, someone would track down Yury on their own, and then where does that leave me? Prison.

Another ring, this one finally mine. My hand's on the receiver, lifting midring. "Hello?"

"I have what you need," Omar says. "O'Neill's in an hour?"

"I'll be there."

I WALK INTO O'NEILL'S sixty minutes later, on the dot. Little bells ring as the door opens, but no one looks up. The bartender's leaning against the bar, pounding out a message on her phone with her thumbs. There's a lone man seated in the center of the bar, hunched over a glass of something amber-colored. A couple's at the table by the front window, deep in conversation.

I walk farther in, let my eyes adjust to the dimness. I scan the room, neon-lit beer signs and old license plates and memorabilia from another decade, and I spot him at the back, alone at a table for two, watching me.

I walk over and take a seat across from him. He has a glass in front of him. Something clear, with bubbles. Tonic, maybe, or soda. He's not a drinker. And certainly not the type to drink while he's on the clock.

He's giving me an even look, hard to decipher. I think there's distrust, though. My hands tighten in my lap. This isn't some sort of trap, is it? Has he told anyone else at the Bureau about our conversation?

"What'd you find?" I ask.

He looks at me for a long moment, quiet. Then he reaches into a bag at his feet, pulls out a single sheet of paper folded in half, lays it down on the table in front of him. I can see a telephone number on it, handwritten in pen, local area code.

"Burner phone," he says, and it doesn't surprise me, even if it disappoints me a bit. "No other call history."

I nod. *Please let there be something. Something I can use.*

"Purchased here in the city, a week ago. Cellphones Plus in Northwest. No CCTV, records are spotty at best. We've never had luck tracing burners from there."

I feel like I'm deflating, hope draining out of me. How am I supposed to find Yury with this?

Omar's watching me, an expression I can't read. Then he pushes the sheet of paper across the table, toward me. I take it, open it. There's a map, a section outlined in red. I look up at him.

"That's the location of the call, based on the cell tower that pinged."

I look back down, examine the map more closely. Northwest D.C. A radius of about twelve city blocks. Yury was close by. I look up at Omar. "Thank you."

He stares at me, then sighs. "What are you going to do with this? Can't you let me help you?"

"You said you'd give me time," I remind him. "Please, just give me time."

He nods, ever so slightly, a resigned nod, his eyes never leaving mine. "Be careful, Vivian."

"I will." I fold the paper back in half, then in half again, slip it into the work bag at my feet, then push the chair back from the table, stand to leave. "Thank you again. Really."

He stays sitting, watches me. I sling my bag over my shoulder and turn, and I'm about to take a step when his voice stops me.

"One more thing," he says. "About that call." I turn to face him. He gives his head a quick shake. "There was no patch-through from Russia."

CHAPTER
17

I DRIVE HOME IN A DAZE. I'M DOING WHAT I NEED TO DO— taking the right route, stopping at red lights, using my turn signal—but it's by rote. Everything around me is a blur.

No patch-through. That means Matt's not in Moscow. He's in Northwest D.C., in that neighborhood outlined in red. With Yury. But why?

And why did he lie to me? Something isn't right. Fear is tapping away at the edges of my mind, trying to break its way inside.

When I get home, Mom's in the kitchen, at the stove. Matt's place. She's wearing my apron, the one I've had for years, which usually sits in a drawer, untouched. The smells that fill the kitchen take me back to my childhood. Meatloaf, the same kind she's been making since I was a kid. And mashed potatoes—from scratch, loads of butter. Not the kind I buy, precooked, microwavable. There's something so familiar about it, so intensely comforting.

I greet her, greet the kids. Paste a smile on my face, nod when I should, ask the right questions. *How was school? How were the twins today?* I'm there, but I'm not present. My mind is on that little box outlined in red. Matt's there, somewhere.

Dad sits in Matt's chair during dinner. It feels odd to see him there, like he doesn't belong. Mom squeezes in on the other side of Ella. Too many people at the table, but we make it work.

Visions of Matt float through my mind. Tied up somewhere, a gun to his head as he talked into the phone, told me he was in Moscow. That's the explanation, right? That's the only one that makes sense, the only way he'd lie like that. I look down at the meatloaf, my appetite gone. Then why am I not panicking? Shouldn't I be panicking?

Mom's asking the kids about their day, trying to direct the conversation, trying to fill any silence with words, with normalcy. Dad's cutting meatloaf into tiny pieces for the twins, and they're shoveling it into their mouths by the fistful, as fast as he can cut.

Ella's answering her questions, chattering away. But Luke's quiet, looking down at his plate, pushing food around with his fork. Not engaging, not eating. I wish I could take this pain away. I wish I could bring his father back, make everything normal once again. Bring back his smile.

Ella launches into a story about the playground, a game of tag. I look over at her, say the right things in the right places, the little phrases that make her think I'm listening, that make her keep talking, but my eyes keep drifting back to Luke. At one point, I look up and see my mom watching me, concern etched on her face. For

Luke, for me, I don't know. I catch her eye and hold her gaze, just for a moment. And I know she wants to take away my pain as much as I want to take away Luke's.

Later that night, three of the four kids are down and I'm tucking in Luke. I sit on the edge of his bed and notice his old stuffed bear tucked in beside him. It's tattered now, stuffing peeking through a tear where one ear connects to its head. He used to carry it around the house, bring it to school for nap time, sleep with it every night. I haven't seen it in years.

"Tell me what's on your mind, sweetie," I say, trying to strike the right tone—soft, gentle.

He grasps the bear tighter. His eyes are open in the darkness, wide and brown and so smart, so much like Matt's.

"I know it's tough with Dad being gone," I say. I feel like I'm floundering here. How am I supposed to make him feel better when I don't know what to say? I can't say his dad will be back. I can't say he'll call. And I certainly can't tell Luke the truth.

"It's nothing to do with you or your brothers and sister," I say, then regret the words. Why did I say that? But isn't that what they say to do, when one parent leaves? Assure kids it's not their fault?

He squeezes his eyes shut, and a single tear leaks out. His chin is quivering. He's trying so hard to hold it all in. I stroke his cheek, wishing desperately I could take his pain and make it my own.

"Is it that?" I say. "Are you worried you made Daddy leave? Because you absolutely didn't—"

He shakes his head firmly. Sniffles once.

"What is it, then, sweetheart? Are you just feeling sad?"

He opens his mouth, ever so slightly, and his chin quivers more. "I want him to come back," he whispers. More tears spill down his cheeks.

"I know, sweetheart. I know." My heart is breaking for him.

"He said he'd protect me." His voice is so quiet I wonder if I heard him correctly.

"Protect you?"

"From that man."

The words make me go still. Fear rushes through me, makes me cold all over. "What man?"

"The one who came to my school."

"A man came to your school?" There's a thudding in my ears, blood pounding through my veins. "Did he talk to you?"

He nods.

"What did he say?"

He blinks quickly, and his eyes get a detached look, like he's remembering something. Something unpleasant. Then he shakes his head.

"What did the man say, sweetheart?"

"He knew my name. He said, 'Tell your mom I said hello.'" Another sniffle. "It was just weird. And he had a weird voice."

A Russian accent, no doubt. "Why didn't you tell me, honey?"

He looks worried, scared, like he did something wrong. "I told Dad."

I swear my heart stops, just for a second. "When did this happen? When did you tell Dad?"

He thinks for a moment. "The day before he left."

IT TOOK MATT AND ME five months to get out of the house together after the twins were born, just the two of us. My parents were up from Charlottesville for the weekend. We'd finally established a bedtime routine; the twins were sleeping in their cribs, a long stretch at night, not waking until midnight or so. It seemed like my parents could hold down the fort for the evening.

Matt said he'd make plans, and I was happy to let go of the reins, looking forward to a surprise. I thought he'd make reservations at that new Italian place, the one I'd been wanting to try, the one that was far too quiet to take the kids.

He wouldn't tell me where we were going until we got there. I thought it was charming, fun, keeping me in suspense. That is, until we got there, and I realized the truth: He knew if he'd told me where we were going, I'd have refused.

"A gun range?" I said, staring at the sign out front, a big ugly warehouse of a building, dirt parking lot crowded with pickups. He pulled the Corolla in, bumped along toward an open spot, didn't answer me. "*This* is your surprise?"

I hated guns. He *knew* I hated guns. They'd always been a part of my life; my dad had been a police officer, wore a gun every day—and I'd spent every day of my childhood worried that a bullet would find him. After he retired, he still carried. It was a sore point between us; I didn't want guns in our house, ever. He didn't want to be without one. So we'd compromised. He could have his gun when he visited, *if*—and only if—it was unloaded, locked in a travel gun safe at all times.

"You need to practice," Matt said.

"No I don't." I'd been proficient long ago, those first years at the Agency when I wanted to check every box, be prepared for any assignment. But I'd let the certification lapse. I was perfectly happy being deskbound, close to home. I hadn't touched a gun in years.

He put the car into park, then turned to face me. "You do."

I could feel anger starting to rise in me. There was absolutely nothing I wanted to do less right then than shoot. This wasn't how I wanted to spend my evening. And he should have known that. "I'm not doing this. I don't want to."

"It's important to me." He gave me a beseeching look.

I heard shots echo inside the building, and the sound made my skin crawl. "Why?"

"Your job."

"My *job*?" I was utterly confused. "I'm an analyst. I sit at a desk."

"You need to be prepared."

I was exasperated at that point. "For what?"

"The Russians!"

His outburst silenced me. I had no idea what to say.

"Look, you work Russia, right?" His tone softened. "What if they come after you someday?"

I saw the worry on his face. I'd never realized before that my job scared him, that he was concerned about my safety. "It's not like that. They don't—"

"Or the kids," he said, interrupting me. "What if they come after the kids?"

I wanted to argue. To tell him that it wasn't like that, that the Russians wouldn't "come after" an analyst, not like that. That they certainly wouldn't come after our kids. Did he really think I'd have a job that would put our kids in any danger? But there was something in his expression that stopped me, that took the argument right out of me.

"Please, Viv?" he said, and gave me that pleading look again.

This was important to him. This was weighing on his mind. This was something he needed. "Okay," I said. "Okay. I'll practice."

IF THERE'S ONE THING about Matt I know for sure, it's that he loves our kids.

From the bottom of my heart, I believe he loves me, too. I may have some doubts; I was, after all, his target. But the kids? There's no question in my mind he loves them. The way he looks at them, interacts with them—that's real. That's why it's been so hard for me to believe that he would have taken off, left Luke to walk home from the bus stop alone, left the other three waiting at day care.

And that's why now it's impossible for me to believe it. Because if he'd heard that someone had brought Luke into this, there's no way he would have run off and left us.

He would have gone after the person who approached our son.

Late that night, when the house is quiet, I pad down the stairs and peek into the living room nook, over to the pull-out couch where my parents lie sleeping. My dad is snoring softly. I can see my mom's chest rising and falling. I walk quietly to my dad's side of the bed. There's a set of keys sitting on top of the end table. I pick it up.

The snores continue, unabated. I glance at my mom, see her chest still rising and falling in a steady rhythm. I walk over to their luggage, set against the wall, and open the largest suitcase. Lift some folded clothes out of the way, rummage around, until I see it. The travel gun safe, buried at the bottom.

I lift it carefully out. I find the smallest key on the ring, slide it into the lock and turn, hear it click open. I freeze and glance over at my parents. Still asleep. Then I open the safe and take the gun out, light in my hands and yet heavy at the same time. I pick up the magazines, the box of bullets. Set everything down on the carpet, close the safe, lock it. I put it back at the bottom of the suitcase, arrange the clothes on top. Our deal is Dad can't touch it while he's here; he'll never even know it's gone.

I place the keys back on the end table, careful not to let them clang. Slide the magazines and the box of bullets into the pockets of my bathrobe, then slip out of the room as quietly as I entered, gripping the gun tight in my hand.

CHAPTER
18

I LIE AWAKE THAT NIGHT WITH THE GUN ON THE BEDSIDE table next to me. I stare at it in the darkness. This is all surreal. The kids are involved now. It might not have been an explicit threat, but the implication is clear: They'll use my kids as leverage. And that changes everything.

I can't stop thinking about that day at the shooting range. Matt wanted me to practice. He specifically mentioned the Russians, too. It's like he knew this day might come, knew I had to be prepared.

I roll on my side, away from the gun, toward the spot where Matt should be lying. The bed seems especially empty tonight, especially cold.

I finally get out of bed. My mind won't shut off, won't let me sleep. I walk through the quiet house. I peek in on the kids, check the locks on the doors and windows, the third time tonight. I find my way to the front hall, pull the folded paper from my work bag. Then I take it into the family room, the room where the kids play, where so much of our life has taken place. I sink down on the couch and unfold it, stare at the map, the box outlined in red.

Yury's there, somewhere. The man who approached my son, who terrified him. And Matt's there, too. Something happened to him. He's in trouble.

I look at the streets, the pattern of them. I find the one outside my old apartment, the one where we met, just inside the red lines. How has it come to this? Who would have ever thought, a decade ago, that we'd one day be here, blackmailed by the Russians, on the verge of losing everything?

I walk into the kitchen, set the map down on the counter. Turn on the coffee maker, listen to the rush of the water heating, the squeal of the coffee brewing. I reach into the cabinet for a mug and see the tumbler. I hesitate, ever so slightly, and then I close the door.

Coffee poured and mug in hand, I turn back to the counter, look at the map once again. I walked those streets, long ago. Matt and I both did. He's there, somewhere. I just have no idea how to find him.

I have no idea what to do.

I drain the last of my coffee and set the mug in the sink. Then I grab the baby monitor from the counter, take it with me upstairs, set it on the bathroom counter. I get in the shower, close my eyes, and let the hot water beat down on me, the steam rise around me, until the air is so thick and hot I can barely see, barely breathe.

"NO ONE IS TO pick up my kids except our emergency contacts," I say to the day care director early the next morning. Ella's little hand is clasped tight in mine, enough that she complained as we hurried in from the parking lot. My other hand is holding Luke's. *I can wait in the car,* he muttered, but I wasn't going to hear it. Not this morning. "That's my parents, and my neighbor Jane."

Her gaze shifts from the bags under my eyes down to my left hand. "If it's a custody issue, we'll need a court—"

"My husband and me and our emergency contacts," I say, gripping the kids' hands even tighter. "Check IDs, if anyone comes. And call me immediately." I write down the burner phone number, then give her my iciest look. *"No one else."*

I drive Luke to school, and he's sullen, because he wants to take the bus. I peer along the length of the fence, down the tree-lined street, then hurry him into the building, my arm around his shoulder. When we're at his classroom door, I bend down so that we're face-to-face. "If you see him again, call me right away," I say. I press a slip of paper into his hand, the number of the burner phone. I see a flash of worry, and in that instant he's years younger, my baby again, and I can't protect him. Hopelessness fills me as I watch him open the door to his room.

When the door's shut behind him, I find my way to the principal's office. I tell him that Luke was approached by a stranger on school grounds, and I use every shred of anger and indignation I can muster. He's used to it from the other parents here, I'm sure. His eyes widen and the color drains from his face, and he's quick to pledge more security along the perimeter of the school, and on Luke himself.

I join the morning traffic, begin the usual commute, the mindless crawl toward the city. And I hate it, because I should be with the kids. But I can't keep them huddled in the house with me forever, and I can't be at school and day care and work at the same time.

The car inches forward, ever closer to an exit sign. It's the one I used to take to get to my old apartment, the one that leads into the northwest section of the city. I stare at the turnoff, the lane that's clear. And when I'm close enough, I turn the wheel and accelerate. Yury's there, somewhere. Matt is, too.

The exit leads onto streets that are so familiar. I wind through them, picturing the red-bordered box in my mind, navigating until I'm inside it. My eyes are scanning the roads, looking for Matt's car, and Yury's. Picking out each and every black sedan, checking the tags. None are a match.

I finally parallel park on a quiet street and start walking. My bag's slung over my shoulder, the gun tucked in a zippered makeup case at the bottom. The morning is warm already. Pleasant. The kind of morning we'd have ventured out in when we lived in this part of the city, walked to get coffee or breakfast, that little diner on the corner we liked.

Memories come flooding back, Matt and me in those early days, those blissfully happy, uncomplicated days. I walk past my old apartment building, stop in the same part of the street where I bumped into him, all those years ago. I picture carrying that box, the collision. I can almost see the coffee stains on the concrete, the smile he flashed at me. Would I change the past, if I could? Make it so I'd never met him? My heart feels like it's squeezed tight. I give my head a shake, keep walking.

I reach the corner where I stood when I saw him next.

The bookstore is long since shuttered, a clothing boutique in its place now. Still, I stare at it, imagine it's the bookstore again, that he's out front, book in hand. The feelings that coursed through me, excitement and relief. Now it's sadness, just sadness.

And the coffee shop, the one where we sat at the table in the back, talked until our coffee grew cold. The Italian restaurant, now a kebab place, where we had our first meal. It's like I'm wandering through my life, and it's a strange sensation, because they're the moments that defined me, that brought me to where I am today, and none of them were real.

And then I see the bank up ahead, the one on the corner with the domed roof. There's a heaviness in my chest as I look at it, the dome glinting in the sun. I never gave the place a second glance, never had any idea Matt was coming here regularly, meeting with the very person I was working day in and day out to find, while the kids sat in day care.

I walk over, find the little courtyard around the side, a grassy square, trees and manicured flower beds and two benches, dark wood and wrought iron. I look at the one on the right, the one that faces the door. I try to picture Matt sitting there. Yury doing the same.

I sit down on it and look around, see what Matt must have seen, what Yury would have seen, too. The courtyard's empty, quiet. I'm suddenly so conscious of the underside of the bench, the place where Yury left Matt the flash drive. I reach my hand under and feel around, but there's nothing there.

I scoot down to the other end of the bench, feel around underneath. Still nothing. I bring my hand back up, slowly, clasp it in my lap with the other. I blink into the emptiness, feeling numb. It's not like I thought I'd find anything, did I? Matt and Yury are together.

It's just that I don't know what else to do. I have absolutely no idea how to find Yury, how to find Matt, how to make everything okay.

I PULL INTO THE parking lot at day care at five, the height of the pickup rush hour. The lot's crowded, cars extending all the way into the third row, the one that's usually empty. I see a minivan pulling out of the middle row, and I wait as it backs up, slowly, timidly, then drives off. I pull into the space and park.

I'm just getting out of the car when I see him. At the far end of the lot, in the farthest row. His car's backed in, and he's leaning against the hood, arms across his chest, looking right at me. Yury.

I'm rooted in place. Terror creeps into my heart. Him, here. And what am I supposed to do, ignore him? Come back out with Ella and let him confront me then?

I force myself to move, to walk over to him. We stare at each other. He's in jeans and another button-down shirt, two buttons open at the top, no undershirt. His necklace catches the light, shiny gold. His expression is hard; none of this fake-friendly stuff anymore.

"Leave my kids out of this," I say, with more confidence than I feel.

"I wouldn't be here if you'd just done what I asked. This would all be over."

I glare at him. "Leave them out of it."

"This is the last time I'm coming to see you, Vivian. The last warning." He holds my gaze, eyes boring into mine.

I hear footsteps approaching and I turn. It's a mother I don't recognize, a toddler on one hip, a preschooler by her side, their hands clasped tightly. She's talking to the older one, not paying the slightest attention to us. They walk to the SUV a few spaces away from Yury's car. We're both silent as she loads in the kids, gets them strapped in, then gets into the car herself.

When her door closes, Yury speaks again. "Obviously the threat of jail isn't enough." He smirks, ever so slightly, and his hand brushes across his hip, touches the holster through his shirt. "But luckily, I have four more points of leverage."

My body goes cold. *Four.* My kids. He's threatening my kids.

The engine of the SUV starts; the sound makes me jump. I take a step closer to him. "Don't you *dare.*"

The smirk deepens. "Or what? You see, I call the shots here." He jams a thumb into his chest, enough to make the gold pendant bounce against his skin. "Me."

The police. I need to go to the authorities. To Omar. Forget the blackmail, forget staying out of jail. I don't care in the least what happens to me. I'd gladly spend the rest of my life behind bars right now, if it meant my kids would be safe.

"I know what you're thinking," he says, and I blink at him, my attention drawn back, away from what I should do, back to what's right in front of me. "And the answer is no."

I look at him, his eyes, his expression. Does he really know? Can he really know what I'm thinking?

"If you go to the authorities," he says, and I realize that yes, yes he knows what I'm thinking, "then you'll never see Luke again."

I'm immobile, frozen in place, as he turns around, gets into his car, the one I'd just driven all over D.C. looking for. I watch as he starts it, pulls out of the spot. There are people all around, parents walking inside, alone, returning to cars toting kids, the smallest ones on hips or in car seats, the older ones skipping along holding hands, little backpacks on their backs. I'm just standing there, staring at the car as it pulls out of the space, out of the lot, and finally turns out of sight.

Then a breath escapes me, a great choking gasp, and my legs buckle, suddenly too weak to hold me up. I reach out to the nearest car to keep from falling. Luke. My Luke. How can this be happening? My God.

I'll do it. I'll do what he says. I picture the flash drive, inserting it into the computer, letting the Russians in, being responsible for the lives lost, those nameless, faceless individuals whose information makes it into the reports I read, I rely on. At least it's not Luke. I picture his smile, his laugh, his innocence. At least it wouldn't be my baby.

Not right now, anyway.

I feel like all the air in my lungs is gone, again.

Because it *would* be my baby, eventually. One of them. It wouldn't be over. He'd know that all he had to do is threaten my kids, and I'd do whatever he wanted. It would only be a matter of time before he'd threaten them again.

I make my feet move. I don't know how I do it, because they might as well be lead. My insides are coiled tight. Everything seems unreal and yet so, so real. I see the front door of the school, but my path's not taking me that way. It's taking me to my car.

I get in and fasten my seatbelt, hands shaking. Then I pull out and away, faster than I should. I turn the way he turned, one hand on the wheel, the other reaching into my bag, pulling out the burner phone. I fumble with it, punch in numbers I know by heart, hold it to my ear.

"Mom?" I say when she answers. I hear Luke in the background, talking with my dad, and relief floods through me, knowing that he's home safe. "Could you pick up Ella from school?"

WE STOOD IN THE farthest lane of the shooting range. I watched Matt load one of the rented pistols, his motions fluid. Shots reverberated around me, loud even through the ear protection I wore.

"When was the last time you did this?" I asked, my voice practically a shout, everything sounding muffled. He'd been shooting before; it was one of those things I knew about him, even if I couldn't remember when I learned it, or the details. Like fishing, and golfing.

"Ages ago," he answered. He flashed me a smile. "It's like riding a bike."

I loaded the other pistol as he got the target ready, a paper one, the outline of a person, little zones we were supposed to aim for. Chest, head. He clipped it onto the pulley system, sent it to the back of the lane. "Ready?" he asked.

I nodded, got into position. Lined up the sights like I'd learned long ago, one eye closed. Racked the gun, moved my finger to the trigger. Pulled back slowly, the voice of my old instructor ringing in my ear. *Let it surprise you.*

Pop. The gun bounced back hard, my hand, my whole arm moving with it. Like riding a bike, indeed; everything had come back to me, quicker and clearer than I could have imagined.

Matt started laughing.

"What's so funny?" I said. I could feel my defenses going up. It'd been years since I'd shot; he could at least give me a chance to warm up.

He pointed to the target. "Look."

I followed his line of sight. There, in the dead center of the target's chest, was a small round hole. "I did that?"

He had a big grin on his face. "Let's see it again. Put it right through that hole."

I took a deep breath, lifted the gun, aimed. Finger on the trigger, slow pull. *Pop.* This time I looked, saw another hole, close to the last one, heard Matt's laugh again.

"You sure you haven't been practicing?" he said with a grin.

It was my turn to laugh. "Let this be a lesson. Don't mess with me."

The grin faded from his face, and he stared at me for a long moment. "Could you do this, if you were ever threatened?"

I looked at the target, tried to imagine shooting a real person. "No," I answered honestly. "I don't think I could."

"If someone threatened you, you don't think you could shoot?"

I shook my head. I couldn't picture myself in a situation where I'd ever have a gun. If I were being threatened, I wouldn't want a gun anywhere near me. Odds were I'd be the one who'd end up shot.

His eyes didn't leave mine. They were searching, penetrating. Making me uncomfortable. So I turned away, back to the target, lined up the sights again. Finger on the trigger. I was about to press down when I heard his voice. "What if someone threatened the kids?"

The target morphed, before my eyes, into a person, a real one, one who was a danger to my kids, one who wanted to hurt them. I pulled back on the trigger, heard the pop. The hole I was aiming for, the first one I made, in the center of the chest, had widened, just the smallest bit. I'd hit it, dead-on. I turned to Matt, my expression as serious as his. "I'd kill him."

IN A FEW BLOCKS, I've caught up. I see the rear of his car, that black sedan, a handful of car lengths in front of me. His brake lights, glowing red, as he stops at a light. I slide down a bit in my seat, a reflex almost, and watch the red spots.

I have the Corolla, thank God. I'm as nondescript as he is. Still, though, he could be watching for me, looking for some sort of tail in his rearview mirror. Could be a habit, even.

I learned how to do this ages ago. One of those classes at work I never imagined I'd use, another box checked. I hang back, keep those cars between us, keep myself out of his sight. I watch the lanes on either side, wait for him to switch, to make a turn, anything.

Finally the sedan pulls into the lane on the right. I stay in my lane, hang back, watch. Now will be the test. Is he watching for a tail? Or is he sure I haven't told a soul, that I'm crumpled into a ball in the parking lot, or dragging myself home, terrified and helpless?

A short time later he turns, and I realize I've been holding my breath. A car behind him turns, too, then another. I could do it, too; there are so many cars following the same path, it wouldn't be alerting. I'm getting closer to the turn, and then I see the sign. The distinctive blue *M*, a right arrow. The Metro's this way.

I look to the right as I approach. The turn leads directly into a parking garage. The sedan is at the gates, stopping for a ticket. I only have a split second to decide. I can't follow him into a garage. Too confining, and besides, it's not like I could follow him on foot, alone. He'd spot me for sure.

I press down on the gas, accelerate past the turnoff. I look as I drive past, see the gate opening and his car driving in. I'm breathing fast now, braking to slow myself. I feel lost, now that he's no longer in front of me.

But I can't be lost. I can't be helpless. I need to fight.

I fumble for the paper in my bag, the one from Omar. Pull it out, open it up, my eyes darting between the road and the paper. I look closely at the little map until I see a blue *M*, a Metro station, in the center of the marked zone.

Then I lay my foot down on the gas.

IT'S A LONG SHOT, really. I know it is. It could have been part of a surveillance detection route—pull into the garage and out again, continue on his way. And even if he actually got on a train, he could have gone anywhere in the city. *Anywhere.*

But I find a spot along the street nevertheless, one with the Metro exit in my line of sight, and I sit. I wait, and I watch. In the silence of the car, I think of my kids. All I ever wanted was to be a good mother to them. And now everything is in jeopardy.

"Please, God," I whisper. "Protect them." I haven't prayed in years, and it seems wrong to be doing it now. But if there's even a chance it could help them, it's worth a shot. Because every second that ticks by, every second I don't see Yury come out of that Metro exit, makes it more likely this won't work. And if this doesn't work, I don't know what to do next.

I cast my eyes up, at the roof of the car, like somehow that'll make God more likely to hear. "I don't care what happens to me," I say. "Please just keep them safe."

And I'm incredibly conscious of the fact that my dad's gun is sitting right beside me, buried deep in that bag.

I ALMOST DON'T SEE HIM when he emerges from below ground. He's wearing a baseball cap now, a faded red Nationals one. A jacket, too—black windbreaker. He's walking my way, on my side of the street, a fact that makes my breathing go shallow, my entire body go stiff, but his head is bent down, the cap the only thing I can see. I watch him from behind a pair of sunglasses, stock-still, silently imploring him not to look up. I don't breathe as he passes, and then I exhale noisily, catch sight of him in my rearview mirror, head still down, body hunched forward.

I keep my eyes glued on him as he gets smaller and smaller in the distance, then panic begins to take hold. I need to follow him. I need to see where he goes. But if I pull out now, I'll lose sight of him. I'll have to double back, follow him down the street, and by then he might already be gone, or he might catch sight of me and it'll all be for nothing.

I turn the key in the ignition with trembling fingers, my eyes still on the rearview mirror, on his back, heading into the distance. My eyes leave him for just a second as I check for traffic, get ready to pull out of the spot. They're back on him a second later, and just as I'm about to pull away from the curb, I stop. He's turned. He's walking up steps. He's at the door of a townhouse. Letting himself in.

A rush of adrenaline runs through me, a burst of relief. I watch until he's out of sight. I memorize the door, blue, the arch above it. White mailbox. Three down from the fire hydrant.

I reach for the burner phone in my bag, tap the last number I called, hold the phone to my ear. Then I set my eyes back on the blue door.

"Hello?" my mom says.

"Hi. It's me. How's everything with the kids?"

"Oh, they're fine, dear. They're all home, safe and sound, happy as clams."

"Thanks for getting Ella."

"Of course." There's an awkward pause. I hear dishes clang in the background. Ella's high-pitched chatter.

"I'm going to be late tonight," I say.

"That's fine," she says. "Take your time. Your dad and I can get them into bed."

I nod and blink quickly, willing the wall of emotion inside to stay put, just a little while longer. I glance over at the bag on the seat next to me, the one that holds the gun. "Tell them I love them, okay?"

Then I angle the rearview mirror down, sink down in my seat, set my eyes back on the blue door, and wait.

CHAPTER
19

IT'S A FEW MINUTES BEFORE TEN O'CLOCK IN THE MORNING when the blue door finally opens. I've already talked to my parents, apologized for being out all night, made sure the kids are okay. I sit up straighter in my seat and watch as Yury steps outside. He's wearing a new hat—a black one this time—and track pants and a dark T-shirt. He turns and locks the door, then walks down the steps, head lowered. He presses a button on one of the keys in his hand, and a car across the street flashes and beeps. Another sedan, this one white. He slides into the driver's seat and pulls away from the curb.

My mind goes immediately to the kids. But he'd given me time after our talk, time to do what he wanted. They're safe, for now.

I take the gun from my bag, tuck it into the waistband of my pants. It's cool against my skin, and hard. Then I reach for the credit card that I laid on the console last night, and the bobby pin lying next to it—one I dug up from the bottom of my bag, another stray from Ella's ballet buns. It's bent now, the way Marta taught me. I hold them tight in my fist as I slip out of the car, then walk quickly toward the house, my own head down, too, like Yury's.

At the blue door, I pause, and I listen. I don't hear anything from inside. I rap my knuckles against the door, once, twice. Hold my breath and listen. No sound. A vision floats through my mind again. Matt, tied up in a chair, duct tape over his mouth.

I take the bobby pin, slide it into the lock, move it around until it makes contact. With my other hand I wedge the credit card into the space between door and frame, apply pressure. My hands are shaking so hard I nearly drop the card. I'm afraid to look around, just praying no one's watching, that my body shields what I'm doing from any passersby.

The lock disengages. Dizzy with relief, I turn the knob and open the door a crack, half-cringing, half-expecting an alarm, something to happen, but nothing does. I open it farther and look inside: a living room, sparsely furnished, just a couch and a big TV. A kitchen beyond that. A carpeted staircase leading up; another, down.

I step inside and close the door behind me. No Matt. But maybe somewhere deeper in the house? And if not, can I at least find the evidence? That file, the one Yury's using to blackmail me?

Suddenly I'm filled with doubt. What if Matt's not here, and I can't find the evidence? Worse, what if Yury comes back? What would he do if he found me?

But I need to try. I force myself to take a step forward, then another.

And then I hear something.

Upstairs. Footsteps.

Oh my God.

I freeze. I pull the gun from my waistband, swing it out in front of me, aim at the stairs. This can't be happening, can it?

But it is. Footsteps, coming down the stairs now. I'm absolutely frozen in fear. I see feet come into view—bare feet, men's feet. I watch through the sights. Now legs come into view, muscular. Athletic shorts that are too big, too baggy. White undershirt. I keep my gun trained on him, wait for his chest to appear, so I can line up the sights.

"That was quick" comes his voice.

Matt's voice.

That fact registers at the same time he comes fully into view. Matt. I take my eyes off the sights, look over the gun, into his face. Impossible. But it's true. It's Matt.

He sees me and freezes, pales like he's seen a ghost. His hair is damp, the way it is when he's just gotten out of the shower. He looks . . . like he belongs here. I keep the gun pointed at him. A storm of confusion is brewing inside me.

"Oh my God, Viv, what are you doing here?" he says, and then he's rushing down the last steps toward me, his face open now, full of relief. I wish he would stop, slow down, give me time to process this, because this isn't right. None of this is right. I had visions of him tied up somewhere. A captive. Not alone, unrestrained, showering in Yury's townhouse.

He's almost to me now, completely ignoring the gun pointed at him, smiling at me like he couldn't be happier to see me. And I lower the gun, because this is my husband I'm looking at, pointing a *weapon* at, but it's almost hard to do, almost like my arms are protesting, or my brain, or something. He wraps me in an embrace, but my body stays stiff.

"How did you find me?" he asks, incredulous.

I still haven't moved my arms, haven't returned his embrace. I don't understand. I don't understand any of this. He pulls away, holds me at arm's length, looks at me intently, his eyes searching mine. "Viv, I'm so sorry. He came to Luke's school. He talked to Luke. I couldn't wait. I had to go. . . ."

I stare at him, his face so open, so honest. The confusion feels like it's starting to melt at the edges, the smallest bit. It's what I thought, isn't it? He left us to protect Luke, to tell Yury to stay away from our kids. So why is my mind still screaming that this is wrong?

Because he's here, alone. He wasn't a prisoner, bound to a chair somewhere in the house; that image that was haunting me wasn't the truth. I look him up and down, the damp hair, the clothes. There's a sick feeling in my stomach. *Why are you still here? Why didn't you leave?*

"He said if I left, he'd kill Luke."

The words send a chill through me.

"Maybe I should have tried . . . I didn't know if I could take him. . . ." He looks ashamed when he says it, and I feel a pull in my chest. "I didn't leave you, Viv. I swear." He looks like he's about to cry.

"I know," I say, as much to convince myself as anything else.

"I wouldn't do that."

"I know. I know." Do I, though?

His eyes search mine, and then something crosses his face, a brief flash of panic. "Yury's going to be back soon. He just ran out for coffee. You need to go, Viv."

"What?"

His voice is urgent. "You need to go. You need to get out of here."

A jumble of emotions swirls inside me. Panic, confusion, desperation. "I need that file. What they're using to blackmail me."

He gives me a long look, one I can't read. "This is dangerous. The kids—"

"Where is it?" I watch him, unblinking. *You've had time to search.*

His eyes are boring into me. Then they soften. "Upstairs."

He did look. He found it. Relief surges through me. "Can you—"

I stop midsentence, pivot toward the door. There's a key in the lock, scraping, turning. I raise my gun and aim at the closed door, the edge that's going to open, any second now. He's back. Yury's back.

I watch the edge of the door through the sights. It opens, and I see him, head down, a disposable tray in his hand, two cups of coffee. He hasn't seen me yet. I keep the sights on him. He takes a step in, starts to close the door.

And then sees me.

"Don't move," I say.

He goes still.

"Close the door." I make sure the sights are in the dead center of his chest. If he makes even the slightest move to leave, I'll shoot him. I swear to God I will. This is the guy who frightened my son.

He slowly, carefully closes the door.

"Hands in the air," I say. I'm surprised by how calm my voice sounds. How commanding, how confident, when I feel none of those things. What I feel is utter terror.

He complies, sort of. Holds his hands in front of him, the tray extended toward me in one hand, the other open to show me his palm.

"Try anything, and I *will* shoot." My voice sounds deadly serious. A dizzying sensation creeps over me, like I'm watching myself in a movie.

He looks at me, impassive, then his eyes shift to Matt. They stay expressionless.

I need to look like I know what to do. I need to stay in control. I try to force my mind to work, to come up with a solution.

"Tie him up," I say to Matt. Yury shifts his gaze back to me. His eyes narrow slightly, but he doesn't make a move.

I don't look over at Matt, but I hear him leave the room. Yury and I stare at each other. There's that hint of a smirk on his face, one that ratchets up my unease. His goal, probably.

Matt comes back moments later. I glance over, and he's carrying a straight-backed wooden chair and a roll of duct tape. Yury shifts his gaze to Matt, looks at him in a way I can't read. I wish he'd talk. I wish he'd say something. It would be better than this silence. My hands tighten on the gun.

Matt sets the chair down and Yury sits, without prompting, gingerly, slowly. He sets his gaze on me and puts his arms behind the chair. No resisting, no fighting back. Matt starts wrapping his wrists with duct tape. Then his ankles. Then his body—first around chest and chair, then lap and chair. Yury keeps his eyes on me. There's a confidence in them, one that shouldn't be there, not when he's helpless like this, not when I have a gun trained on his heart.

When Matt's done, he sets down the duct tape and turns to me, his expression blank. No fear, no anger, nothing. I lower the gun, but I keep it at my side. "Can you get the file?" I say to him, and he nods, heads up the stairs. I watch him go, and I have a strange sensation that I shouldn't have let him out of my sight.

Yury watches him go, too, then turns back to me. Another smirk flickers across his lips. "You think that's going to make this all go away?"

The question makes my chest tighten. "Yeah, I think it will."

He gives his head a shake. Doubt creeps over me. But if the evidence is gone, then at least I won't be in jail. He won't be able to blackmail me. The rest I can figure out later.

I hear Matt's steps on the stairs and glance up. My fingers tighten around the gun at my side, my muscles tense, ready to move. All I can picture is him coming down these stairs moments earlier, apparently at ease. He comes into view, fully dressed now, and my eyes go straight to his hands. There's nothing in them but a slim stack of papers. My legs feel suddenly weak.

What am I thinking? This is Matt. I loosen my grip on the gun, watch as he comes closer, wordlessly extends the papers. I take them from him with my free hand, look down at the first page, a screenshot that I recognize. It's the exact same set of printouts Yury left in our mailbox. But this isn't right. This isn't all they'd hold on to.

"Where's the rest?" I say, looking up.

"The rest?"

"The digital copy."

Matt gives me a blank look. "That's all I found."

There's a sinking feeling in my chest. I fold the papers in half, stick them into the waistband of my pants, against my back. Then I turn to Yury. "I know you have another copy. Where is it?" I try to keep my voice hard, but I can hear the panic creeping into it.

He's still staring at me with that hint of a smirk. "Of course there's another copy."

I'll find it. I don't care how I have to threaten him, what I have to do to him. I take a step closer, and he tilts his head to watch me. "But it's not here. I don't have it."

I go cold.

"Oh, Vivian. You thought you outsmarted me." It's a full-blown smirk now. Patronizing. "Someone got us these search results, remember? Someone with access to Athena, to all your sensitive information. Someone on the inside."

Nausea ripples through me.

"My friend has a copy. And if anything happens to me, those papers go straight to the FBI."

THE ROOM FEELS LIKE it's spinning. "Who?" I say, and my voice sounds foreign, like it belongs to someone else. "Who has the copy?"

Yury smiles, a content smile, one that breeds fury inside me. Destroying that evidence was my last hope. I had actually started to believe that it might work.

"It could be a bluff," Matt says, and I don't turn around. It's not. I can tell by the look on Yury's face that it's not.

"Who?" I say again, and I take a step closer, raise my gun. Yury's face shows no fear.

I feel a touch, one that sets all of my nerves on fire. I swing the gun around, and it's Matt, behind me. His hand's on my forearm. He lets go, raises both palms in the air. "It's just me, Viv," he says calmly.

I keep the gun trained on him. He looks down at it, then back at my face. "It's okay, Viv. I just want you to think. Don't be impulsive."

My brain feels broken, like it can't process what's happening. *Don't be impulsive.* "He threatened Luke," I say. I turn to Yury, aim the gun back in his direction. "I'll kill him."

Yury's expression doesn't change.

"What good would it do?" Matt asks. I stare at him. He doesn't want me to shoot Yury. Because he's on Yury's side? "You won't learn anything if you do that."

Why is he so calm? But I try to process the thought. It's true, what he says. If I shoot Yury, I'll never know who has that other copy. Maybe there's still a sliver of hope, a chance that I can find that evidence.

Matt gives me a sympathetic look, then puts a hand on my arm, pushing the gun down gently. "Viv, we have him," he says quietly. "He can't hurt the kids."

I search Matt's face, and I know he's right. Yury's here, restrained. The threat to my kids is off the street, finally. If I call the authorities right now, he'll be in prison for life. He's a Russian spy, one who directed a cell of deep-cover agents. He won't have the chance to get anywhere near my kids.

The gun feels suddenly heavy in my hand. "So what do we do now?" Do we call the police, even though Matt and I would both spend the rest of our lives behind bars?

Uncertainty flickers across his features. "Maybe if you just do what they asked, insert that flash drive . . . ," he suggests, a glimmer of hope on his face, and I feel like the floor has dropped from under me. This again? Is he really still stuck on this? Why is it so important to him?

"It won't protect them."

"Yury said—"

"They'll ask for something else. They'll threaten the kids again."

"You don't know that. And anyway, this would buy us time. . . ."

My throat feels incredibly tight. All these conversations we've had about inserting the flash drive. He's desperate, almost. Why does he care so much, why does he want so badly for it to happen, unless *he's* really part of *them*?

"And then what?" I say. "Matt, this is a man who *targeted our kids*. He told you he'd kill Luke. You really want to just let someone like that go?"

He shifts his weight from one foot to the other, looks uncomfortable. And I can't take my eyes off him. In my mind I see him walking down those stairs, relaxed, about to chat with Yury.

I see him promising me he didn't tell the Russians anything about Marta and Trey. Lying to me. And I believed his lie. I believed it was the truth.

I feel like, for the first time, I'm seeing who he really is.

Something changes in his face, and I have that unsettling feeling again that he knows exactly what I'm thinking. "You really don't trust me," he says.

I voice the thought at the forefront of my mind. "Okay, maybe you couldn't leave. But shouldn't you have done *something*?"

He twists his wedding band around his finger. "I tried to call you once. . . . Your phone was off. . . ." He's struggling to get the words out. "Yury found out what I did. He came back with Luke's backpack. Said if I tried anything else, next time . . ."

Luke's backpack. That's why it was missing. They were *that* close to my son. At his school, in his classroom. Reaching into his cubby, the place he stores his lunch. And their message couldn't be more clear: They can get to him, whenever and wherever they want. I look over at Yury, who's watching us with a smile.

I feel like I'm going to be sick. Of course Matt didn't do anything after that. How could he? Luke's life was in danger.

I force my mind to focus. It's not just the fact that he's here. It's everything. The lie about Marta and Trey. Suggesting *again* that I insert the flash drive.

"Nothing I say is going to make a difference, is it?" he asks.

"I don't know." I hold his gaze, hold my ground. "I think you want very much for me to do what he asked. And I'm trying to understand why."

"*Why?*" He gives me a look of total disbelief. "Because I know these people. I know there's no way out." He reaches out for me, then drops his hand. "And because I don't want anything to happen to our kids."

We stand, staring at each other. He's the first one to break the silence. "If I was on their side, Viv, if I wanted it so badly, why didn't I do it to begin with?"

"What?" I say, but it's more to stall than anything, because there's a perfect clarity to his question.

"I gave you a flash drive. You inserted it. Why go through all this, if that's what I wanted? Why wouldn't I have just given it to you to begin with?"

I can't answer him. He's right. That doesn't make sense.

"Or why didn't I lie to you? Tell you the second flash drive was nothing, just another server reset?"

If he had, I would have done it. I would have inserted the drive.

"I'm on your side, Viv," he says, softly. "I just don't know if you're on mine."

My mind feels like a jumbled mess. I don't know what to think, what to do right now.

And then my phone starts to vibrate, deep in my pocket. I fumble for it and see the number. Luke's school.

He should be there by now, right? He must not have arrived. Oh God, what happened? I should have called my parents, checked in, made sure they got him on the bus, maybe even driven him there. Kept him safe. I hit the green button.

"Hello?" I say.

"Hi, Mom."

It's Luke. I exhale a breath I didn't know I was holding, feel my world spin. And then a new torrent of panic crashes over me. Why's he calling from school? "Luke, honey, what's wrong?"

"You said to call if I saw him again."

"Who?" I say, an automatic response, but even as the word comes out of my mouth, I know.

"The man. The man who talked to me at school."

No. This is not possible. "When did you see him, Luke?"

"Just now. He's outside. By the fence."

This can't be. I glance at Yury, who's listening to all of this, a smile still on his face. "Luke—are you sure it's him?"

"Yeah. He talked to me again."

I can barely force out the next words. "What did he say?"

He lowers his voice, and I hear the tremor in it. "He said to tell you time is running out. What does that mean, Mom?"

Full-blown panic takes hold. I look at Matt, and I know he heard the conversation. There's a flash of anger on his face that looks almost animal, and in that instant he's my husband again, the man who'd do anything to protect us, to keep our family safe.

"Go," I say to him, covering the mouthpiece with my hand. He glances at Yury, then back at me, looks uncertain. "I'll be fine. Go take care of Luke." He'd never let anyone hurt the kids; of that I'm sure. We exchange a look, then he grabs the phone from me.

"Luke, you stay where you are," he says. "Don't move, buddy. I'll be right there. Dad's coming to get you."

CHAPTER
20

THE DOOR CLOSES BEHIND MATT, THEN THERE'S SILENCE. I'm trembling, fear and anger and desperation churning inside me. This won't end with Yury in prison. Whoever's at Luke's school right now just made that clear. Someone else already knows. Someone else is a threat.

Calling the authorities won't protect my kids.

Will anything?

Yury's watching me with an amused expression. I bend down to his level, look him in the eye. "Who is threatening my son?" I say in a way that sounds frightening, even to me. How could I have been so wrong? If there's one thing I've had drilled into me, in my job, it's never to make assumptions. And yet didn't I do exactly that? Heard there was a man, someone with an accent, and assumed it was Yury.

An accent. That's what Luke said, right? Wasn't that why I thought it was Yury? I struggle to think back to the conversation, remember Luke's exact words. *He had a weird voice.* God, I don't even know for sure it was a Russian accent.

Is it the person that Yury said was on the inside? No
one I know of with access to Athena has an accent. Could
it be someone higher up in management, someone in IT?

Or could it be another Russian agent?

"Who is threatening my son?" I say again. He says
nothing, just mocks me with his eyes. And then instinct
takes over. I bring the grip of the gun down hard against
his forehead, as big a shock to him as to me. I've never
hit anyone in my life. "I will kill you," I say, and I mean it.
If it would protect my kids, I'd kill him in a heartbeat.

He sneers at me, squinting, a welt already forming
on his forehead. The force of the blow, the way his neck
snapped back with it, has left the opening of his shirt
askew around his neck. The pendant on the gold chain
has slipped out from under his shirt, catches the light.
It's some sort of gaudy cross. "Why not?" he says. "You
don't have anything to lose."

Rage simmers inside me. "Who?" I jam the gun into
his temple. Whoever it is, he'll probably be gone by the
time Matt arrives. How on earth will we find him?

"Could be any number of people. I have so many
friends I can call on." Yury smirks. He's toying with me.
I turn away from him, so he can't see my face, can't see
the desperation, the terror that I'm feeling.

So many friends. There's a thought swirling around
in my mind, slowly forming into something distinct.
Whoever Yury has on the inside knows Matt's identity.
And shouldn't they be hiding his identity from everyone,
if the cell's really so compartmented?

And what about all the agents at my wedding? All

gathered in one place, at one time. Maybe it's not as compartmented as we think. Maybe our understanding of the program is flawed. Maybe . . .

Dmitri the Dangle. His name suddenly fills my mind, crowds out all else. Dmitri the Dangle, the walk-in who claimed there were dozens of sleeper cells in the U.S. The man we thought was a double agent, someone the Russians sent to us bearing false information. But he was right, wasn't he? If there were that many agents at my wedding, he was right.

He was telling the truth.

I rack my brain, trying to remember what else he said. What other claims didn't fit with what we knew, so we ignored them, chalked them up to being false leads?

He said the sleepers' names were stored on the handlers themselves. On their bodies, at all times.

I look at Yury. My mind is churning, fitting together the pieces of a puzzle I didn't even know existed. Names stored on handlers' bodies at all times. And what we've always believed to be true, based on all our other intelligence: names stored electronically. Something clicks in my mind.

Could it be? I pull my eyes away, up to his face, and my breath catches. It is. I see it in his face, the realization that I *know*. There's a helplessness there, the same kind I've been feeling for weeks now. He's bound to the chair, can't hide it, can't protect it. The smirk's gone now.

I take a step toward him, then another, until I'm standing over him, and he has no choice but to stare up at me, exposed and vulnerable. I can see the fear grow in his eyes. I take hold of the pendant, look at it, the contours of the golden cross, the size of it. Turn it over, see four tiny screws.

I clasp my fist around it. I look him in the eye as I pull down with one swift, forceful yank. His neck jerks forward, then back again as the chain snaps, cascades down around my hand.

"This is it, isn't it?" I say, and before I can say another word, I hear a click behind me, a gun being cocked.

CHAPTER
21

I GO COMPLETELY STILL. SOMEONE ENTERED, AND I DIDN'T hear. We didn't lock the door behind Matt, did we?

Yury's craning his neck around me to face the door. His eyes are glued on something, someone, whoever just entered. There's recognition on his face. A slow smile creeping to his lips. And it sends panic shooting through me. I'm going to die. I'm going to die here, right here, right now.

I'm frozen in place, waiting for the shot. I can't bring myself to turn around, to see the person who's going to kill me.

Yury's smile is even bigger now. I see his teeth, crooked on one side, yellowed. He opens his mouth to speak. "Hello, Peter. It's good to see you."

PETER.

I hear the name, but it doesn't seem real. It can't be, can it? I turn around, slowly. Pleated pants, loafers, glasses—and a revolver pointed right at me. Peter.

Instinctively I drop my pistol, raise my hands, back away from him.

Omar said there was a mole in CIC, someone who worked with me. Yury said they had someone with access to Athena. I should have connected the dots.

But Peter? *Peter?*

"Vivian, I think you know Peter?" Yury says, and starts laughing, a crazy, manic laugh. He's enjoying this.

My eyes are still on Peter. He lowers the gun to his side, his arm at an awkward angle, like he doesn't quite know what to do with it.

"Those search results you took, Vivian?" Yury says. "I told you they didn't matter. Because our friend Peter here has another copy. Don't you, Peter?"

"How could you?" I whisper, ignoring Yury, my focus entirely on Peter.

He blinks at me, says nothing.

"I have to say, your timing is wonderful," Yury goes on. "I was just talking about you."

Peter's eyes don't leave mine. I'm not sure he heard what Yury said. "When you didn't show up this morning, Vivian, I had a feeling you might be here," Peter says.

Peter's the mole. He's been working for the Russians, helping them blackmail me. "How could you?" I say again.

He pushes his glasses up with the index finger of his free hand, opens his mouth to speak, shuts it again. Clears his throat. "Katherine."

Katherine. Of course Katherine. Katherine's the only thing that mattered to Peter more than his job, his country. He pulls his glasses off, uses the back of his other hand—the one with the gun—to swipe his eyes. The gun flails, the barrel pointing in all directions. I'm not sure he even remembers he's holding it. And his finger's still on the trigger.

"That clinical trial . . . ," he says, putting his glasses back on, adjusting them on the bridge of his nose. "She didn't get in."

Didn't get in? I stare at him, need him to continue. In the chair behind me, Yury is silent.

"She had a couple of months to live, at most. There's no way to describe what that's like, hearing that news. . . ." His voice wobbles. He shakes his head, clears his throat. "One day she was fine. We had the rest of our lives to look forward to. And the next day, that news. *Two more months.*"

I feel a pang of sympathy for him, one that very quickly dissipates. This isn't Peter, my mentor, my friend. This is someone standing in front of me with a gun, ready to kill me.

He blinks, refocuses on me. "Then someone showed up at my door. One of them." He nods at Yury. His voice stays flat. "Promised to get us the drugs from the trial, if I'd work for them."

"So you did it," I say.

He shrugs, a hopeless shrug. There's shame in his gesture. At least there's that. "I knew it was wrong. Of course I did. But he was offering the most valuable thing in the world to me. Time. Time with the one person who meant everything to me. How can you put a price on that? How can you say no to that?"

He's pleading, like he needs me to understand, to forgive him. And in a way, I do. As much as I hate to admit it, I do. They hit him where he was most vulnerable. They did the same to me, didn't they?

"I never told Katherine. She wouldn't have let me do it. I told her that they let her into the trial after all. I vowed that when it was all over, I'd come clean. I'd tell security exactly what I'd told the Russians. I'd right every wrong I'd committed."

A rush of something surges through me. Hope? It's over now, isn't it? Katherine's gone. "The drugs worked, for a while." Yury's listening with rapt attention, like he's hearing all this for the first time, too. "Then he gave me the flash drive. Told me to load it on to the computer in the Restricted Access room." Peter pushes the glasses up on his nose. "I refused. Telling them about Marta's drinking, or Trey's boyfriend, that's one thing. But giving them access to our systems . . . to the identities of covert agents, Russians who are working for us . . . there's no way I could do that."

Peter's jaw clenches tight. "He threatened to cut off her drugs. And then he did it. She died four weeks later."

My mouth opens and a rush of air escapes. My heart goes out to him once more, imagining the agony of those weeks, knowing what his decision cost them both. And then a newfound surge of hatred for these people. These monsters.

"They think I won't say anything," Peter goes on. "They think there's no way I'd go to the authorities now, because I'd guarantee myself a place in prison for the rest of my life. What they don't realize is that my life isn't really worth living anymore."

Yury looks like he's been hit. Stunned, speechless.

Peter ignores him. There are tears in his eyes. "I didn't want to go on, but I had to. I had to fix what I'd done." His voice quivers. "Especially what I'd done to you."

"To me?" I breathe.

"I told them we were almost into Yury's laptop. My guess is that's when they loaded Matt's picture on, for you to find."

It makes sense. That would explain why the files weren't encrypted. Why it was photographs, nothing more. It was a setup.

They knew exactly how I'd act. That I wouldn't turn Matt in. That they'd be able to manipulate me. They knew it, even when I didn't.

"I'm responsible for getting you into this," Peter says quietly.

I should say something, but I don't know what, can't find the words. This is too much to process right now.

And then I see Peter's eyes focus on something behind me. A mask of fear settles over his face.

"Drop the gun," I hear. Matt's voice.

I turn, and there he is, standing at the edge of the living room. Beyond him, I can see that the door leading from the kitchen to the patio is ajar. He snuck in through the back. A pistol is in his hand, by his side. His gaze is locked on Peter.

There's a dull pounding in my head, like none of this can really be happening, none of it makes sense. He shouldn't be here. He should be at school, picking up our son, keeping him safe. "Where's Luke?" I ask. "Why are you back already?"

He doesn't look at me. I'm not sure he even heard me.

"Matt, where's Luke?"

"I called your parents. They're getting him."

How did he know my parents were at the house? And why didn't he go himself? None of this is right. "Why?" I manage to ask.

"They're closer. They'd get there faster." He holds my gaze, his expression soothing. "They were glad to help. And I couldn't leave you here alone. Go on, Peter. Continue."

But Peter is silent. His hands are clasped in front of him, the revolver on the floor at his feet. I look over at Yury, who's taking it all in. The fear I'd seen just moments ago is gone, replaced with the smug look that terrifies me, even though I'm too confused to understand exactly why.

Matt speaks again. *"Continue."* His voice is brittle.

"Yury's right, Vivian. I downloaded the search results before the systems reset. I'm the reason they're black-mailing you." Peter's expression hardens. "But he's wrong about something. I didn't keep a copy." He reaches into his front pocket, and Matt raises his gun.

"Matt, stop," I say. I can hear the panic in my voice.

"It's okay," Peter says. He's already pulled something out of his pocket, something small. "It's just this." He holds out a flash drive, dangling from a silver key ring. I stare at it, watch it sway back and forth, suspended in the air, and wait for him to explain. There has to be an explanation. I trust him. He's been my mentor for years.

"It's the pictures you found, minus Matt's. That's all I kept." He extends the flash drive out to me. "There's no evidence you've ever seen them. Nothing they can use to blackmail you."

Peter takes a step closer to me, the drive still suspended from one hand. "Do what you want with this, and with the identity of the fifth sleeper." He casts a quick glance at Matt. "I trust you'll make the right decision, Vivian, whatever that is. But they're not going to manipulate you the way they did me."

I pull my eyes from him to the drive. Then I reach for it, take it from him. Matt's watching me, his expression unreadable. Peter's words keep ringing in my head. *I trust you'll make the right decision, Vivian, whatever that is.*

I look down at the gun in Matt's hand. My mind flashes back to the shoe box in our closet, to finding the empty space where it had once been hidden. And then realization hits.

"You had a gun this whole time." The words come out before I can process them, filter them.

"What?"

"Why didn't you shoot Yury? Why did you stay?"

"Jesus, Viv, are you serious?"

"You said you weren't sure if you could take him. But you had a *gun*."

"I'm not a killer." He looks incredulous. "And what good would it have done?"

"He threatened our son. He brought you Luke's *backpack*."

I watch the emotion on his face morph into hurt. "My God, Vivian, what's it going to take for you to trust me?"

I can't answer that. We stare at each other, unblinking, and I see his jaw tighten, his nostrils flare, just the smallest bit.

A sound pulls my attention away. Yury is chuckling. "This is better than the movies," he says with a laugh. *He believes Matt's on his side.* The revelation hits me like a slap, leaves me feeling like the wind's been knocked out of me.

And then Yury's smile vanishes, just like that. His face becomes like stone. "The boy dies tomorrow," he says, his eyes burning into mine. The words draw all the air out of the room, they're so unexpected, so *terrible*. "If you don't do this, Luke dies tomorrow."

There's no doubt in my mind that he means it. Suddenly it's just me and him, this man who intends to kill my child. I'm paralyzed, can't tear my eyes away from his face.

"And then another one after that. Ella, maybe." There's a look in his eyes now that makes my stomach turn. "Although she's growing into quite a pretty girl. I might save her for last. Start with the twins, let her get a little older first . . ."

My vision's blurring, all the strength in my body gone. I manage to turn toward Matt, the only person who could possibly understand the depth of my terror right now. I open my mouth to speak, but all that comes out is a strangled, anguished plea.

Something changes in his face. A look of resolve settles over it, and inexplicably, I know what's coming. I watch Matt lift his gun.

And then there's a shot.

MY EARS RING; EVERYTHING is muffled, fuzzy. The blast reverberates in my head. I blink, try to focus. This isn't real. This can't be real. Matt drops the gun. His hands fly up in front of him, like he doesn't know what to do with them. There's a look on his face I've never seen before. Revulsion and disbelief, like he had no idea he was capable of what he just did. He takes a gasping breath, then another.

Yury's slumped in his chair, head lowered. Blood darkens the center of his shirt, creeping, staining it at the edges, even as I watch.

Reality hits me a moment later. Matt just killed someone. My husband just took someone's life. A monster's life, but a *life* just the same.

"You need to leave," I hear. Peter's voice. I can barely hear him through the ringing in my ears, the hammering of my heart. "The Bureau's been on my tail. They'll be in here any minute."

The FBI. Here. Oh my God.

"You need to leave," Peter says again, this time with more urgency. He reaches down, picks up Matt's gun.

I need to leave. But I can't move.

And then there's a sound behind me, pounding. A loud blow, then another, and then the door bursts open. Figures in dark tactical gear enter, crouched low, rifles raised and aimed. They're shouting. *"FBI! Hands in the air!"*

I raise my arms high above me. I see the vests, the large block letters. The barrels of the rifles, pointing at Peter, at me.

Just Peter and me. Matt's gone.

"Drop your weapon!"

I look at the agents, and there's a face I recognize. Omar. He's aiming at Peter, yelling. They're all yelling.

"Drop the gun! Drop the gun!"

Matt's gun is still in Peter's hand, at his side, that awkward tilt of the arm. I can't read his face. There's more yelling, more instructions to put the gun down, put hands in the air. Then I hear Peter's voice over them: "Let me talk. *Let me talk.*"

The yelling quiets. The agents go still, each in a shooting stance, arms extended straight in front, guns aimed—two at Peter, one at me. Peter sees it, too. "She's done nothing wrong," he says. He's calm, astonishingly calm. "She's here because of me. I needed her to hear me explain."

The gun stays trained on me.

"It's okay, she's one of us," Omar says. After the slightest hesitation, the barrel swings away from me.

"Peter, drop your weapon," he orders.

"I need to talk." Peter shakes his head. "I need you to listen." The glasses have slid down his nose again, but this time he doesn't slide them back up, just tilts his head down, looks over them. "I did this," he continues, gesturing to the chair with his empty hand. "I killed this man. Yury Yakov. He's a Russian agent." His eyes are full of desperation. "I worked for him. I'm the mole."

Omar looks stunned. My eyes dart back to the gun in Peter's hand. "I told the Russians about my coworkers. I'm the reason Marta and Trey were pitched. Maybe

others, too. I told them we were investigating Yury. That
we were about to gain access to his computer." His forehead is damp; light's reflecting off the sweat, glistening
there. "And then I inserted a USB drive into the computer in the Restricted Access room. I erased the search
history from Agency servers."

I suck in a breath. I think back to that day, to bumping into him at the door. He knew. And now he's con-
fessing to it. Protecting me.

And then the truth hits me: There's a reason he's con-
fessing to everything right now, right here. There's a
reason he hasn't dropped the gun. *"No!"* I scream. "I'm
sorry," he whispers, his eyes still on me. Then he raises
the gun.

I see it happen, hear it happen. Yelling. A hail of bullets. Peter, sagging to the floor in front of me, blood
flowering out around him.

Screaming, a dull sound at first, louder as my hearing
returns, until I realize that it's coming from me.

CHAPTER

22

I SIT ON THE COUCH IN YURY'S LIVING ROOM, PERCHED ON the edge, my hands gripping the cushions on either side of me—overstuffed, drab brown fabric. There's a wail of police sirens outside, several of them, out of sync, a grating symphony. Flashing lights, too; they cast a pattern on the wall, a little show of dancing blue and crimson splotches. I watch it, because otherwise I'd look at the sheet that covers Peter's body, and I can't do that.

Omar's beside me, close but not too close. I can feel his eyes on me. His, and those of the other agents in the apartment, the host of others that have now swarmed in. They're tagging, photographing, milling about and talking, stealing glances my way.

I think that Omar's waiting for me to speak first, and I'm doing the same. Waiting to hear him Mirandize me. I'm intensely aware of the folded printouts in my waistband, the evidence that would get me locked away for the rest of my life.

"Can I get you anything?" he finally says. "Water?"

I shake my head. My eyes are still on the lights on the

wall. I'm trying to sort through everything that's happened, trying to make sense of it all. I have the hard copy of the evidence, and Peter destroyed the backup. Yury's dead; he can't accuse me of anything. And Peter confessed to my worst mistake—inserting the flash drive.

"We're going to have to talk about this, you know," Omar says, his voice gentle.

I nod, my mind working. Is he asking me as a friend and colleague? Or as a suspect? I could pretend I just found out that Matt's a sleeper, that Yury told me. Let the Bureau look into it. It's a chance to make things right. To turn Matt in, like I should have the very first day this began. He'd understand. It's what he told me to do, to begin with.

Luke dies tomorrow. But if I don't insert the flash drive, they'll go after Luke. I have no idea who's threatening him, and I can't tell the FBI about it without telling them everything, implicating myself. I can't get thrown in jail when Luke's in danger like this. I don't trust the Bureau to find the guy who's threatening him. Not in time.

"Could you start by telling me why you're here?" Omar presses.

I look away, and without thinking my eyes land on the sheet covering Peter. Omar follows my gaze, then nods, like I've just answered his question. "That call the other day. Was it from him?"

My eyes stay on the sheet. I'm not sure how to answer. I need a story that fits with everything that happened. I need time to figure that out, and I'm out of time.

"Or Yury?"

I blink. What would make the most sense? What did I tell him about the call? I struggle to remember. *Someone's wrapped up in it . . . someone who's important to me.*

"Vivian," Omar says, his voice so gentle it's almost tender. "I never should have given you that info. Not without knowing what was going on."

"It's okay," I stammer. What does he know? What did I tell him that day?

"I should have trusted my gut, figured out why you needed it." He shakes his head.

"You did me a favor."

He looks away, back over to the sheet. A raw sadness twists his face. Peter was his friend, too, wasn't he? "You were trying to help him," he says. It's a statement, not a question.

I swallow. *Now.* I need to say something. "He was my mentor. My friend."

"I know. But he was a traitor."

I nod, on the verge of tears, emotion threatening to crest over.

"We had him under surveillance. Suspected he was the mole. We watched him come in here. And then when we heard the shot . . . What did he say, before we arrived? Did he explain *why* he did it?"

"Katherine," I say. "They used Katherine." It's all I can choke out. There will be plenty of time to explain more later. That part I want to explain, *need* to explain. Peter wasn't a bad guy. They took advantage of him, coerced him. Used the thing that was most important to him, in all the world.

"They get you where you're most vulnerable," he murmurs.

I listen to the wail of the sirens outside. "He planned from the beginning to make things right. That's what he was trying to do." I shudder. He did make things right, didn't he? At least for me. Admitted to my biggest sin, setting back the servers. Kept Matt's identity hidden. Even came up with the four pictures I erased, the ones I felt so guilty about hiding.

The four pictures. The flash drive. I pat the outside of my pocket, feel it in there. I reach in and pull it out, extend it toward Omar. "He gave me this. Said the pictures of Yury's sleepers are on here."

Omar's gaze locks onto it. He hesitates, then takes it from me, swings around, calls for a colleague. Within minutes, there's a laptop on the table in front of us, and Omar's inserting the drive. I watch as pictures appear on the screen—the woman with the orange curls, the man with the round glasses, the two others. The four I erased. They're all here. And Matt's not.

"Four?" I hear the other agent say. "Only four?"

"Strange," Omar murmurs. "Should be five, right?" He looks at me.

I blink at the screen and nod absently. I'm vaguely aware that the agents are having a conversation, something about the significance of four versus five, theories for why there might only be four. A sleeper died. Retired. The program isn't quite as robust as we believe.

I can feel Omar watching me. A long look, intense. One that sets my nerves on high alert.

There's more conversation, more discussion, and eventually an agent comes over, scoops up the laptop, disappears with it. The other agents drift away.

"I'm going to let you go home," Omar says. He lowers his voice. "And tomorrow, Vivian, you're going to tell me everything. *Everything*. Is that clear?"

Tomorrow. *Luke dies tomorrow*. I nod, because I can't make my voice work right now.

He leans in closer, his eyes searching mine. "I know there's more to this than you're letting on."

I'M STILL BADLY SHAKEN by the time I get home. The gunshots won't stop echoing in my mind. I'm still picturing Peter's face as he apologized, as he lifted his gun, as he fell. But most of all, I'm hearing Yury's words, the threat to my son.

Matt's in the front hall when I walk in, and it's jarring to see him here, in our house. It feels wrong, almost like he doesn't belong. I stop and we stare at each other, neither of us speaking, neither of us making any move toward the other.

"Why didn't you leave when Peter said to?" he finally asks.

"I couldn't." In my mind I picture the agents storming in, then turning around and seeing he wasn't there. My eyes search his. *Why did you leave without me?*

"I thought you were right behind me. When I got outside and realized you were still in there . . . I was terrified." The words ring true, but the emotion doesn't quite reach his eyes. "What happened in there?"

I shake my head. *Too much to tell you right here, right now.*

"Are you okay?" His voice is flat, like he doesn't much care one way or the other. And it dawns on me: He blames me. He blames me for the fact that he killed someone. And he's furious with me.

"Yeah."

His expression doesn't change, and I'm about to say something else when I hear Ella. "Mommy's home!" she yells. She bounds into the hall, runs over, hugs my legs. I lay a hand on her head, then crouch down to her level, give her a kiss. I look up and see Luke hanging back. I let go of Ella, walk over, and give him a hug, relief coursing through me. Thank God he's okay.

And then Yury's words run through my head, unbidden. I squeeze him even tighter.

I walk into the family room. My dad's on the couch, and my mom's on the floor, struggling to her feet. There's an elaborate Lego town spread out in front of her. "Oh, honey, you're home," she says. There's concern on her face. "I can't believe you worked all night. Do they make you do that often? That's not healthy, working all night like that."

"Not often," I say.

"And with Luke sick and everything," she goes on, shaking her head. I glance at Luke, whose head is bowed, then at Matt in the kitchen, who shrugs slightly, avoiding my eyes. I guess they'd have to lie, though, wouldn't they? They had to give my parents some reason why he came home from school early. There's an awkward pause, as we all just stand around, looking at one another.

"Well," my mom finally says. "Now that Matt's back, we can get out of your hair." She gives Matt a smile. My dad's looking at him from the couch, no smile, naturally. He's never been one to let things go easily, if he thinks someone's hurt me.

I glance at Matt, but he's still not looking at me. They can't leave. Not yet. "Actually," I say, "if you guys could stay a little longer . . ." My mom's smile fades. Dad's expression hardens. Both of them look at Matt, like he's about to take off. "If you can't, I understand. I know you've got work and—"

"Of course we can stay," my mom says. "Anything you need, honey." Her eyes dart again to Matt. It's okay; I can make this right later. I can make all of this right. "You know, your father and I could use some fresh clothes. Why don't we head back to Charlottesville tonight, come back in the morning."

"You can do laundry here," I say.

She ignores me. "And the house. We should check on the house." She wants to give us privacy, doesn't she?

"If that's what you want to do," I say. I don't have the strength to argue. And besides, it'll be easier for Matt and me to talk if they're gone.

They leave a short time later, and then it's back to just the six of us. I lock the door behind them, then check the locks on the other doors, and the windows, too. As I'm drawing the blinds, I hear Matt in the kitchen. "What should we have for dinner tonight, princess?" His tone is light, but I can hear a hollowness in it.

"Mac and cheese?" comes Ella's voice.

"For dinner?" Matt says. There's a beat of silence,

and I look over, into the kitchen. She's bobbing her head up and down, a grin on her face.

Matt turns to Luke. "Buddy, what do you think?"

Luke looks up at me, like he's waiting for me to say no. When I stay quiet, he turns back to Matt and shrugs, a smile pulling at the corners of his lips. "Sure."

"Mac and cheese it is," Matt says, reaching down into the cabinet for a pan. There's an edge to his voice, one I hope the kids don't notice. "Why not?"

"With peas?" Ella says brightly, like she's bargaining. That's usually the compromise when we have mac and cheese for lunch. A side of peas.

"We don't need the peas," Luke chides, his voice hushed. "He already said yes."

Ella's little brow furrows. "Oh."

Caleb starts fussing, so I put him in his high chair, set a couple of crackers on his tray. Chase sees them and starts whining, throws his arms out toward me, his chubby fingers spread wide. I pick him up and set him down in his own chair, with his own crackers.

Luke and Ella drift off into the family room, and I watch Matt at the stove. His back's to me, and he's quiet and stiff. *Because I'm not a killer,* I picture him saying. He turned into one, though. And he blames me for it.

"Do you want to say anything?" I ask. I see him go still, but he doesn't turn around, doesn't say a word.

I feel even more desperate, even more hopeless, seeing him like this. How can I deal with this threat to Luke when Matt won't even look at me, won't speak to me? How can I be so close to losing everything, all at once?

"I didn't ask you to do it," I say quietly.

He spins around, a wooden spoon in his hand. "You made it clear what you expected."

"What I *expected*?" This isn't fair. He can't be putting this all on me. He heard what Yury said about Ella—

He lowers his voice even more. "You wouldn't trust me unless I did it."

"Why *should* I trust you?" I practically explode. It's loud enough that the kids can hear. Luke and Ella go quiet in the family room, their play paused.

"Mommy?" Ella says tentatively. "Daddy? Can you stop fighting, please?"

Matt and I exchange a long look. Then he shakes his head, turns back to the stove. We don't say another word.

CHAPTER
23

WE GET THE KIDS FED AND BATHED AND INTO BED, AND then we fall back into our normal routine—Matt cleans up the kitchen, I pick up the toys in the family room—except none of this is normal, because we've just been through hell, and there's a threat to the kids, and Matt won't even look at me.

I watch him, see the top of his head, the little spot on the top where the hair's starting to thin, just the smallest bit. He's scrubbing something in the sink. I sit back on my heels. "We need to talk."

He doesn't turn. Keeps scrubbing.

"Matt."

"What?" His head jerks up and he gives me a look, one that's sharp and pained at the same time. Then he looks back down.

"We need to talk about Luke," I insist, and I hear the desperation in my voice. I need to talk to him. I need a partner in this.

His hands go still, but he doesn't look up. I can see the rise and fall of his shoulders with each breath. I focus on that spot where his hair's thinning, so different now than it was a decade ago, when we first met. So much is different now.

"Fine." He turns the water off. The rush stops, and there's only a slow drip, the last droplets finding their way into the sink.

I exhale, grateful for this opening, then force my mind to focus. "Did Luke say anything else about the man who talked to him at school?"

He swings the dish towel over his shoulder, walks into the family room. He perches on the armrest of the couch, his body tense. "I pressed him on it. Had him tell me everything he could possibly remember. It was a Russian accent, for sure. I pulled up some audio clips on my phone, different accents. There was no question in his mind." There's a coldness to the way he's speaking. I try to ignore it, try to focus.

"Okay." Russian accent. Another Russian agent. There's a thought pricking at the edges of my mind. *The ringleader.* Could it be? Could Yury have reached out to his handler? Asked for help?

"And appearance: He said dark brown hair, brown eyes. Average height and weight . . ."

It makes sense, though. Almost more sense than anything else. Yury's not supposed to have contact with any other Russian agents; no one except the ringleader.

". . . wearing jeans last time, black pants this time. Button-down shirts both times. A necklace . . ."

A necklace. He continues to talk, but the words are a blur. My mind's churning again. "A necklace?"

He pauses midsentence, whatever the sentence was. "Yeah. A gold chain."

Without thinking, my hand lands on the front pocket of my pants, feels the hardness of the pendant inside. And then just as quickly, I pull it back to my lap, clasp it with the other. My eyes find Matt's—do I look as guilty as I feel?—and I see confusion in them. Hurt. Like he knows I'm not telling him something, that I don't trust him enough to do so.

He stands and turns away from me. "Wait," I say. He stops, and for several long moments I don't know what he's going to do. Then he turns back around.

"I lied to you, Viv. And I am truly sorry, from the bottom of my heart." His chin quivers, just the smallest bit. "But I have let you hate me for weeks. I can't do it forever."

"What's that supposed to mean?" It feels like a good-bye, and how can it be, when we need to get rid of this danger, protect Luke from this threat?

"I thought we were strong enough to get through this. But I'm not sure anymore." He shakes his head. "I'm not sure you'll ever trust me."

Confusion swirls inside me. *Should* I trust him? He lied to me, for years. But I understand why he did it. He was trapped. And ever since I discovered the truth, he's been nothing but honest.

I picture him walking down the stairs in Yury's apartment, fresh from the shower. But he was there because he couldn't leave. Because Luke was in danger. The only reason he was even there in the first place was to protect Luke.

He didn't leave us, like I'd feared. He'd gone to keep our kids safe.

And he didn't tell the Russians about Marta and Trey, either. Peter admitted to that.

"I murdered him, Viv. I murdered him and you *still* don't trust me."

I remember the horror on his face when he realized he'd killed Yury. And not because it was *Yury,* but because he'd killed a man.

He did something he'll regret for the rest of his life. And he did it for me.

"I'm sorry," I whisper. I reach an arm out toward him, and he just looks at it. The gulf between us has never been this wide.

The way he's looking at me, the hurt that's there, is so intense it frightens me.

I think I trust him. The reasons *not* to trust him seem to be evaporating. And I need him on my side right now. It's what's best for Luke. For all of us.

My fingers find their way into my pocket, grasp the pendant. I pull it out and extend it toward him, almost like an offering, a way to prove my trust. "I took this off Yury, right before Peter arrived."

He says nothing, and his expression stays wary.

I turn the pendant over, find the four tiny screws on the back. "Could you get a screwdriver?"

He hesitates, then nods. Leaves the room, comes back moments later with a toolbox. I pull out the smallest screwdriver. It fits. I loosen all four screws, remove them, then use my fingernail to pry open the edges of the pendant. It comes apart in my hands. Wedged in one side is a mini flash drive. I give it a shake, and it falls out, into my hand. I hold it up to the light, then look at Matt. "I think the names are on here."

"The names?"

"Yury's five sleepers."

He gives me a blank look. And then it clicks: He doesn't know what I know. I hesitate, but only for a second.

"Each handler has the names of his five sleepers in his possession. If something happens to him, the replacement's supposed to find the names, contact Moscow for a decryption code, take over. It's how they protect the sleepers' identities."

His brow furrows. "Why don't they just ask Moscow for the names?"

"The names are not in Moscow. They're only stored locally."

He's quiet, and I can almost see the wheels turning. "They're not in Moscow?"

I shake my head. I can see the truth is dawning on him.

"So when we were told the new handler would get in touch with us . . ."

"That's only if they find the names," I say.

"And that's why we have those plans for recontact, if a year passes."

I nod. "Because if the replacement can't get the names, it's the only way they have of getting back in touch with you."

"I had no idea," he murmurs. He takes the flash drive from me gingerly. Holds it between thumb and forefinger, studies it, like it somehow holds all the answers. Then he looks up at me. I know we're thinking the same thing. If these are the names, Matt could stay out of jail.

Yury's dead. The blackmail's gone. The five names are gone. Whoever Moscow sends as Yury's replacement won't be able to get his hands on the names. He'll have to wait for the sleepers to make contact. And if Matt doesn't, then he'll be free, once and for all.

It would be enough to keep us both safe, to keep anyone from finding out who he is and what I did. It would be a sweet victory if not for the cloud hanging over us. It doesn't matter in the least if Matt's safe, or I'm safe. Someone's planning to hurt our son. Our children. And I have no idea who.

Then a thought hits me with such tremendous force I'm breathless. *But Luke might.*

THE LOBBY'S EMPTY WHEN I arrive, except for a lone security officer near the turnstiles, one who looks vaguely familiar. My footsteps echo in the cavernous space as I approach. I nod at her as I badge in, pass through the turnstiles. She nods back, expressionless, watching me.

I walk through silent halls to the door of my vault. Touch my badge to the reader, enter my PIN. There's a beep, then a click as the lock disengages. I push open the heavy door. It's dark inside, and silent. I turn on the lights, flooding the space with harsh fluorescent lighting, and walk to my cubicle.

I unlock my desk drawer and pull out the file, set it on the desk, near the corkboard pinned with pictures of my family, drawings by the kids. It's thicker even than I remember, full of research into possible candidates for the ringleader. *Pictures* of possible candidates.

I sit down, pull the file in front of me. Start sorting quickly, separating out the pictures and bio data from the other research, winnowing the pile by almost half. Luke might recognize someone. If we can identify him, we can protect the kids. It's no longer a nameless, face-less threat. It's a person, one we can go after and destroy.

But the pile—it's still too big. How can I hide all this? My bag is too dangerous. All I need is for the security officer to stop me, rummage through it. I haven't come this far to get caught smuggling out classified material. My gaze drifts from the file to the picture of Yury, pinned to my cubicle wall, and my mind drifts, too. The necklace. On his body, at all times, just like Dmitri the Dangle said. *On his body.*

I stand, grab the pile of papers, head for the table in the back of the vault that houses the printers, the copier. There's a thick roll of tape there. A large envelope. I grab both. I slide the papers into the envelope. Pull up my sweatshirt, stick it flat against the small of my back, start wrapping tape around myself.

If anyone catches me like this, it's game over. All of this will be for nothing. But it's also the only way I can think of to try to figure out who the threat is. The Bureau would never show Luke a bunch of classified photos. So it's worth the risk, isn't it? Of course it is. And besides, they're not looking for people smuggling out paper. They're looking for electronic media. The odds of them finding this on me are slim, aren't they?

I pull the sweatshirt back down. This might work. It actually might. I walk back to my desk to get my bag, sling it over my shoulder. I'm ready to leave when the drawings catch my eye. The one Luke made, me in the cape, an *S* on my chest. Slowly, I sink down in my chair and stare at it. Supermommy. That's how Luke sees me, isn't it? For all my faults as a mother, he still sees me as a superhero. Someone who can solve any problem, take care of him.

I think about the man who visited him at school. Who threatened him. How frightened must my little boy be? How much must he be craving a superhero right now, someone who can protect him, fight off the evil, fight the bad guys. "I'm trying, buddy," I whisper.

And then my gaze shifts to Ella's drawing, the one of our family. Six happy faces. That's the whole reason I'm in this mess, isn't it? Trying to keep those faces happy, all six of us. Is there still a way to have that? Gears are turning in my head, shifting, trying to sort through how this all might play out, how I can possibly keep my kids safe and keep my family together, at the same time.

And then I have an idea.

I bend down to the drawers below my desk, the heavy metal ones bolted to the floor. I spin the dial, first one way, then the other. Find the numbers. Unlock it, pull out a drawer. Flip through the hanging files until I find the one I'm looking for. Inside, a report, red cover sheet, long classification string at the top. And another, farther back, just like it.

I open them up, first one, then the other. I scan until I find what I'm looking for. A long string of numbers and letters, and then another. I copy them down on a Post-it, fold it, and tuck it into my pocket. Then I head for the exit.

IT'S THE SAME SECURITY officer on the way out. She's at the desk near the turnstiles, a small television on in front of her, one of the twenty-four-hour news channels. She looks up as I approach.

"Leaving already?" Her face is serious.

"Yes, ma'am." I flash her a smile. I try to place her. I used to see her here in the mornings, I think.

"Just a quick visit in the middle of the night?"

"I couldn't sleep."

"Some people turn on the television."

My heart's pounding now. "I know. Nerdy analyst here." I raise my palms in mock surrender.

She doesn't laugh, doesn't smile. "I'm going to need to take a look in your bag."

"Of course."

She walks over, and I'm sure she'll be able to hear my heart thumping, see my hands shaking. I fight to keep my face impassive and hold the bag out for her, open. She peers in, then sticks her hand in, moves a few things out of the way to get a better look. I catch sight of a pacifier, a baby food pouch.

Then she pulls a wand from her belt, starts wanding my bag. "You work nights now?" I say, trying to pull her attention off the search, onto me. Trying to make myself appear less suspicious.

She takes the wand off the bag, holds it near my head, runs it down the front of my body, close enough that it's touching me. I start to panic. That packet of papers against my back is thick. Too thick.

"The pay's better," she says. "My oldest is off to college next year."

She moves the wand to the other side, starts to run it up the back of my legs. I hold my breath, a shiver running through me. Higher and higher, almost to my lower back now, almost to those papers. Just before it hits, I step away, turn to face her.

"Do you like it, working nights?" I say, with my best conversational look, one I hope looks natural, because I'm absolutely terrified right now.

I wait for her to tell me to turn back around. The wand's still in her hand, but she hasn't made a move toward me.

"We do what we need to do for our kids, right?" she says, scowling.

I hold my breath, hope she won't remember she didn't finish with me, or won't care. Then she tucks the wand back in her belt, and the relief makes me dizzy.

My body's gone weak, and the papers taped to my back seem suddenly so heavy. "We certainly do."

Then I take my bag and head for the exit, without looking back.

LUKE SITS ON THE edge of his bed between Matt and me. We're closer than we need to be, almost like we're trying to give him strength, trying to let him know he's safe, that he's not alone.

He's in his baseball pajamas, the ones that come up a

little short at the ankles: another growth spurt. His hair's sticking up in the back, the same way Matt's does when he wakes. He's still groggy with sleep, his eyes heavy.

"I need you to look at some pictures," I say gently.

He rubs one of his eyes, squints in the light, peers at me in confusion, like he's not entirely sure if he's awake or dreaming.

I rub my hand in slow circles against his back. "I know this is strange, buddy. But I'm trying to figure out who talked to you at school. So we can find him, and make him stop."

A shadow crosses his face, like he's realized that he's awake, that this is real, but it's the reality he wishes didn't exist. I wish it, too. "Okay," he says.

I pick up the papers from beside me and lay them in my lap. On top is a photograph, a headshot of a man with a serious expression. I watch Luke as he looks at it. I keep rubbing his back, wishing I didn't have to do this, make him sit here and relive the fear of being confronted by a stranger.

He shakes his head, doesn't make a sound. I turn the page over, facedown on the bed, and a new picture takes its place. A surge of guilt runs through me, showing him these faces that will probably haunt him, the same way they haunt me.

He looks at it quietly, the same amount of time. I catch Matt's eye over the top of his head, see my guilt reflected on his face, the same question that's running through my mind. *What have we done?*

Luke shakes his head again, and I go on to the next one. I watch him, the profile of his face. He looks so serious, so much older than his years, and I feel an over-whelming sense of sadness.

I flip through page after page. He looks at each one carefully, methodically, for the same amount of time before he shakes his head. Soon we've fallen into a rhythm. *One second, two seconds, three seconds, shake head, flip the page.*

We're nearing the end of the pile now, and desperation is starting to take hold. What do I do next, if this doesn't work? How am I going to find the man who's threatening him?

One second, two seconds, three seconds, shake head, flip the page. One second, two seconds, three seconds . . .

Nothing. No shake of the head.

I go still. Luke is staring hard at the picture. I'm afraid to even breathe.

"This is him," he says, so quietly I almost can't hear him. Then he looks up at me, those wide eyes, like saucers. "This is the man."

"Are you sure?" I say, even though I know he is. I can see the confidence, the determination on his face. The fear.

"I'm sure."

CHAPTER
24

I STAND IN THE KITCHEN, MY BACK AGAINST THE COUNTER, mug of steaming coffee in one hand, the picture in the other. Anatoly Vashchenko. I stare at him, the long face, the receding hairline. I'm looking at the face of the ringleader. The man who's a threat to Luke. To all of my kids.

I turn the picture over, look again at the text on the other side. The bio data, everything I was able to dig up on Vashchenko that we could use to track him down. It's short, one of the shortest in the pile, barely any text at all. My eyes focus on one line in particular. *Travel to U.S.: None known.*

None known.

I blink at the words, willing them to change. But they don't, of course. They stare back at me, taunting. Obviously he's traveled to the U.S.; he's here right now. And if we don't have a record of him being here, he's using an assumed identity.

Which means we have no way to track him down.

Luke's asleep, and all is silent, except for the occasional clack of typing from the family room. Matt, on the laptop, working on decryption. Typing, then a long pause. More typing, more silence.

I take a sip of coffee, taste the bitterness on my tongue. I feel like I'm deflating inside. I found the ringleader; I actually did it, and what does it matter? I don't have enough to track him down, to *do* anything about it, certainly not in time. *Luke dies tomorrow.* I can't get those words out of my head. He's out there, menacing Luke, and I'm powerless to stop it.

Powerless to stop it, on my own.

The thought's in my head, clawing its way to the front. I'm trying to push it back, push it away, keep it from fully forming. But I can't. It's the only way.

I leave the picture on the counter and walk into the family room, mug between both hands, trying to warm them. Matt's on the couch, leaning forward, his laptop open on the coffee table in front of him. A flash drive's attached, a little orange light lit. He glances up as I enter, his face tight, tense. I sit down beside him, look at the screen, the jumble of text, indecipherable to me, the characters he's typing, a string of them.

"Any luck?" I say.

He sighs, shakes his head. "My encryption code's not enough. It's multilayer, pretty complex stuff."

"Do you think you can crack it?"

He looks at the screen, then back at me, regret and frustration all over his face. "I don't think so."

I nod. The fact doesn't surprise me, not in the least. They're good, the Russians. They've designed this so no one can break in. Not without the other decryption codes.

"What do we do now?" he asks.

I search his face. I need to see exactly how he's going to react, to all of this. Because I think I trust him. I think there's an explanation for everything. But I need to be sure. "We go to the authorities."

His eyes widen, just the smallest bit. I can read surprise, but little else. "What?"

"It's the only way to keep Luke safe."

"But we know who it is—"

"And that's all we know. We have absolutely nothing that can help us find him. Nothing. But the authorities, they would."

His eyes haven't left mine. I see hopelessness, desperation. "There's got to be some other way—"

I shake my head. "We have a name. A Russian name. Nothing on his alias, his location. Maybe if we had more time . . ."

I watch him process the information, the way I've been forced to. It's the only way. We can't track him down on our own. Not in time.

"Luke dies tomorrow," I say quietly. "What if he comes for Luke, and we can't stop it?"

The crease in his forehead deepens. He's still thinking; I can see it.

"You're right," he says. "We need the help."

I wait for it, the next question, the one I know is coming. Because this is when it'll really matter, his reaction. I need to see how he'll react when I say it.

"So what do we tell them?" he finally asks. And I hear the unspoken part of the question, the one I've been running through my mind, as well. *How do we get their help without implicating ourselves?*

I look up, meet his eyes, memorize the expression, wait to see how it'll change. "The truth."

"What?" He stares at me in utter confusion.

I watch him closely. "We tell them everything."

There's a flash of something in his eyes. Disbelief, I think. "We'll go to jail, Viv. Both of us."

I can feel emotion welling up in my chest, an intense pressure. Being in jail would mean life as I know it is over. I wouldn't be there for the kids. I'd miss their childhoods. Their lives. They'd hate me for leaving them, for turning them into a media spectacle.

He blinks at me, and the incredulity morphs into frustration. "You're just giving up? Now, when we're so close?"

"I'm not giving up." I'm not, that much I know for sure. I'm just finally *standing* up, doing what's right, what I should have done a long time ago.

"After all of this—"

"All of this was for the kids," I interrupt. "And this is *still* for the kids."

"There's got to be another way. Some story—"

I shake my head. I need to stay firm here. Because he's right. There probably is another way. Another lie we could tell. I could sit down with Omar, spin a tale that he might buy, that might be enough to keep us out of jail, to keep Luke and the other kids safe. "I don't want any more stories."

I don't want something that's going to bury us deeper, spiral us further down in deceit. I don't want to spend the rest of my life looking over my shoulder, waiting for the other shoe to drop, terrified I've made the wrong decision, that my children are still in danger. I want them in witness protection. I want them safe.

"And I don't want to take any chances. They won't understand how much danger the kids are in, how much of a threat Vashchenko is, or even *why* he's threatening the kids, unless we come clean," I say. "We need them protected. This is what's best for them."

"Both their parents in prison? *That's* what's best?"

A cloud of doubt is forming over me, because honestly, I don't know. But in my gut, I feel like this is right. It's the way to keep them safe. And besides, how can I be the mother I need to be, if I let the rest of my life be a lie? How can I teach the kids right from wrong? All the times I've chastised them for fibbing, all the times I've told them to do what's right, they're all running through my mind like a movie reel. And Peter's words. *I trust you'll make the right decision, whatever that is.*

"Maybe it is," I say. I'm still holding on to a fragment of hope that it won't happen, both of us in jail, but I can't tell him that, not yet.

And I know, deep down, that we probably will end up behind bars. But maybe what's best for them isn't us all being together, after all. Maybe it's making absolutely sure they're safe. That we're teaching them to do what's right, even if it's difficult. Maybe someday they'll look at everything I've done, everything Matt's done, and they'll understand. But if we keep going like this, keep living this lie, another ten, twenty years, or until whenever the authorities finally catch up with us, then what? How will we be able to look them in the eye again?

I pull my phone out, lay it carefully down on the ottoman in front of us. I see Matt look at it.

I take a deep breath. "I trust you. I hope you can see
that now. But you can still leave. I won't call until you're
on a plane out of here."

He looks at the phone a moment longer, then his
gaze shifts to me. "Never," he whispers. "I'd never leave
you." He reaches for my hand. I feel his fingers encircle
mine, warm and so familiar. "If you think this is what
we need to do, then we'll do it."

This is Matt, my husband, the man I know, the man
I love. I was wrong to ever doubt him. So very, very
wrong.

I let go of his hand, reach into my pocket, pull out
the little square of paper. Unfold it, lay it down on the
ottoman, the two long strings of characters visible to us
both. "There's one more thing I want you to do."

DAWN IS BREAKING WHEN Omar arrives at our house,
alone, just as I asked. I greet him at the door and usher
him inside. He enters warily, one cautious step forward,
then another, his eyes looking around the room, taking
everything in. He doesn't say a word.

I close the door behind him, and then we stand awkwardly in the hall. I feel a flash of regret for calling him
here, an urge to back out. There's still some time to get
out of this. Then I lift my chin. It's the right thing to do.
It's the only way to keep my kids safe.

"Let's go sit down," I say, nodding in the direction of

the kitchen. When Omar doesn't move, I start leading the way. I hear his footsteps behind me.

Matt's already sitting at the kitchen table. Omar sees him and stops, eyes him, then gives him a nod. Still doesn't say a word. I scoot Chase's high chair out of the way and drag Luke's chair to the end of the table, gesture for Omar to sit. He hesitates, and then does so, lowering himself into the chair. I sit in my usual spot, across from Matt. I glance up at him and suddenly I'm at the table weeks ago, the day I learned the news that would change my life, all of our lives.

There's a folder in front of me at the table, the paper I need nestled securely inside. I see Omar's eyes land on it, then travel up to my face. "What's going on, Vivian?" he says.

My voice, my body, everything suddenly feels paralyzed. Is this really what's best for the kids?

"Vivian?" he says again, confused.

It is. It'll protect the kids. I can't do it on my own. I can't keep them safe.

I slide the folder over to Omar, my hand trembling. He puts a hand on it, his eyes on me, quizzical. He hesitates, then opens it gingerly. I see the headshot, the one Luke identified.

"Anatoly Vashchenko," I say quietly. "Yury's handler. The ringleader."

He's staring at the picture. He finally looks up at me, his face like a question mark.

"He needs to be arrested immediately. And I need protection for all my kids until it happens."

His eyes shift from me to Matt, and back to me again. He still hasn't said a word.

"He threatened Luke," I say, my voice cracking. "He's a threat to my kids."

He exhales softly, his eyes locked on me. He gives his head a shake. "What the hell's going on, Vivian?"

I need to get this out, all of it. "He'll have a necklace. A pendant. A cross, I think. There should be a flash drive embedded inside. It'll have the names of his five handlers."

Omar blinks. He looks stunned.

"Matt can walk you through the decryption process," I add softly. "His code, ours from Moscow, the one from Dmitri the Dangle."

I glance at Matt, who nods grimly. Once I gave him the other decryption keys, it hadn't taken long for him to get into the folder, to find the five pictures. The same five I saw that day at work, a lifetime ago, but with text this time: addresses, occupations and access, instructions for signaling meetings.

I actually didn't expect to see the same faces, the other four. Once I realized the pictures were planted, I felt sure the others were fake. But maybe I shouldn't have been surprised. Maybe it was proof of their arrogance, their confidence that they knew exactly how everything would play out.

"The handlers all have them, too. With the names of their five agents," I say. I set down Yury's necklace, the heavy gold cross. The flash drive's tucked back inside, the screws tightened. "The fifth name's in here."

Omar's eyes widen ever so slightly. His jaw's gone slack, his mouth open in an unconscious O. I've stunned him. He shifts his gaze to Matt, and Matt nods. "Viv didn't know," he says. His voice breaks, and my heart breaks to hear it. "I kept it from her."

Omar turns back to me.

I feel like I owe him some sort of explanation, but I don't know what to say. "They get you where you're most vulnerable," I finally settle on. "With us, it was our family."

His eyes are disbelieving.

"He would have come in from the cold," I say softly. "Years ago."

Omar looks away. Something changes in his face. "Exactly the kind of person I thought we might find."

He hasn't made a move for Yury's necklace. I place my index finger on the pendant, slide it closer to him. What's going to happen next? That flicker of hope is still there, but it's so faint, so very faint.

In any case, it was the right thing to do. It's the way to keep the kids from harm.

More likely, he's going to call for backup. Place us under arrest. My parents should be back soon, but now I wish I'd insisted they stay the night. And the kids, the poor kids. What if we're gone by the time they wake up?

He's still staring at the necklace. There's a strange feeling creeping over me, that glimmer of hope intensifying. Maybe this'll work. Maybe it'll be enough.

Finally he places his own index finger on the necklace, but instead of pulling it toward himself, he pushes it back to me. "You'll be needing witness protection, then," he says.

A tingling sensation runs through my body like electricity. Did this actually succeed? I look down at the necklace, back in front of me now. He doesn't want it. He's not going to take it, to see the fifth name. Matt's name.

I'm trying to wrap my mind around the words, trying to understand if this is really happening. I look at Matt and see his confusion. We didn't talk about this; it seemed so unlikely, and if there really was a chance of it working, I didn't want to jinx it.

"Witness protection?" I say, because I don't know what else to say.

It takes Omar a minute to respond. "You just gave me enough information to disrupt the entire cell. Certainly the Russians wouldn't take kindly to that. And if they're *already* threatening Luke . . ."

I look down at the flash drive. I shouldn't get my hopes up. Not yet. Maybe he didn't understand. That Matt's the fifth sleeper, that I knew about it. That we both belong in jail.

"I've done some things wrong. I'll tell you everything—"

"Everything we've been investigating," Omar says, holding up a hand as if to stop me, "everything we attributed to a mole, or to a Russian agent with access to CIC, Peter confessed to." He drops his hand, looks from me to Matt, then back again. "I'm confident that the fifth sleeper hasn't done a thing to harm national security."

Oh my God. This is really happening. Omar's going

to let us go. It's what I hoped. It's what I thought might possibly keep us out of jail, keep our family together. Give them enough. Information for freedom.

It only works, though, if he can keep the kids safe. "The kids—"

"Will be protected."

"That's the only thing we care about."

"I know."

I'm quiet for a moment, still trying to process everything. "How will it work?" I finally ask.

"I'm going to walk myself right into the director's office with information that'll disrupt the entire cell. He'll give me what I want."

"But—"

"I'll say Matt admitted to being a sleeper. That he gave me the ringleader's name, gave me his encryption code, let me know about the necklaces. And that, in exchange, we're going to protect him and his family."

"But what if someone finds out—"

"We'll keep it in compartmented channels. Highest classification."

"Can you—" I begin, and again he cuts me off.

"It's Russia. Everything's compartmented." I hear the words I myself have spoken so many times, the ones I know are true. The ones that mean maybe, just maybe, this could work.

"Will the director agree?" I ask, my voice almost a whisper. Even if Omar wants to do this for us, there's no guarantee he can, right?

He nods. "I know how the Bureau works. I'm confident."

Hope is radiating through me. Hope that maybe we'll be safe, and together, after all. I look at Matt and see the same emotions mirrored on his face.

"What now?" I finally ask.

Omar smiles at me. "Pack your bags."

CHAPTER
25

I SIT IN THE SAND ON THE LITTLE CRESCENT BEACH AND watch the kids. Chase is running along the edge of the surf, sturdy little toddler legs churning across hard-packed sand, a seagull skipping along in front of him. Caleb stands behind him, blond curls glistening in the sun. Watching, squealing in delight as the gull takes to the sky. Ella's farther up the beach, packing sand into bright turret-shaped buckets, concentration on her face, an elaborate sandcastle in front of her. And out in the ocean is Luke, belly-down on a boogie board, waiting for the next wave. Water glistens off his back and the legs that seem to lengthen by the day, tan from the sun and the hours spent out here in the surf.

A warm breeze blows by, swaying the fronds of the palms that dot our little beach. I close my eyes and just listen for a moment. The soft crash of waves, the rustle of the palms, the sounds of my kids, content and happy. The most beautiful, mesmerizing symphony that could possibly exist.

Matt comes up behind me and sits down in the sand next to me, close, his leg touching mine. I look at them, our two legs, both tanner than they've ever been, almost brown against the fine white sand. He smiles at me, and I at him, and then I turn back to watch the kids, content to sit in companionable silence. Luke catches a big wave, rides it in, all the way onto the sand. Caleb takes a tottering step, then another, then sinks down to the sand and scoops up a large shell, examines it.

Twenty-four hours after we sat at our kitchen table with Omar, we were on a private plane, heading for the South Pacific. At first, when Omar said to pack our bags, the thought was terrifying, packing up our lives into suitcases, knowing that anything we left behind, we might never see again. And so I focused on the things most important to me, the things that were irreplaceable: photos, baby books, that kind of thing. As it turns out, that's all I really needed. All the other *stuff* in our house—the closets full of clothes and shoes, the electronics, the furniture—well, I still don't miss it. We started over here, simply. Bought the essentials. We have one another, and our memories, and that's all we really need.

My parents came with us. Omar offered it up as an option, and I went to them with it, even though I didn't think they'd do it, didn't think they'd want to be ripped away from all they knew. But once they heard they wouldn't be able to communicate with us for a year, maybe more, there was no hesitation. *Of course we'll come,* my mom said. *You're our child. You're everything to us.* And that was it, decision made. One that I understood completely.

And things between Matt and me are solid again. *I forgive you,* he said, the first night in the new house, as we lay in an unfamiliar bed. If he could forgive me for doubting him, for making him feel like he had to kill to earn my trust, surely I could leave the past in the past. I curled up into his arms, the place I knew I belonged. *I forgive you, too.*

I hear a helicopter in the distance, the faint whir of the propellers. I watch as it comes into view, growing more distinct as it approaches, louder, the gentle whir becoming a rhythmic *thump-thump-thump.* The kids have all stopped what they're doing to watch. It passes right over us, so loud that Ella and Luke cover their ears; Chase and Caleb just stare in wonderment.

Helicopters aren't something we see here. They settled us on a remote part of the island, two houses set on bluffs overlooking the ocean, bookending a little crescent stretch of beach below. I never knew how Omar managed to do it—the houses, the living expenses, all of it. He told me not to worry, that after all we'd done for our country we deserved it. And I didn't press it. It was the first time in as long as I could remember that I didn't have to worry about money.

I look up at my parents' house now and see my mom step outside. She slides the glass door closed behind her and starts walking down to the beach, the breeze billowing her long skirt around her legs. I turn around and see the helicopter hovering above the bluffs behind us, coming down slowly, perpendicular to the ground, for a landing.

Matt and I exchange a look. Wordlessly we both stand,

brush the sand off. We wait for my mom to reach us. "Go ahead," she says. "I'll keep an eye on the kids."

The sound from the propellers quiets as we trudge up the hill to our house, over white sand dunes that slide away with each step until we reach the wooden stairs, dusted with more sand. We walk up until we reach the top, the patchy grass that passes as a lawn, the square two-story house with the sharply slanted roof, terraces all around. I see Omar approaching the house from the direction of the helicopter, wearing khaki cargo pants, a flowered Hawaiian shirt. He breaks into a smile when he sees us.

We reach the front of the house at the same time. I embrace him, hugging hard, and Matt shakes his hand. There's something oddly thrilling about seeing him here; he's the first person from back home we've seen in a year. He warned us, told us we'd be on our own for a year, possibly longer, but still we were unprepared for the strange sensation of being completely cut off from everything—the people we knew, the routines, even things like email and social media. He'd given us a cell-phone, but with strict instructions to power it on and use it only in case of emergency. Short of that, we were just to wait. Wait for him to make contact. And now, here he is, a year to the day later.

"Come on in," I say to him, opening the front door and leading the way. The house is airy and full of light, all white and blues. And it feels more like home than our home ever did. Seashells adorn the place, ones we've gathered from walks on our beach. And photographs. So many photographs. Black-and-white shots of the kids, of the palm trees, of anything that catches my eye. It's nice to have time for hobbies again. Most of all, though, it's nice to have time for my kids.

I lead him into the family room and sit down on the couch, a well-worn blue sectional, the one we all crowd onto for movies and game nights. He sits on the opposite side. Matt comes in a moment later, a pitcher of lemonade and two glasses in his hands, and sets them on the coffee table. He gives me a smile. "I'll give you two some privacy," he says. I don't stop him, and neither does Omar.

When he's out of the room and we hear a door close upstairs, Omar leans forward. "So how's life here?"

"Wonderful," I say. And I mean it wholeheartedly. I'm happier than I've ever been. I don't feel trapped anymore, stuck in a life that's just happening to me. I feel in control of my life. And my conscience is at peace. I'm going to finally have the life I want.

I pick up the pitcher and pour lemonade into each glass, ice cubes clinking against the sides.

"School? I know you were worried about that."

I hand him a glass. "We've been homeschooling. It's not a long-term solution, but it's been working. The kids are actually learning a ton."

"And Caleb?"

"Doing so well. Walking, even saying a few words. And he's healthy. You were right, the cardiologist on the mainland is fantastic."

"I'm glad. You have no idea how often I think of you guys. How much I've wanted to check in."

"Me too," I say. "There's so much I want to know." I pause. "How have you been?"

"Great, actually." He takes a sip from his glass. "I'm the new deputy director, you know." He's trying—and failing—to contain a grin.

"That's amazing."

The grin breaks free.

"And you deserve it. Totally."

"Well, this case did a lot for me. Not gonna lie."

I wait for him to say more, but he's quiet, the smile slipping away. My mind drifts to Peter and I wonder if his has, too. Finally I speak. "Can you tell me anything about the cell?" It's a question that's been at the forefront of my mind for a year now. I'm desperate to hear what he has to say.

He nods. "You were right about Vashchenko. He was the ringleader. We tracked him down pretty quickly. Found the flash drive embedded in the pendant, just like you said. And decrypted it with the keys you gave us."

I clasp my hands tightly in my lap and wait for him to go on.

"From there, we arrested the other four handlers. Three days later we had a major operation, arrested all twenty-four members of the cell."

"We heard about it," I say. It was a major news story, even here, although everything I read about the operation said twenty-five operatives. Alexander Lenkov was identified as one of those arrested, though details about him were scarce, and the only photograph released was pixelated enough to be indistinct. Luckily I don't think anyone would have recognized him as my husband. "What's going to happen to them all?"

He shrugs. "Jail, prisoner swap, who knows." He eyes me for a moment. "I'm sure you read that most of them are claiming they were framed? That they're actually political dissidents, enemies of the state, that kind of thing?"

I nod and smile. "At least they're consistent, I guess."

He grins, then turns serious again. "The Bureau finally approved the 'Come in from the Cold' op. We got two recruits that way, so far. We're working on using them to disrupt another cell. And we're using your algorithm to try to find other handlers. There's a huge amount of resources devoted to it, FBI and CIA."

I'm quiet for a moment, letting everything sink in. They disrupted an entire cell, and they're making progress on finding others. I shake my head in wonderment, and then I ask the other question that's on my mind, the one that's more pressing, that frightens me far more. "And Matt? Do they suspect him?"

He shakes his head. "No indication the Russians know he's still out there, or that he had any involvement."

My eyes flutter closed. A weight lifts itself off my shoulders, freeing me. It's what I'd hoped; the news stories seemed to credit the disruption to Peter, described as a longtime CIA analyst preyed on because of his wife's illness, then blackmailed. And to a Bureau agent identified simply as "O."

"And as for you," he goes on, "you're listed as taking a temporary leave of absence. It's pretty well known in CIC and the Bureau that it has something to do with this case, and there's a rumor going around that the

Russians blackmailed you and you resisted. But no one at the working level knows the details."

"Who knows the truth?"

"Me. The directors of the FBI and CIA. That's it."

I can feel my tension draining away. This conversation couldn't be going any better if I'd written it myself. But at the same time, what does that mean for us, here? I feel a surge of sadness, like everything around me is tenuous, might be pulled away in a heartbeat. I'm almost afraid to ask the next question. "So what now?"

"Well, from everything we've seen, it's safe to return. We can get you back into your house, your job. . . ."

My mind drifts, even though I don't want it to. The kids, at day care all day. Seeing them just for brief snippets in the morning, and again at night—if I'm lucky. I try to push away the thought.

"We'll iron out all the details in the coming weeks. We'll get Matt some new documents—birth certificate, passport, et cetera. Something that'll hold up to any scrutiny." He pauses, looks at me expectantly, so I offer him a weak smile.

"We'll make the transition back as smooth as possible, Vivian. Nothing to worry about. And we'll do some amazing work together, you and I. More disruptions . . ."

He trails off, looks at me with a strange expression on his face. "That's what you want, right?"

I don't answer immediately. It's odd, being in this moment. Because for the first time, it's actually my choice. I'm not trapped in a job that I'm no longer sure I want. No one's manipulating me, pressuring me to do anything. I can do whatever I want. I can choose.

"Vivian?" he presses. "Are you going back?
I blink at him, and then I answer.

MATT AND I HAD celebrated our ten-year anniversary at the beach, just as we'd hoped. We sat in the sand on the crescent beach and watched the kids play, toasted with plastic cups of cheap sparkling wine as the sun slipped closer to the horizon, bathing our world in reds and pinks.

"We're here, after all," he said.

"Together. All of us."

I listened to the crash of the waves, the squeals and giggles of the kids, and I remembered the last time we'd talked about it, the plans for our anniversary, a trip to an exotic beach. It was the morning I found Matt's picture, just before everything fell apart. I was transported back to my cubicle, the high gray walls, the ever-present feeling of floundering, of failing, of being torn between two things that were so important to me, each of which demanded more time than I could give. My throat tightened, just thinking about it.

I dug my toes deeper into the sand and looked at the horizon, the sun sinking ever lower. And I said the only thing that was on my mind in that moment. "I don't want to go back to the job." It was out of the blue, really, because we hadn't talked about work, not since we'd left the States. "I mean, if it's even an option." It felt good, saying what I wanted. Making a choice. Being in control.

"Okay," Matt said. Just that. *Okay.*

"I want to sell the house," I said, pushing further.

"Okay."

I turned to face him. "Really? I know you love the house—"

He laughed, shook his head. "I don't love the house. I hated it, in the beginning. Hated that I talked you into it just so you'd be trapped in your job."

The words felt like a blow, one I should have seen coming. I curled my toes deeper in the sand and looked back at the ocean.

"I love the memories we've made there," he added. "But the house itself? Nah."

I tried to process the thought, the realization—once again—that so much of what I believed to be true wasn't really true.

"I love *you*, Viv. And I want you to be happy. Really, truly happy, like you were when we first met."

"I'm happy," I said, but the words rang false. Was I? Being with the kids, with Matt, I was happy. But there was so much about my life that *didn't* make me happy.

"Not the way you deserve to be," he said softly. "I haven't been the husband I want to be."

I should have said something, should have argued. But I didn't. The words didn't come. I think maybe I wanted to see what he was going to say.

"When you went back to work after Luke was born . . . That day you came home and said you couldn't do it. Couldn't leave him. There was nothing I wanted more than to say, 'Don't.' To say we'd sell the house, I'd get a second job, whatever. It killed me to tell you to hang in there, to stick it out. I knew how unhappy it made you. I knew. And it killed me."

I felt tears spring to my eyes, thinking back to that day,

one of my lowest. I watched the kids through the blur. A game of tag, Luke sprinting so fast, Ella keeping up. Chase toddling behind, trying so hard. And Caleb, sweet Caleb, standing, taking a few hesitant steps, laughing.

"There are so many times I've let you down. When I convinced you to work Russia. When we found out it was twins. I was so focused on keeping our family together, so afraid they'd order me to leave. I put that above being there for you. And I'm sorry for that. From the bottom of my heart."

I watched the sun slip below the horizon, the ball of fire disappearing. The brilliant reds and oranges had given way to deep pinks and blues, streaks in the sky.

"I haven't liked the person that I've been. But I want to rebuild. I want to start over, to be the husband I know I can be. The one you deserve."

The kids were still running in the sand, oblivious to the sunset, to our conversation, to the choices we needed to make. Their shrieks trailed over, mixed with the sound of the waves.

"What do you want, Viv?" Matt asked.

I looked over at him, his features muted now in the dusk. "A fresh start."

He nodded, waited for me to go on.

"I want time with the kids."

"I want you to have that. We'll make it work."

"And I don't want any more lies."

He shook his head. "Neither do I."

I ran a finger through the sand, drew a wavy line. "Is there anything else I should know? Anything you're still hiding?"

He shook his head again, more adamantly this time. "Everything's on the table. You know it all."

We were quiet for a few moments, then he opened his mouth to say something, closed it again. I could feel his hesitation.

"What is it?"

"It's just . . ."

"What?"

"Well, the job. You've worked so hard to get where you are, and you're doing such important work. . . ." He gave his head a quick shake. "Now's not the time to talk about it. I just want you to make the right choice, the one that'll make you happy."

Then he shifted so that he was facing me. He took my hands, stood, pulled me up to my feet with him. His words were echoing in my head, the ambivalence I'd felt for all those years creeping back into my conscience. Then he pulled me close, gently, his hands on my waist. And I realized he was right about one thing, at least; this wasn't the time to talk about it. I'd have a year to think. I wrapped my arms around him.

"Remember our first dance?" he said softly.

"I remember," I said. And in that moment, I was transported. The two of us, on the dance floor, swaying to the music, his hands around my waist. Feeling warm and happy and so, so in love. Surrounded by tables full of people, one familiar face after another.

"Look around," I had said to him. I pulled back slightly so I could look at his face. "Isn't this amazing? Everyone we love is here. My family, your family. Our friends. When is this ever going to happen again?"

He didn't look. He stared at me, intense.

"Look around," I prompted again.

He didn't. "You and me," he said. "That's all I see. That's all that matters. You and me."

I'd stared at him, confused by his intensity, the urgency in his voice. He pulled me closer, and I rested my head against his chest, anxious to escape that look.

"The vows I said to you, I meant every word," he told me. "No matter what happens in the future, never forget that. If things get . . . rough . . . just remember. Everything is for us. Everything I do, for the rest of my life, it'll be for us."

"I won't forget," I murmured, certain I never would, and at the same time wondering if the words would ever make sense.

And as we swayed on the beach to the music of the waves, I put my head on his chest again, just as I did all those years before. I felt his warmth, heard his heartbeat. "I didn't forget," I whispered.

"Everything I did, I did it for us," he said. "For our family."

I turned my head to the side so that I could see our kids, now hardly more than shadows against the darkening sky. "So did I." I pulled him closer. "So did I."

"I'M GOING BACK," I SAY.

The words sound right. The decision sounds right.

The fact of the matter is, I've missed it. I've missed the thrill of opening up new intelligence reports, the anticipation, the feeling that a big break might be right around the corner. That any minute, I could piece together a puzzle that would help my country.

I *did* work hard to get where I am. And it's part of my identity, part of what makes me *me*.

"You had me worried there for a minute," Omar says. I see the relief on his face. "They're giving you even more access, you know. We'll be able to accomplish a lot together. Start our own back channel, share information between our agencies, all that data that's needlessly restricted. We can really make a difference."

That's what I want, isn't it? Always have, ever since joining the Agency. But I don't feel the anticipation I thought I'd feel. The excitement. I don't feel much at all.

"I might be deputy director, but my heart's always going to be in Russian CI."

I nod. A sense of unease is creeping over me. Did I make the right decision? It wouldn't be too late to change my mind.

"And besides, you owe me." The way he says it, the smile that doesn't quite reach his eyes, I'm not entirely sure he's kidding. But the truth is, I do owe him. All those times he protected me, broke rules for me, shared information he shouldn't have. I'd be in jail if it weren't for him. Matt and I both would be.

We sit in silence for a few awkward moments, then he cocks his head, gives me a long look. "Are you sure this is what you want, Vivian?"

My mind goes to the kids, even though I don't want it to. But my babies aren't babies anymore. I had a year at home with them, that time I'd always wanted. I try to push them from my mind.

A year ago, I would have said no. But the more time that's passed, the more certain I've become. All the reasons are there. It's the right choice.

"I'm sure."

I CLOSE THE DOOR behind Omar and stand for a moment in the silence. There's a sadness settling over me, a vague sense of regret. And it doesn't quite make sense, because I've had plenty of time to think this through.

I hear Matt come into the room and don't turn. He comes up behind me, wraps his arms around my waist. "So?" he says. "Did you make a decision?"

I nod. There's still a hint of uncertainty in my mind, a sense that maybe I've chosen wrong, but he warned me I might feel that way, the last time we talked about it. "I'm going back."

He lowers his head into the space between my neck and my shoulder, the spot that always sends a shiver running through me, and I can feel him smile. "I think you made the right choice."

EPILOGUE

OMAR WALKS HIGH ON THE RIDGELINE, THE OCEAN TO HIS left, helicopter straight ahead, set down on a barren stretch of dirt and patchy grass. He pulls a cellphone from his pocket. Presses a button, holds it to his ear.

"*Zdravstvuj,*" he says in greeting. And then he listens.

"*Da,*" he says as he walks. Another pause, and then he switches to English. "She's going back. I'll make the necessary arrangements." He listens to the response. "A few months, maybe. But it'll be worth the wait."

He glances behind him, a quick glance, just to be sure there's still no one there.

"I'll see what I can do," he says, and then a moment later: "A long game, indeed." A smile pulls at the corners of his mouth. "*Dosvedanya.*"

He takes the phone away from his ear, presses a button. He's close to the helicopter now, and the pilot's started the propellers. They begin to whir, slowly at first, and then faster, until there's an almost deafening *thump-thump-thump.*

Without breaking his stride, he throws the phone down into the great expanse of ocean below, where it falls swiftly toward the jagged rocks. He jogs the next few steps, until he's at the helicopter, swinging himself inside. And then it takes off, lifting high into the air.

He watches below as it turns out toward the ocean. Sees the crescent beach, Vivian and the four kids. She has one of the twins on her hip, leaning her head close to his, pointing to the helicopter. The other three surround her, their play momentarily paused as they watch the sky.

He sees their house, the little box with the angled roof. Matt, on the back terrace, watching the copter approach, forearms leaning on the rail and shirt billowing in the breeze.

On the terrace, Matt's eyes stay locked on the helicopter as it gets closer, the pounding of the propellers growing ever louder. He watches as it passes in front of the house with an almost deafening roar, and in the instant it's right in front of him, he could swear he sees Omar, that the two of them make eye contact, just for a moment.

His eyes don't leave the helicopter as it continues on down the coast, the rumble gradually fading until he can hear the waves crashing, once again. A smile creeps to his lips, not the disarming, open smile that his family's always seen, but something else entirely. An expression that would make him look like a stranger, if anyone saw it.

He watches the helicopter fade into the distance, and a single word escapes his lips, one that's whispered, almost like a secret, "Dosvedanya."

ACKNOWLEDGMENTS

None of this would have been possible without David Gernert, who helped shape the initial manuscript into the book it is today, and the whole team at The Gernert Company, especially Anna Worrall, Ellen Coughtrey, Rebecca Gardner, Will Roberts, Libby McGuire, and Jack Gernert.

Heartfelt thanks to the brilliant and incredibly kind Kate Miciak, who improved this book tremendously. I'm beyond grateful to Gina Centrello and Kara Welsh for making my dreams come true, and I'm lucky to be working with an amazing group of people at Ballantine and Penguin Random House, including Kim Hovey, Jennifer Hershey, Cynthia Lasky, Matt Schwartz, Scott Shannon, Theresa Zoro, Sanyu Dillon, Susan Corcoran, Michelle Jasmine, Kristin Fassler, and Quinne Rogers. Thanks also to Kelly Chian, Julia Maguire, Alyssa Matesic, and everyone who worked behind the scenes to help publish the book.

Sincere appreciation also goes out to Sarah Adams and the team at Transworld, Sylvie Rabineau at WME, and Carolyn at the PRB.

And a big thanks to my whole family, especially my mom for believing in me, Kristin for her advice and ideas, Dave for his support, and my dad for his enthusiasm.

Most of all, to my boys: I love you to the moon and back. And to my husband, the best friend and partner I could ever ask for: The best decision I ever made was to say yes.

ABOUT THE AUTHOR

KAREN CLEVELAND is a former CIA analyst. She has master's degrees from Trinity College Dublin (international peace studies) and Harvard University (public policy). Cleveland lives in northern Virginia with her husband and two young sons. This is her first novel.

karen-cleveland.com
Facebook.com/KarenClevelandAuthor